Playing for Keeps

ALSO BY JENNIFER DUGAN

Hot Dog Girl

Verona Comics

Some Girls Do

Melt With You

The Last Girls Standing

WITH KIT SEATON

Coven

Playing for Keeps

JENNIFER DUGAN

G. P. Putnam's Sons

G. P. Putnam's Sons
An imprint of Penguin Random House LLC, New York

First published in the United States of America by G. P. Putnam's Sons,
an imprint of Penguin Random House LLC, 2024

Visit us online at PenguinRandomHouse.com.

Library of Congress Cataloging-in-Publication Data
Names: Dugan, Jennifer, author.
Title: Playing for keeps / Jennifer Dugan.
Description: New York: G. P. Putnam's Sons, 2024. |
Summary: A baseball pitcher and a student umpire fall for one another
against league regulations and must keep it secret.
Identifiers: LCCN 2023036103 (print) | LCCN 2023036104 (ebook) |
ISBN 9780593696866 (hardcover) | ISBN 9780593696873 (epub)
Subjects: CYAC: Lesbians—Fiction. | Dating—Fiction. | Baseball—Fiction. |
High schools—Fiction. | Schools—Fiction. | LCGFT: Lesbian fiction. | Novels.
Classification: LCC PZ7.1.D8343 Pl 2024 (print) |
LCC PZ7.1.D8343 (ebook) | DDC [Fic]—dc23
LC record available at https://lccn.loc.gov/2023036103
LC ebook record available at https://lccn.loc.gov/2023036104

ISBN 9780593696866
1st Printing

Printed in the United States of America

LSCH

Design by Nicole Rheingans
Text set in Milo Serif Pro

To anyone who's ever felt suffocated by the weight of others' expectations. We can catch our breath together.

CHAPTER ONE

Ivy

IT'S AN unreasonably hot August day, but I stand here anyway—focused, determined . . . and sweating my ass off in my long black pants and a bright yellow shirt that looks good on exactly no one. I both look and feel like a glorified, over-heating bumblebee.

At least my whistle is cool.

There's not too much time to dwell on things as the players thunder down the field around me, rushing this way and that, chasing the black-and-white ball down to the goal. I watch them carefully while I run through the rules in my head. I'm always watching for a handball, a foul, or a player inching their way offside. I take this game seriously—unlike some of my coworkers.

As if on cue, one of the players, #10, a Messi in the making, comes careening down the side, capturing the ball out of the air with one of the best first touches I've ever seen. He dribbles a few steps, waiting for the defenders to show their hands, and then, with a little shimmy, he sends the ball flying over their heads in a perfect rainbow before darting around them to continue his attempted path to victory. I chase after, always keeping the players in my sight. With the ref shortage, I'm usually the only one officiating games, and this one is no different.

Number 10 is fast, but the defenders are faster *and angrier*—no one likes a show-off, especially when they're on the opposing team. They chase him down, yanking his jersey back just as he starts to shoot, and then shove him into the turf. It's a dirty foul inside the box, and I rip the yellow card out of my pocket as I blow my whistle. I hate calling plays like this, but these kids left me no choice. That play wasn't just dirty; it was *dangerous.*

The ball rolls free from the tangle of players currently shouting at each other on the turf, and the goalie scoops it up. I blow my whistle hard again and separate the teams, who are two seconds away from an all-out brawl, and ignore the way half the crowd stands up and screams at me that it was an accident, while the other half applauds me. Calling a PK, or a penalty kick, in a tied game like this with less than a minute on the clock is as close as you can come to calling it. But rules are rules, and it's my duty—and my honor if I'm getting cheesy about it—to uphold that. If you don't want the penalty, don't do the foul.

I take the ball from the goalie, set it up right on the line, and then nod toward #10. "On my whistle," I say, and jog backward to where I can see the entire field of play. A few players from the defending team try to make a wall and block things—they always do even when they know it's not allowed—but I wave them off. Shots like this come down to two people only, player and goalie, and everyone knows it.

I blow my whistle again, loud and shrill, breaking the silence that's wrapped around us, as players and spectators alike pray for their desired team to win. Number 10 lowers his hand and jogs into a perfect kick that sends the ball sailing into the upper right-hand corner of the net. Unstoppable.

The goalie jumps anyway, slamming into the ground with a force that has to hurt, while #10's team crowds around him in a sea of purple jerseys. I blow the whistle three times, letting everyone know we're at time: game over, purple team won. And then I race over to the table between fields where I stashed my bag.

It's usually best, in my experience, for officials to get out of Dodge after a call like that. Right or not, in a high-intensity game, there are a lot of feelings on the line.

"Hey, Ref," a man yells, jogging toward me.

I sling my backpack over my shoulder, pretending I don't hear him, and then speed walk down the center of the field. I make a point to wave to Aiden, who is currently reffing a game of his own—even though we aren't really friends—just so the guy chasing me knows that someone else has eyes on us. Aiden glances behind me and waves back with a frown.

Great. Now he's going to have to keep an eye on me *and* ref his game. I hate it. He shouldn't have to do that. People should respect us, respect what we do. There wouldn't be games without us—which they should know since so many are getting canceled or rescheduled. *A lot* of people have quit the job, tired of dealing with reckless players and overzealous spectators.

The man currently weaving between soccer fields and yelling at me to stop running isn't the first angry soccer fan I've dealt with, but it never gets any more fun . . . or any less scary. People are unpredictable.

"Hey," he says again as I reach the parking lot. I realize too late that leaving the area where there were tons of witnesses to head to the parking lot where I'm a lot more isolated was a terrible idea. Shit.

Well, now that flight's clearly out, I guess fight it is. I turn to meet him head-on. I've been screamed at before. I've had people spit on me, yell at me. One even tried to slap me. I've been called every derogatory name in the book. I've been told women shouldn't officiate. Just last week I was called a "dumb bitch" for the dozenth time. I handled it then, and I'll handle it now. And, most importantly, rule number one, I'll never let them see me cry. No matter what.

"You know there's a ref shortage, right?" I say, lifting my chin to meet his eyes. "So maybe chasing one down to scream at them in the parking lot isn't the best idea if you want to keep having games here. I know U8 soccer is *so* brutal," I deadpan, "but come on, man. They're second graders. It's not that deep."

Did I mention today's game was with literal children? They don't even have all their adult teeth yet, but their parents are convinced every one of them is god's gift to the sport. Half of them won't even make it past rec, but that's none of my business.

"I wasn't chasing you," the man says, staring at me, but then my words must register because his annoyed face falls. "Oh, no. I guess I kind of was, but it's not what you think!"

I raise my eyebrows. Having an angry parent rethink their position is definitely a first for me.

"Here," he says, and holds out my yellow card. "You dropped this on the field when you were breaking up the argument. I wanted to give it back in case they charge you to replace them. We're not all monsters on the sidelines, you know."

I take it from him, bewildered, just as Aiden comes jogging up. His game must have ended right after mine. I hope I didn't distract him too badly. "Everything okay?" he asks, looking between me and the man. The man nods at him and then heads back to where his kid is waiting. "What happened?" Aiden asks as soon as we're alone.

"Weirdly, nothing," I say, wiping the sweat off my forehead. "I dropped one of my cards, and he just wanted to give it back. When he started chasing me, I guess I just freaked."

"Lucky," Aiden says. "I got a can of Gatorade thrown at me just before halftime for calling a foul on a kid who slide-tackled another kid *and then bit him*. The mom was like, 'How is that a foul?' and I was like, 'Get your rabid kid out of here.' First time I ever red-carded a six-year-old. Man, these people think it's the World Cup, but these kids are barely potty-trained."

I laugh. I can't help it; this job is too much sometimes.

Becoming a pro ref is my biggest dream, sure, but even I am willing to acknowledge that it can get a little dicey sometimes.

I know it sounds weird. Most people dream of being a professional athlete or a rock star or an astronaut or something. But a few years back, after some *extenuating circumstances*, I realized I wanted to go pro in a different way. I wanted to be a ref.

I want to follow in Sarah Thomas's NFL footsteps. She's incredible: the first woman to officiate a major college football game, the first woman to officiate a college bowl game, and if that wasn't wild enough, the first woman to ever be hired as an official in the NFL. Cherry on top of the sundae? In 2021, she went on to become the first woman to ever officiate in a Super Bowl—2021! We're not talking about the Dark Ages here. Sarah is kicking down doors and breaking through ceilings that up until embarrassingly recently seemed to be made of solid steel.

I may have a picture of her on my wall. Or five. Mia, my best friend, thinks I have a crush, but it's not that. Or at least it's not *just* that.

A lot of my friends do this as a part-time job or to work off some of their club dues or field rental fees for their own sports, but not me. This is what I want from life. Sure, refs deal with a lot of hate. We're often accused of favoring one team or the other, even if that's obviously not true. But our work is important. We keep it fair, we keep it moving, and we keep it as safe as we can.

The people doing it on a national stage, like Sarah Thomas or Carl Cheffers, who work during the most-watched televised sporting events, are badasses on a whole other level. The shit they have to deal with, the pressure they're under . . . I can't even imagine. Look at me—I consider myself great under pressure, yet I'm one step away from crumbling under the weight of the college stress my mom is putting on me. Let's just say, my parents don't fully understand the whole *I want to be a ref* thing and are suggesting—nay, demanding—that I come up with a backup plan.

It's gotten so bad that the other day at dinner, I almost yellow-carded my mom. Me and her . . . it's complicated. She just doesn't get it—get *me*—at all. She's constantly shoving colleges down my throat and riding me about "wasting" my potential. Which is bullshit because I have every intention of meeting what I consider my potential. She just doesn't agree with what that looks like.

She's one of those people who buy into the whole *those who can't, ref* idea. She doesn't see it as "a viable path to success." The fact that I gave up being the one kicking the ball to be the one standing on the sidelines drives her up a wall. "Think of the scholarships you're missing out on" is a constant refrain, even though god knows there's not tons of money in college soccer.

The truth is, though, I actually was really good at the sport when I was younger. I'm no Rapinoe or anything, and I don't know that scholarships would have been in my future even if I hadn't quit, but I was the best defender we had in the local club, and I can juggle over a thousand times without dropping the ball. It just wasn't for me, especially after my brother . . .

Whatever. Needless to say, I realized pretty quickly that my priorities had changed. When the coach would ask me to study film, instead of watching plays and looking for where I could improve as a player, I'd find myself focusing on the refs, what they were doing, what they were seeing, if the lineman made the right call or the wrong call, analyzing what call I would make in that situation or how to defuse tensions by being fair. Pretty soon I hung up the cleats and grabbed my flags.

I started working for the same club I used to play for. First, I was just in charge of running scoreboards at big games, but Harry, the owner of this place, said he saw something in me. He asked me what I wanted to do—actually asked me *and listened*—and before I knew it, I was a lineman for youth soccer. Now I'm generally the one in the thick of it, standing in the center of the field getting in the mix. It's exhilarating and exciting in a way playing just isn't to me anymore. I've worked my way up from having to take extra shifts at the snack bar to being scheduled nonstop on the field. When we're short, Harry trusts me to be the one to run the game alone. It feels good. It feels like I'm making a difference. It feels like finally I can control something in my life. My mom accused me of hiding out on the fields, but the truth is I thrived at a time when the rest of my family was falling apart. I found my calling.

Down came the Neymar and Alex Morgan posters, and up went my queen, Sarah Thomas. Okay, sure, so they don't actually have posters made of her, but I ripped some images from newspapers and the internet and had them blown up and printed on card stock. Close enough.

But it's a very long road from here to *her*.

Refs go through years of training, starting out in little kids' games, like I am, progressing into the high school level and varsity if you get lucky. On to juco and then working your way through the college rank, and then, if you're really lucky and you work extremely hard, you go pro.

I get my mom's concern, and I get why some of my friends think I'm bananas for this. A lot of people think this is just a shit job for retirees or kids looking for a buck, but it's not. My boss, he gets flown all over the country to ref major competitions, mostly soccer showcases. He's constantly sought-after and has built a reputation for being fair and knowledgeable. Every fancy tournament that parents are paying thousands for their kid to attend wouldn't happen without people like Harry and me.

My phone buzzes in my hand. Speak of the devil, he's calling me now.

"Hi, Harry," I say cheerfully. Aiden's eyebrows scrunch up, and he leans closer nosily.

"Hey, Ivy, you mind swinging by the office before you head home today?" Harry asks. "I've got something I'd like to discuss with you."

"Sure," I say, a little bit nervous. Harry grunts and hangs up. He's efficient like that, not one to worry about pleasantries or even saying goodbye.

"What'd he want?" Aiden asks, leaning against my car as I unlock it and toss in my bag.

"I don't know. He just asked to see me. I'm gonna head up now."

"You think you're getting fired?" Aiden asks, and I know he's teasing . . . but also not.

Aiden's *almost* as passionate as me about officiating. Most of the people our age who work here are content where they are, but Aiden knows that my opportunities come at the expense of his and vice versa. We're each other's biggest motivators and fiercest competition. He makes me better at my job, and I appreciate that, even though we're basically the definition of frenemies.

Like he'll come running to help me out with an out-of-line parent, but he'd probably be just as likely to trip me as to help me up when we're working together in a game, if he thought it would give him a bigger chance to shine. The major difference is that he's not in it for the long haul; he's in it for the hook.

The hook. If I never hear that phrase again, it will be too soon. Ever since last spring, my mom has constantly been on me. "You're going to be a senior, and we need *a hook* for those college apps! We need to set you apart! Maybe you could write an essay about your brother or—" I cut her off there. I am not turning my brother's death into a college application essay. I know she didn't mean it like that—losing Nicky to cancer a few years back almost destroyed her—but sometimes she's so desperate to find a silver lining, or for something good to come out of it, that she blurts out the most inappropriate things.

So yeah, Nicky isn't my hook, but Aiden seems to think being an official is going to be his. He reads all the same books my mom does, like *Who Gets In and Why* and *The Exceptional Applicant.* He took the SATs six times to try to superscore and got increasingly frustrated when, no matter how many tutors he paid for, his score stayed basically the same. He's obsessed with the idea of getting into a "low acceptance" school, like bragging rights are half the battle or something. I think the pressure has gotten to him, even if he's the one putting it on himself, which is why I'm not flipping him off right now for suggesting that there's some universe where I could be getting fired right now and he wouldn't be.

"Doubt it." I shrug and then jog toward the building and away from Aiden's disappointed frown.

Harry's office is on the closed-off second floor, over the snack bar in the indoor portion of the sports dome. The sports multiplex boasts state-of-the-art indoor and outdoor turf fields used for soccer, football, and lacrosse, as well as a secondary set of baseball fields in the back.

"Hey," I say, knocking twice on his open door as I walk in and drop into the seat across from him. Harry is gruff and down to business, but I think he's a softie at heart. He was one of the only adults in my life who noticed how screwed up I was after Nicky died, and instead of yelling at me to get back on the field when I so clearly was breaking down, he offered me a place on the sidelines.

He's never been anything but kind to me since, and while our relationship is pretty strictly boss and employee, he's been there for me more than once when I needed it. Then again, I'm probably one of the only refs who never misses a game or calls out for something better to do. There *is* nothing better to do in my opinion.

"Hi, Ivy," he says, leaning back in his chair with a smile. "I'd say have a seat, but you already did."

I smile and make a show of settling in and kicking my leg up over the arm, which earns me an eye roll, but a friendly one.

"I saw you out on the field for a little bit today. You got a lot of heart. Your calls are pristine and unquestionable."

"Thanks," I say, and I mean it. Coming from him, a reffing legend, that means a lot.

"You're eighteen, right?" he asks, looking over a folder on his desk. I realize it's my personnel file. I didn't think I'd be getting fired, but now I'm nervous.

"Y-yes?" I say, and it comes out sounding more like a question.

"You sure?" He laughs.

"Yes," I say, sitting up a little straighter. "Got the teasing and bullying to show for it." And that part's true too. I got held back in first grade. No, I didn't fail, or rather, I guess I sort of did. But that's not why I repeated the grade. In fact, the school wanted me to move ahead with my peers, but my parents fought it. They said I wasn't going to be chronically behind just because of school policy.

I had needed glasses badly. They helped, but even with them—and the contacts I started wearing in middle school—I was never a star student. School is just hard for me, boring, and I can't think of anything I'd like to do *less* than stay after for extra help. That's another reason I love reffing so much. The only things I need to study are plays and coverage, and I'm damn good at it. No one has ever called me stupid on the field—well,

12

aside from the unhinged parents, I guess, but they don't mean it in the same way the kids at school did when I was little.

"I know you're in it for the long haul, Ivy, and an interesting opportunity has presented itself to me. The ref shortage around here right now is unprecedented."

"It's no wonder with the way parents act." I think back to Aiden and the Gatorade and shake my head.

"Well, our umpire friends over on the baseball and softball side are having the same problems."

"Makes sense," I say, not sure where this is going.

"I've got a friend who runs the premier baseball league asking if we can spare some refs to come ump their games for the fall ball season. They're renting those back fields from us. I thought of you right away, maybe Aiden too, and Phil if he can get his wife to agree to any more time."

"I hate baseball," I say, slumping.

"It'd be a favor to me. And they pay double what I do. Don't get that in your head, though. The important thing is that you'd be officiating at a higher level and showing off how adaptable you are. You do a good enough job, and I'll recommend they keep you on for the college showcase at the end of the season too. It's a pretty big deal, and I think you could get it. Lotta coaches and colleges at those things. Nice connections to make if you want to ref in college."

I roll my eyes. While Harry is ridiculously supportive of the idea of me working to go pro as an official, he also has my mom's back and says that I need to either get a bachelor's or go to trade school. I think it's the only reason my mom still lets me work here. She and Harry have *an understanding*, which means they gang up on me sometimes, or he agrees to take me off the schedule for stuff like the SATs, even though I don't want him to.

Still, I sit up a little straighter. Double pay? A chance to ref in front of colleges? Holy shit, this could be the break I've been waiting for.

"Did I say I hate it? Because I meant I love it. I love baseball. It's suddenly my favorite sport. I just love the sound of a ball cracking against a bat."

Harry grins. "I thought you might feel that way. I already sent your packet over to them this morning, and you're on their schedule for this weekend. There'll be a crash course on umping Friday night, and they'll pair you up with someone more experienced to show you the ropes Saturday, but I suggest you start studying the rule book tonight."

"That was risky," I say, shaking his hand and then standing up to leave. "What if I had said no?"

"You were never going to say no." He laughs and goes back to the papers on his desk.

And he's got me there.

CHAPTER TWO

June

THE SWEAT stings my eyes under the absurdly hot August sun, and I squeeze them shut for a second, willing the pain away as I wind up and release ball after ball to my ever-patient catcher, Javonte.

I'm good at that—pitching, I mean. Although willing away pain is a very close second.

"I love you, June, but I need a break," Javonte says, pulling off his catcher's mitt and pushing up his mask. "It's hot as balls out here." He stretches out his hips and raises his arms up over his head. He's a tall Black boy, seventeen like me. We're both about to start our senior year. He's the best catcher in a three-hour radius, almost guaranteed to go pro and already getting verbal offers from colleges, and he's my best friend on the entire planet.

I follow his cue and stretch out too, rubbing my shoulder. It's still sore despite the cortisone shot I got in it the other day. I wish I could take a real break, but I glance over to the parking lot, where my dad is sitting in his car, air conditioner on full blast, watching me. Yes, it's hot. Yes, I'm tired. But there's no way I'm getting out of here anytime soon. I follow Javonte over to the dugout where we stashed our bags, and I swear I can *feel* my dad frown even without looking over.

Javonte drops onto the bench and kicks his feet up onto a little rail as he shuffles through his bag and pulls out a water bottle. He passes it to me, and I take a long swig before passing it back. I should be grossed out, germs and all that, but Javonte and I are together 24-7 in this lead-up to college recruiting, so if one of us gets a cold, it's everybody's cold anyway.

The two of us have been joined at the hip since we both wobbled onto the T-ball field as kindergartners. The way our parents tell it, he hit a solid ball off the tee and was making a home run, and I ran all the way from the outfield to tackle him at second, not realizing that as the last hitter he had to run all the bases anyway . . . and that there was no tackling in baseball. I didn't even *have* the ball. I just wanted to stop him.

Javonte cried. And then I cried.

Then my dad scooped me up and told me letting the last batter run all the bases even if they got out was a bad rule anyway, and my mom told him to "chill," which was how she said calm down, because she was weird like that.

Mom always brought tons of snacks, so after the game she had me walk over to Javonte and offer him a bag of Mini Chips

Ahoy and apologize. I was just excited, I told him, and he said it was okay, he wasn't really mad, just embarrassed, and that we should switch to the same team so I didn't do it again. I wouldn't have anyway, but even then, I think we both knew we were meant to play together.

The next thing you know, Javonte and I are having playdates every weekend, Dad's teaching him how to hit without a tee, Mom's teaching me to pitch, and his parents and my parents become best friends and somehow convince our town league to shuffle some players so we can be together.

I kind of come from a legacy family when it comes to throwing and hitting balls, and the league wanted my parents to keep donating and volunteering, so they allowed it. My dad was a minor-league baseball player until he couldn't be anymore. He was always waiting for the big call-up to the majors. To his credit, he did get to play a couple games with the Astros once when someone was injured, but that was long before me. By the time I came into the picture, he was already resigned to the minors and coaching varsity baseball on the side.

My mom was a softball pitcher. She played all the way through grad school and was one of the top pitchers in the country for a while. After she graduated, she took a year or two to play pro and then decided one of them needed a steady job and it clearly wasn't going to be Dad. So she made use of her advanced degree and eventually opened up a solo practice as a speech therapist for nonverbal kids.

It's possible that the only thing Dad loved more than baseball was Mom, although she would have denied it. I do think he was secretly grateful that she never made him choose, and sometimes I wonder if she just wasn't sure if he would pick her or the ball and decided it was better not to even raise the question. She loved pitching and she loved making me into a little mini version of her, but softball didn't have her heart the way baseball had Dad's. She was happy to work, happy to have the 9-to-5, and happy to be home to tuck me in every night.

Javonte's parents, on the other hand, were the opposite of my parents and their athletic history in every way. Javonte's dad is an accountant, and his mom is a children's book author, and they both loved to joke that if you saw them running, you'd better run too, because it meant something bad was chasing them.

I used to roll my eyes—that was a worse joke than my dad makes—but secretly I liked it. I liked that every weekend they weren't stuck hiking or at minor-league games or practicing and practicing and practicing. I liked that their house always smelled like cookies, and that no one ever said, "Eat like the athlete you are," when I came over for dinner.

But still, despite their differences, our parents became a frequent foursome, and as luck would have it, Javonte and I became best friends too. That lasted right up until seventh grade, when my mom got the diagnosis we had all been dreading since she'd found a lump: breast cancer.

Javonte's mom, Mel, was there right up until Mom's last breath. Held her hand through all the years of treatment, through hospice, and then helped me pick the dress for her to be buried in when Dad was too broken up to do it.

Our parents are still friends, but in more of an *it takes a village to raise a child* way than, like, because they want to hang out with Dad.

I have dinner at Javonte's most nights now, because Dad found a job working on third shift—not because he had to, but because he wants to be able to come to all my practices and games, and to work out with me after school every day. Most days he sleeps until three, then meets me at the ball field all afternoon, then goes to my evening games. After that he goes home and naps for two hours while I get takeout or go off to Javonte's for a home-cooked meal, and then he goes to work. He gets home right when I get up to go to school, and we have breakfast together quick.

It's kind of cool in some ways, kind of sucks in others, but I think we're all just doing our best. We never really got out of survival mode after Mom died, and over the years it's become more of a way of life than something that needs any changing.

Javonte nudges my ankle, and I realize he's holding his bottle out to me again. I shake my head and sigh. I need to get back out there before Dad gets out of his car. Javonte frowns but puts his cap back on and grabs his mask.

"Come on, then, Junie," he says as he drags the mask back over his bright white smile. "Mom's making steak and potatoes today, and I'm not gonna be late because you didn't hit your pitch quota."

He's teasing me, and I know it. He would wait if my dad kept me here even longer, but he's right that I don't want to be late either, because that sounds like heaven.

DAD'S SITTING ON his car by the time Javonte and I have finished practicing and picked up all the balls. Tuesdays are rest days for the team, but Javonte and I always practice on our own. Sometimes some of the other guys will join us if they have nothing going on, but apparently, they have a lot of important *Call of Duty* games to attend to. I don't blame them. If I had a PlayStation, I would probably live on it too, which is probably why Dad won't buy me one. Well, that and the price tag.

Still, the guys on the team are like my brothers, so they let me sneak some turns when we're hanging out. I've been on their team since I was little, so they aren't weird about having a girl on the team or anything, and they'll come for anyone who is. Plus, I've definitely proved myself over the years. I'm better than most. Better than all, locally, I would say, but some guys on the other teams might disagree.

They keep it to themselves, though, when I pitch a no-hitter.

I know girls usually play softball, and I have nothing against them. Softball girls are just as intense about their sport as I am about mine. They're kick-ass athletes through and through, but after T-ball, there was no way I was splitting off from Javonte. At first the coaches agreed through elementary school but said I would have to go to softball for JV and varsity at school and possibly even club. That was fine with me; back then, middle school and high school seemed like some faraway time and place I would never get to. And then when my mom got sick, there was no way anyone was booting me off the team, ever. I worked my ass off with my dad until I wasn't just as good as the boys—I was better.

I *earned* my spot. And guess what? Turns out there isn't any rule about girls not being able to play baseball. You don't even need to get special permission like they did that one time the soccer whiz at our school joined the boys' team for better competition her senior year. (That girl's going to the Olympics one day, mark my words.)

Would it be easier for me to get a college spot as a softball player than as a baseball player? Sure. Do I think that's stupid? Yes. I shouldn't have to give up a sport that I love just because I'm a girl—and I'm not the only person who thinks like that. There are a few awesome women already paving the way on "men's" college teams, and groups like Baseball For All out there advocating for all the girls who don't believe baseball is just for boys.

So yeah, I stayed with my guys, striking out every jerk who doubted me—and there were *plenty* of them over the last few years. We never had any of that bullshit hazing. Nobody ever made me feel like I didn't belong. In fact, they make a hobby out of roughing up anybody who messes with me on the field— legally, of course, or at least when the umps aren't looking. These guys are my family, just as much as Mel is, or maybe even my dad. And working this hard is getting us on the radar for a lot of college scouts, so I owe it to them to keep working, just as much as I owe it to myself and to my parents.

Parents. Plural, still.

My mom did that whole *leave your daughter letters for her to open after you die* thing. So at key moments, an envelope appears in my room, pinned neatly to my bulletin board. Dad must have a stash somewhere. I kind of hate them, even though I would never admit it. I'm sure I'll appreciate them later, but right now every time I open one, it just makes Dad cry, and then I feel like crap, and then I feel guilty about not wanting to open them, which makes me cry. Plus, I just know there are letters for when I get married and for when I have kids, and . . . what if I don't?

I know it's supposed to be this great sentimental thing, a connection to my mom across my life, and I love her for thinking that way, but I don't love that I have to live up to her clearly defined expectations even when she's gone. Like, it's kinda hard not to stress when there's an envelope from your dead mom labeled WHEN YOU PLAY YOUR FIRST COLLEGE GAME waiting to be opened.

What if I don't make a team? What if I fail out of college? I'm haunted by what-ifs. Do I just leave the letters in her hatbox, forever unopened, if I don't make it? Do I have to feel like I've not only wasted my talent but also failed to fulfill her dying wishes?

It's heavy. Too heavy sometimes.

I throw a ball at the fence, hard, and my dad shakes his head and hops off his car hood, jogging toward me.

He thinks I was teasing him, not chasing away thoughts, and I decide to let him believe that. I'm not the only one worrying about living up to Mom's dying wishes, and I know it. Dad's got

22

his own box of letters. I peeked once, and they say things like WHEN YOU FALL IN LOVE AGAIN and WHEN YOU SCARE OFF JUNIE'S FIRST BOYFRIEND.

We've both got our crosses to bear in this family.

"You looked good out there," he says, taking the bucket of balls from my hands. "How's your shoulder holding up?"

I know what he wants me to say.

"Good as new," I lie. The cortisone shot helps, but it doesn't get rid of the pain. The doctors think it's bursitis or some other overuse injury, but if they think I can slow down just as college coaches are starting to talk to me, just as my team is trying to qualify for a tournament that's going to have every recruiter I could dream of in attendance, they have another thing coming.

"Awesome," he says, tugging me in for a quick one-armed hug. "You think I could hit a few, then, quick, before we go?"

And oh, I see it's Nostalgic Dad today. Better than Depressed Dad by miles—I don't know if I could take another bad night comforting him over Mom right now—but still, I'm tired. I told him once he should join a men's league instead of relying on me to pitch for him, but he scoffed at that, saying it was for people who couldn't make it and just wanted to relive their high school glory days. I didn't bother pointing out that he didn't make it either—that would have been cruel.

I pull the bat out of my bag and toss it to him, heading back to the mound. Javonte looks at me and shakes his head, resigned to the fact that we're going to be late for dinner. Again.

CHAPTER THREE

Ivy

I EXPECTED the umpire uniform to suck a little extra with all the additional padding we have to wear. I expected the weight of the face mask to make my neck ache. I expected to be hot. I expected to get a headache from concentrating so hard to make sure I was an excellent ump. I even expected some of the guys on the team to be assholes about a girl officiating and the more experienced umps to be up my ass the whole time, worried I didn't know what I was doing despite the fact that Harry recommended me.

Expecting it means I can prepare for it, plan for it, and figure out a way to keep my cool in its face.

What I *didn't* expect, though, was for there to be an extremely attractive girl throwing balls at about seventy-five billion miles per hour, striking out boys left and right, like some kind of varsity all-star Black Widow. She's got several inches on me, and if that didn't kick-start the telltale *someone's got a crush* flutters in my belly, then her deep brown eyes and perfectly executed high ponytail did.

I practically trip over my feet as I step onto the field, trying not to notice the way her chestnut hair literally gleams in the sun as she warms up. Hell, I didn't even know girls *could* play premier travel fall ball—my bad for missing *that* little regulation or lack thereof. But with this new information, and this athletic goddess in front of me, I think baseball just became my new favorite sport.

So yeah, maybe I smirk a little and chew my gum extra cute as I trot onto the field in pads that make me look like a giant bumpy rectangle, just to make sure she's looking . . . but she's not. One of the boys on her team, a Black kid with a tight fade, narrows his eyes as I pass him, though. He gives me a little nod, which I return, and then elbows her. I realize he's probably her boyfriend, and my heart sinks. I wonder if he picked up on my flirting.

Not that I was flirting! I was simply chewing gum with an amused and open expression on my face. Because that is one regulation I *definitely* didn't miss. Players and officials can't date. Talk about a conflict of interest. Harry even makes us sign a whole code of conduct about it in our new-hire paperwork, and this league had me sign something similar last week.

But still, a girl can *lightly* enjoy herself on her jog to home plate, can't she?

I'm going to like this new job very, very much, I think as I settle into position.

Unfortunately, that bright and hopeful feeling only lasts until the eighth inning. Then I want to die. No, I want to murder. Specifically, I want to murder the extremely hot girl throwing balls at my face—well, not my face. She's not quite that wild. But close enough. She throws a pitch that she thinks is a strike, and I call a ball. Right as her catcher—the maybe-boyfriend from earlier—jumps up to argue with me about it on her behalf, I feel another ball go whizzing by. This one hits the fence just about six inches from my head.

I turn back around, furious. She's standing on the mound with a smug look on her face and a *who, me?* attitude in her eyes. Suddenly, I'm transported back to the U8 soccer championships, thinking of all the parents and players who don't show us any respect and . . . No, nope, I'm not doing that. I shove my hand into where my pocket should be, fully intending to pull out a red card out of habit, only to realize too late that (a) these pants don't have pockets and (b) even if they did, they don't have red cards in baseball. Fuck my life. Instead of being intimidating, I just look like I'm angrily rubbing my hip.

I shake my head to clear it and then stalk toward the mound, only to be met by the other official, an older Brazilian man I recognize from when he hangs out around the snack bar with Harry. Gabe, I think his name is. Gabe blocks my way, crossing his arms, and okay, it's not like I was going to hit her or anything.

"She's done," I say, trying to step around him. I can see her behind him, chewing gum and blowing pink bubbles, with her eyebrows raised at me, as if I'm something suspicious, and maybe a little bit boring, not an actual honest-to-god officiating body she'll have to answer to.

"Take a breath, Ivy," Gabe says. He's probably in his late forties, with scruff on his jaw and enough tan and wrinkles to suggest sunblock is not part of his skincare regimen.

"She just threw the ball at my head."

"Near your head," he corrects.

"Still!"

"Okay, let's think for a second. What do you want to do here? She's kind of the draw for the club. People are here to see her play." I swear I hear her chuckle at that.

"It's a premier game, not the World Series," I remind him. "The girl might be good for the snack bar profits, but it's not like anybody's here paying for a show. She's out. Unsportsmanlike conduct. They're up by four anyway; it's not like we're deciding the game."

Gabe sighs but steps aside and lets me continue my march toward her.

"You're out!" I yell, gesturing for her to head off field. This is met with a scoff.

"You can't get out when you're not hitting. Jeez, I knew you were new, but I didn't think you were *that* new. Pitchers don't get out. We're the ones throwing the ball."

I take a deep breath, trying to decide if she's being deliberately obtuse or if she really thinks I'm so naive that I would try to give her an out on the pitching mound. Jesus, I really can't tell with her.

"I'm not giving you an out, or calling you out. I'm kicking you out. Of. The. Game," I say through my teeth. "You're done for the day."

"What?" she says, stepping closer. "You can't throw me out of the game! Gabe, tell her she can't throw me out of the game."

The other umpire shrugs. "Technically, she can."

The pitcher crosses her arms, stomping her foot for good measure, and I have to stifle a laugh. "Well, tell her not to, then." He pinches the bridge of his nose as we both stare at him.

"If we wanted girl drama, we would go over to the softball fields," a player from the other team calls out. Caleb, I think is his name. His older brother used to be friends with mine. Good friends. Max was always at the hospital keeping Nicky company. Maybe I can let this one slip. "I know you guys are probably on the rag, but can you—"

Scratch that.

"Bro, shut the fuck up," the catcher says to Max's little brother, which, dammit, can't be allowed either, even though he's backing me up and I fully support it.

"Hey, watch it," I say, giving the catcher a warning just to seem like I'm being fair. And then I swing toward the opposing dugout and the boy who just decided to be nasty. Damn, I wish I had a red card. My fingers itch beside me, and I curl them into a tight fist. "Show some respect and watch your mouth, Caleb, or I'll tell your brother all about how this 'girl on the rag' struck you out in three balls. He'll really get a kick out of that, I bet." And yes, I do make air quotes.

"How do you even know my name?" he asks, like that's what matters here.

"I'm Nicky's sister, remember? Now go take a seat before I evict you from the game too."

He looks rightfully sorry as his coach drags him from the fence and shoves him back onto the bench. Beside me, Gabe lets out a huff that sounds suspiciously like a laugh, but when I look at him, his face is still stoic.

The pitcher's coach and catcher have joined us now, turning this convo into a full-on meeting, and fuck, this is not how I wanted my first game to go. After what Caleb just said, there is nothing I want to do more than leave this girl in to keep decimating his team, but rules are rules.

I turn back to the pitcher and take a deep breath. "Look, you can't throw a ball at an official, even if you think it's a bad call. You're out for the rest of the game."

She clenches her jaw, and I can see her fingers tighten around the ball. I keep eye contact, daring her to throw it again.

Her coach says, "Gabe?" and now I'm ready to throw a ball at *his* head because Gabe and I have the same exact fucking rank here right now and he shouldn't be trying to undermine me.

Fortunately, Gabe shakes his head. "It's the right call, Bobby. Unsportsmanlike conduct. Even with the masks we wear, your girl could have really hurt someone." I bristle at the term *your girl* even if Gabe is backing me up on this call.

The coach frowns and then puts his arm around the pitcher, walking her off the field. I don't miss the way she casually flips me off as she walks by, but everyone else seems to, so I let it go. Man, any desire I had to make out with her after this—even though I couldn't have anyway—is gone, gone, gone, thanks to her flippant, immature attitude.

You would think she'd be a little cooler to another girl trying to break into a ridiculously male-dominated field—same team and all—but no.

She has to know that baseball isn't exactly friendly to people who aren't men on the officiating side either. You can practically count on one hand the number of women officiating in the minor leagues, and none of them have ever made it to the majors. It's messed-up.

Okay, maybe I was daydreaming a little during the seventh inning stretch that this pitcher would become a wildly successful MLB player, and I would become the first woman umpire in the majors, but that fantasy went out the window with the flip of her middle finger. Her temper is an embarrassment to the sport, regardless of gender.

Screw her.

OTHER THAN THE scorching sun making my life a living hell, the last inning and a half manage to pass pretty easily and without drama. No one else mouths off or tries to kill me with a baseball. No one argues with my calls except for one jackass in the stands, and even he only shouts when they're for the home team—apparently my calls for the away team are A-fucking-plus to him. He must be one of the player's dads.

Gabe slips me some cash at the end of the game, my share of the officiating fee that apparently the teams pay in cash in this league, and then he heads out to his car.

I would follow him, but I'm feeling nasty and dehydrated, and I happen to know that Harry prides himself on always having gloriously clean locker rooms and showers, including private fancier ones for refs.

Since I'm meeting my best friend, Mia, after this for celebratory pizza, I make the split-second decision to head inside and clean up here. I always stash some toiletries and a change of clothes in my backpack; I've gotten too used to impromptu sleepovers with my friends to risk not.

It'll be a good reset from the annoyance of dealing with the girl on the mound—June, apparently, based on the way her team cheered her name as she walked off the field. Her father (I'm assuming) definitely just called me a piece of shit as I walked by. At least the man sitting next to him told him to knock it off and mouthed "I'm sorry" to me. Baseball parents, man, they might be a close second to soccer parents on the overly emotional scale.

This particular day cannot end soon enough, and I'm suddenly grateful to Harry for only scheduling me for one game today on my first day switching sports. Next weekend, I have a triple-header.

It's an eight-minute walk under the hot sun from the ball field to the building proper, and when I finally find myself standing in front of the "officials only" locker room, I'm feeling fully fried and daydreaming of a nice cold shower, and maybe a spin in the massage chair, even though you have to fill it with quarters to get it to work.

What I'm not daydreaming about is finding the pitcher inside, gingerly pulling off her jersey. She turns toward me as the door swings shut behind me, a scowl replacing her wince as I desperately try not to notice that she's now just standing here in her sports bra. A shiny purple Nike bra that looks almost iridescent.

And why did I hate her again? I suddenly can't remember. But I *do* remember that I should not be noticing her bra. I should not be noticing *her*. I should not be—

"Get out of here!" she yells, and, ah yes, now I remember why. Because she sucks.

CHAPTER FOUR

June

"THIS IS the officials' room. You get out," the ump says so rudely that I have to fight the urge not to throw my glove at her. If my shoulder wasn't absolutely killing me, all bets would be off.

"Listen, Ump—"

"Ivy. My name is Ivy, not Ump," she says, somehow still sounding super furious with me even as she introduces herself.

"Listen, *Ivy*," I say, adding extra emphasis like she's a small, confused puppy, "there are, like, a million baby lacrosse players in the girls' locker room. There must be a tournament here somewhere."

"That sounds like a *you* problem," Ivy says, stomping past me and throwing her bag onto the couch by the mirror. "You're a player. This is the officials' lounge. Leave."

I make a big show of looking around the room. "Sorry, but you only have the ability to throw me out during games, and this doesn't look like a ball field, so get over yourself."

She crosses her arms. "True . . . unless I go to the front desk and explain that there's a squatter in here or tell Harry, my boss, who owns the place and made this locker room for us."

I sigh and rub my shoulder. "Why do you even care?"

"Because you can't just do whatever you want. You were a huge asshole on the field. I could have really gotten hurt by that ball!"

"No, you couldn't have, because I have impeccable aim and control. If I wanted to hit you, I would have. I just wanted to make you jump a little, which is all I did."

Ivy huffs, yanking her dirty-blond hair out of its bun and letting it fall to her shoulders. "You think that's better?"

"Better than a ball to the face? Yeah, don't you?"

She flashes her hazel eyes at me. "There shouldn't have been a ball flying at my face to begin with!"

"If you don't want balls flying at your face, then don't stand behind home plate. Okay, new girl?"

Ivy narrows her eyes at me. "You're unhinged."

"That pitch was a strike, not a ball, and you know it."

Ivy stares at me in disbelief, and yeah, I'm being rude to her, and maybe I'm taking out a little extra frustration on her today, but I'm pissed, and I'm sore, and I just got thrown out of a game for the first time in my life. The lacrosse kids in the locker room were giving me a massive headache; I just came here looking for a little peace.

Nobody ever even uses this one. I sneak into it all the time; it's *way* nicer than the players' locker rooms. Besides, umps usually rush out as soon as the games end to dodge angry parents and players. How was I to know that the most annoying girl in the world was going to show up for a spa treatment or whatever it is she's doing?

Ivy shakes her head. "It was not."

"It was too," I say. I raise my arm up a little too fast and high in exasperation. "Shoot." I wince, pulling my arm close to me and rubbing at the offending shoulder.

I hope she didn't notice, even though it would be pretty impossible to miss. When I glance over at her, her expression has changed from annoyance to concern, so yeah, didn't get that wish. Ivy takes a step forward as if she's going to touch me, and then seems to realize that I'm standing here in nothing from the waist up but a sports bra and seems to change her mind.

I ignore that little flip-flop in my belly at the thought of her hands on my skin, reluctantly realizing that this Ivy girl is unfortunately kind of cute when she's not in oversized pads kicking me off the mound. I can't help but catalog the way her sun-kissed freckles blend perfectly with the stray specks of dust and clay dotting her skin, like maybe she was made to be on the field just like I was.

Whatever. Now is not the time.

"Are you okay?" she asks, worry evident in her voice.

"I'm fine," I grit out, because my brain has caught up to the butterflies in my belly, and I remember that all I want is for this girl to go away and leave me alone. The last thing I need is to be caught fraternizing with the enemy. Well, I guess the other team is the enemy, but any kind of game official is a close second in my book.

"You don't look fine," she says. "What's wrong with your shoulder? You're a lefty, yeah? Isn't that your throwing arm?"

And there are those stupid butterflies again, swirling up from my stomach, making a quick pit stop in my heart before lodging themselves in my brain and whispering thoughts like *She noticed you're a lefty* and *She sounds worried* and *If she wants to play doctor, you should let her.* I do my best to shove them down and grumble out a quick "yeah," ignoring her first question entirely.

"Hang on," she says, and starts digging through her backpack.

Great, she's probably getting her phone to call the front desk and get me escorted out.

Instead, she pulls out a can of Biofreeze and tosses it to me, frowning when I wince again as I catch it. Oh, Biofreeze, my faithful friend. The younger, hipper version of Bengay or Aspercreme, a tingly little menthol thing that promises to cure all of life's aches. I go through this stuff like most people go through water, even though it doesn't really help anymore, and my range of movement has become so bad I literally can't even reach where it needs to go.

"Why do you have this?" I ask.

"You're welcome," she says pointedly.

"Thanks, why do you have this?" I ask again. I guess repeating myself is just going to be our thing.

Not that we are going to have a thing, because we definitely aren't. She threw me out of the game. She's the enemy, I remind myself.

"I fucked up my knee a few years back, just a really bad sprain, but it acts up sometimes. I figured it might today when I was crouching over near the catcher, so I made sure to bring some. Why don't you have any?"

I don't have the heart to tell her that if a cortisone shot doesn't take the pain away, this bottle of menthol gel isn't going to do anything either. Instead, I lie. "I forgot it."

"Seems like you forget a lot."

"Like what?" I ask, my hackles rising.

"Manners, game rules, pain relievers . . . You need ibuprofen?"

I shake my head. "You're really rude, you know that?"

"Says the girl who threw a ball at me to make me jump." She smirks, still watching me, and I realize she's probably waiting for me to use the Biofreeze and toss it back.

There's just one problem. I can't. My hurt shoulder is definitely not going to allow me to bend the way I need to apply it the right way. It seems like a lot of effort for minimal payout.

"This stuff is pricey. I can just use mine when I get home," I hedge, setting it down on the bench beside me. I reach for my tank top and start pulling it on, but she doesn't make a move to get the Biofreeze. It's unsettling how she keeps watching me, like she can see right through me.

"Do you need help?"

"Isn't it more fun to help someone *undress*? I've got this," I say, trying to catch her off guard with some teasing. It doesn't work. She ignores my comment and comes over to pick up the bottle.

"Turn around."

"It's fine. I—"

"Turn around," she says again, this time followed by an impatient sigh. Part of me wants to defy her, but another part is jumping up and down at the prospect of her hands on me. I study her face for a minute, and, positive she's not going to let this go, I reluctantly turn around.

"You don't have to do this, you know. I'm fine."

"Yeah, so fine you can't even put this on by yourself."

I jump as the ice-cold gel hits my skin, and she honest-to-god shushes me, and then keeps squeezing more out. The warmth of her hand massaging it in sends the tingles from my shoulder straight to my brain. Her hands are firm, even though I can tell she's trying to be gentle, and it feels so confusingly good that I let her keep going even though I know it's not really going to help.

My shoulder needs rest. Actual rest and real ice and an anti-inflammatory stronger than generic ibuprofen could ever hope to be.

I lean back a little into her touch, though, feeling some of the stress and tightness melt out of me. It does feel kind of good, kind of nice, even if this *is* the annoying umpire. I mean, I'm not ready to take her off my list of enemies, but maybe I *won't* spend the night shoving needles into an effigy I make of her, like I had previously planned to.

A sharp knock on the door has us both startling apart, and I meet her eyes in the mirror, wondering if she felt the same thing I just did. The little electric swirl of butterflies that don't quite replace the hate so much as confuse it. She looks just as guilty as I do, and I smirk. Looks like the feeling is mutual. Good. If nothing else, maybe I can use this to get some plays called in our favor next time.

Another set of knocks has me scrambling to pull my tank all the way back on. I scrunch my nose up at the way it sticks to the cold, sticky Biofreeze that she's now rubbed all over my shoulder, neck, and upper back.

"Hey, June!" Javonte calls from the other side of the door. "You in there?"

"Be right out!" I call, shoving my things into my bag and slinging it over my unhurt shoulder.

Ivy is making herself busy pulling out her toiletries and a change of clothes.

"Hurry up. Your dad is flipping out in the lobby about you being pulled from the game," he calls. "I tried to calm him down but . . ."

"Crap," I say. I wrench the door open a little too hard, and it flies back wide enough for him to see Ivy.

"Is that the—"

"Yep," I snap, not even looking back toward her or saying goodbye. Whatever moment we just had is definitely over now.

For good. I yank the door shut behind me, fighting against the slow-close hinge with my sore arm, then march after Javonte toward the lobby.

Dad has the boy at the front desk big-eyed and terrified as he unloads on him about the "crap ref," yelling things like "Don't you know who my daughter is?" I used to love when he went to bat for me like this. Like when I was in second grade and one of the coaches wasn't giving me enough pitching attention, even though I was better than the boys. Dad tore into him until the coach apologized and said he was *lucky* to have me.

That was cool. This is mortifying.

"Dad," I say, tugging on his arm. "Dad, come on, let's go."

"I want to talk to someone about what happened on the field today," he says, pulling his arm back.

"Come on, Clint," Javonte says, trying to help me defuse the situation. "We can talk about it with Coach if you want."

Dad seems to come back to himself at that moment, shaking his head at the kid and then turning to face us. "You're right. This kid can't do anything. Where's Bobby?" He strides confidently out of the lobby and toward the parking lot, where in the distance I can see Coach throwing buckets full of baseballs into the back of his car.

"Poor Coach." Javonte slings his arm around me, careful of my shoulder.

Most people don't know the extent of how my arm feels. I downplay it for Dad and Coach, and definitely don't share it with the team—not because they wouldn't care, but because they'd worry too much, and that wouldn't be good for anyone at this point in our baseball careers. But Javonte is different. He catches everything. He's *always* caught everything.

"So . . . that ump was kinda cute, right?" he says, walking me out to the parking lot.

See? Everything. Even if I don't tell him.

"I didn't notice," I lie, but the look he gives me tells me he's not convinced.

CHAPTER FIVE

Ivy

WE'RE NOT even halfway through dinner when my mom starts.

"I signed you up for a college visit at Penn State," she says, scooping her second helping of asparagus.

My dad goes still, knowing that these are fighting words. I glance at my little brother, Sammy, but he's still playing with his mashed potatoes, blissfully unaware. Good.

I flick my eyes to my mother and then down at my plate, trying to decide if her timing was strategic—she knows I won't make a scene in front of Sammy—or just an unfortunate coincidence. Then she adds, "And I signed you up for another SAT prep class too. I still think we can hit 1400 if we really, really try."

I set my fork down and raise my eyebrows at her. "Oh, are you taking it?"

My mom gives me a blank look, unimpressed.

"You said *we*, so . . ."

My dad lets out a huge sigh and mumbles something that sounds like "Here we go" under his breath.

"I said *we* because if I don't stay on you, you don't do anything! You've barely looked at any schools. You don't even know what you want to major in. You refused to take any honors classes this year—what am I supposed to do with that?"

"I don't know." I shrug. "Maybe accept that it's not that important to me? I'm not driving hours to go walk around your alma mater just so you can try to pressure me into applying. I'm more than happy to stay local while I figure stuff out. I've been making real inroads here lately. God, Harry just pulled me up for baseball, and now you're trying to send me away. Why can't you just, for once, pretend to give a shit about what *I* want. I don't even think you hear me anymore."

"Language," Dad says, picking my brother up from his seat and carrying him—and his dinner—into the living room. The familiar sounds of Sammy's favorite Nick Jr. show flood the room seconds later as my mom aggressively shovels more potatoes onto her plate, letting the metal spoon clang against the ceramic dish.

"Just because I don't agree with you, doesn't mean I don't hear you," she seethes. "Officiating is not a career, and I am not going to have you throw away your future because Harry can't keep employees."

"That's not true!"

"You're smart, Ivy," she says through gritted teeth. "Too smart for this. It's time to stop messing around and focus.

You've had all of high school to 'figure stuff out.' You're eighteen for god's sake! Some people don't even get to . . ." She trails off, shaking her head.

Right. That's what this is really about. That's what it's *always* about. My dead brother didn't live long enough to go to college, so now I need to go for the both of us. I take a deep breath and stare down at my plate. The urge to go absolutely nuclear on her is tempered only by the fact I can tell she's near tears.

She's always near tears, though. Sometimes I just want to grab her and shake her and say, *I'm still here. I still matter. Sammy matters. We are not just stand-ins for the kid you lost, the brother I lost too.*

Sammy, poor little Sammy. Yes, thinking about my two-year-old brother as a replacement kid makes me nauseated, but sometimes it really feels that way. Like they only had him because Nicky died. If he hadn't, I would've stayed the doted-on baby of the family, instead of becoming the big sister and the chronic disappointment. I could have stayed the free spirit while Nicky remained the constant overachiever that he was.

Nicky had big dreams, he did. He'd wanted to be a doctor for as long as I can remember, and after he got sick, he decided to be an oncologist specifically. He would have done it too. I know it.

Maybe I would have been someone totally different too, if I hadn't had to pick up the mantle as the surviving child before I even figured out who I wanted to be. I know I didn't want to be that; no one wants to be that. The way people looked at me when I went back to school after the funeral. I wasn't just Ivy anymore; I was Ivy-with-the-dead-brother.

"Mom," I say, grabbing her hand, because I'm not a total fucking monster. "Can you just try to trust me on this? Please? I'll take the stupid SAT classes, but I'm not going on the college tour, okay? Can we just find some middle ground here?"

She squeezes my hand back and looks up. "If you don't tour the schools, you won't know which one is the right fit."

"Oh my god, Mom," I groan, standing up to clear my plate. "I can't do this with you right now. I've got a game to run in the morning."

"Ivy—"

"Good night, Mom," I say, even though it's barely 6:30. Once I make it to my room tonight, I'm definitely, definitely not going to leave it again. Not when she's like this.

I'M AT THE field first thing the next morning, ready for the day's slate of games.

I'd be lying if I said I didn't keep an eye out for June every time I'm scheduled to work these days. I might tell myself it's out of a sense of self-preservation—I don't want to face her wrath again and risk another ball flying at my head while I stand there unaware—but mostly I'm just . . . curious.

Curious about the girl with the temper, curious why she's playing through an injury that so obviously hurts, curious where she gets off with her attitude, and—as ridiculous as it

45

sounds—curious why a girl would choose to play baseball instead of softball.

Look, I know. Reffing in general—and umping in particular—is dominated by men. If anyone should understand her call to baseball, it should be me. I'm fully, totally, one hundred percent on board with women playing any and every sport. But I still want to know what drew her to it and all that.

There's a lot of pressure on girls to conform, to become nice women, to do what's expected. Smile more, whiten your teeth, lose the weight, don't be too loud or too funny or too much. Make yourself less so the boys can feel like more. Don't wear spaghetti straps or you might tempt them. Hold yourself accountable for the both of you, so they don't have to.

Needless to say, to see girls like me and June thriving is kinda cool. I want to know the story there—simple as that. I've been watching enough these last few weeks to know that her team really loves her. She's not trying to be one of the guys, though. In fact, I've seen her call them out for being gross or sexist more than once. She's not trying to ditch her womanhood to fit in. She's comfortable and confident in it, and the boys she plays ball with seem to respect it.

While she may not be one of the guys, she is definitely one of the team. I watch the way they rally around her, celebrating her strikes and cheering her on, the way they high-five her and wrap her in big swinging hugs after she closes out an inning with no hits. It's kind of infectious, and in another universe—one where I didn't have to maintain an air of objectivity—I could almost imagine myself being tempted to get right in there with them, high-fiving her.

But still, she makes it clear that we are not friends, Biofreeze be damned. Every chance she gets, she shouts over a supposed bad call, and I play my part, dishing out as much as I take.

She seems eager to avoid me too, which is why it's weird that today of all days—when everyone was scheduled for triple-headers because of late-season makeup games, and I've been at the field for five hours—I find her in the officials' locker room again.

June glances up when she sees me, her eyes red-rimmed like she's been crying or something, looking so pitiful it makes my heart drop and almost, *almost* makes me forget how awful she was to me today on the field, getting in my face twice, her dad egging on the other parents to scream at me when I called a player out on second—who was clearly out by a mile, I might add. This gave the other team a chance to rally and almost make a comeback, which led to a chorus of accusations that I once again was favoring the underdog.

I don't get it. I don't understand them screaming at me for supposed bad calls against their team, yet when they're against the other team, my calls are apparently perfect. I go from enemy number one to "Finally, a good call." It's not lost on me that the only good calls are in their favor.

I shut the door quietly as she goes back to hanging her head. My cleats squeak and grind against the cheap vinyl floor designed to look like hardwood and doing a terrible job of it. I drop my bag onto the couch across from her, reminiscent of our first meeting. It feels like that was years ago—but really it's been barely three weeks. Too soon for her to have forgotten where she is, and too soon for me to have forgotten her rudeness.

"I don't suppose you would get out?" she asks quietly, wiping at her nose.

I sigh, because of course she would open with that instead of *Hi* or even *Hey, can I hide in here and cry for a while? Do you mind?*

"There another tourney or something?" I ask, thinking back to her excuse last time.

"No," she says, but doesn't offer me anything more.

A wave of frustration passes over me, but I tamp it down because she's wiping her eyes even faster now, her tears coming at a more regular pace. I dig through my bag, pulling out the Biofreeze again and the ibuprofen that I may have added after the last time I saw her. I even have one of those boxed squeeze-and-shake ice packs, but I can't decide if that would cross the line from prepared to creepy, so I leave it there for now.

"Here, let me know if you need help," I say, tossing them onto the bench. "I'm hitting the shower, though. I'm kind of in a hurry today."

June nods but doesn't make a move toward the things I've set beside her or acknowledge me in any real way, and what's her problem? Her team won; they swept all three games today, mostly thanks to her. Shouldn't she be out celebrating or something? Or at least being less of a tool to me?

I don't wait around, though—*Not my circus, not my monkeys,* as my mom loves to say. Usually, she applies it to situations where her coworkers fuck up or something, but I think it fits here too. I. Don't. Care. Whatever June's drama is today, it's not my problem.

Okay, maybe I sneak a glance back at her while I wait for the water to heat up, but that's just basic human curiosity—nothing more. She's still sitting there, wiping at her eyes, and I frown so hard I can feel it in my belly. I don't like sad, subdued June. It feels wrong somehow, like someone took a drawing and smudged it all up or added a stick figure behind the *Mona Lisa.* June is supposed to be crisp angles and acidic comebacks, not this soft, smudged girl who can't stop crying.

She looks up at me, like she felt me watching her or something, and I practically leap into the shower stall, my towel still on and getting soaked. Shit, shit, shit. I toss the wet towel out, and it hits the ground with a sopping squelch.

Great. Now I'm trapped, naked, with my nemesis. I guess worst case I can pick the soaked towel up off the floor—I shudder at the thought of the last time this floor was cleaned. Or I could walk naked through the locker room, just letting it all hang out like I'm an old man at the Y, like it isn't weird or going to kick up my insecurity or anything. Fuck it, though. Either way, that's a problem for future me. Yes, by *future me,* I really only mean five-minutes-into-the-future me. But still, not right-now me, at the very least.

I grab my toiletries and make quick work of washing my hair and body. I try to figure out if I could yell loud enough for Mia to hear me. She's right out in the lobby, waiting to whisk me away to a house party being thrown by this guy Devon she's talking to. I don't really know him; he's some varsity basketball player from our school who seems, like, *rich* rich based on everything Mia's told me about his place—a heated outdoor pool, a hot tub, *and* a basketball court?

I run some quick numbers on the odds that I could project my voice loud enough to carry through the concrete walls of the locker room, over the din of the lobby and snack bar, and through the headphones that Mia is no doubt wearing, because god knows if she goes more than five minutes without music she'll die. It doesn't take long to realize that the odds of that happening are, like, negative zero or something. Whatever's worse than no chance at all is the chance that I have.

The water turns cold, and I shut it off, deciding that standing there dripping in the air-conditioned locker room can't be any worse than the ice pellets that were just hitting me from the showerhead. And Jesus, you would think a sports facility would invest in some better water heaters.

I peek out of the shower stall, hoping that she's gone, but of course she isn't. June is still sitting there on the bench, exactly where I left her. It doesn't even look like she's touched the Biofreeze. Is she in that much pain still that she can't apply it alone?

The rustling of the cheap curtain makes her look at me again, and I jerk my head back. Fuck. What do I do now? I spend another few moments in existential panic before June's voice cuts through the silence of the room.

"Are you . . . okay in there?" she asks, clearly uncomfortable.

"Yeah, great!" I lie, rolling my eyes at myself. Why can't I just ask her to bring me a towel? Why am I being so stubborn about this? I slip my head out from behind the shower curtain again, only to find her still staring at me. I pull back in and drop my head back. What is wrong with me? What is *wrong* with me? This is silly. This is ridiculous. This is immature. I open my mouth to ask her to bring a towel over to me, but before I can, she cuts me off.

"Then stop acting so weird," June says. "It's annoying." And yeah, okay, that's why I didn't want to ask her for help.

I take a deep, frustrated breath and then snatch my soaked, probably germy towel up off the floor. I hiss at the cold when I wrap it around myself. June is still watching me, so I do my best to act natural while I drip across the locker room floor, grabbing my clothes out of my bag and heading to the changing room. I stop and pull a fresh towel off the rack as I pass by, practically ripping the soaking wet towel off me the second I'm in the changing room and flinging it over the door.

The fresh towel is blissfully warm, since the stack is right over the hand dryers that get unnaturally hot, and it chases away the shivers. I spare a moment to snuggle in and thaw out, and then I dress as quickly as I can, wrapping my hair up with the dry towel to avoid any more cold drips. I grab my makeup bag and head to the mirror, doing my best to ignore the way June's eyes follow me from place to place.

"You know you didn't have to use the wet towel," June says, smug. No doubt proud of herself for figuring out my issue.

"Yeah, and you don't have to be such an asshole, but here we are," I say, flicking my eyeliner just right to create a wing so perfect that even Ariana Grande would be jealous.

"You're a real pot of sunshine and rainbows yourself," she grumbles.

"What is your problem?" I ask, turning around quickly to face her.

"My mom died," she says, just like that, and I drop my eyeliner. The room is silent other than the sound of it clattering to the floor and rolling to her foot. Neither of us makes any move to grab it.

"Seriously?" I ask, sure I must have heard her wrong.

She lifts her chin, meeting my eyes. "Yes, my mom died. You want to know what's wrong? That's what's wrong," she says, wielding her words like weapons.

I shift uncomfortably against the counter, feeling the Formica digging into my back. I don't know how to respond to this. I don't know how to handle this at all. This girl in front of me, who seemed soft and smudged a little while ago, has gone razor-blade sharp, and I'm scared to say the wrong thing.

I settle on "Well, that sucks," and her shoulders drop, just a hair, the slightest hint that maybe that wasn't the wrong thing to say after all.

"Yeah, it does," she says, and looks away. She kicks my eyeliner back toward me, still not meeting my gaze, and I pick it up, turning to finish my other eye.

"That's why you're hiding in here?"

"I'm not hiding."

"Fine, is that why you're *sitting* in here?"

"I just needed a minute."

"Okay," I say, trying to give her some space, but her eyes meet mine in the mirror and they're angry now.

"*Okay?* Is that all you have to say?"

"What else should I say?" I ask, reaching for my lip gloss and desperately trying to hold on to my mom's old adage. *Not my circus, not my circus . . .*

"How about *sorry?*"

"Is that really what you want to hear? Because when my brother died, everyone was so sorry all the time, and I hated it."

"Your brother died?" she asks, her words coming out in a whoosh.

"Yeah, three years ago. Leukemia."

"Breast cancer," she says. "Five years ago, today."

Five years ago. Shit. She was young when she joined the *watch someone you love waste away* club. I wouldn't wish that on anyone, ever, not even her.

"Fuck cancer," I say, zipping up my makeup bag and grabbing my hairbrush. "It's not fair."

"No, it's not," she says, letting out a shaky breath. "Do you ever wonder . . ."

I wait to see if she's going to finish that sentence, but she doesn't, so I just pack up my stuff and get ready to leave. I know that Mia is waiting for me. Mia and this house party and beer and not having to think about Nicky, who would have been twenty-one in just two months. Who dreamed of being a doctor and died skeleton-thin surrounded by them. I hate that the closest he ever came to working in a hospital was dying in one. Mia, Mia, Mia. I just need to get on the other side of the door. The door that feels like it's closing in on me. Everything becoming too heavy and too tight.

"Do you ever wonder if you're letting them down?" she asks, her words cutting through, making my hand pause on the door and drop to my side instead of ripping it open.

She's looking at me so earnestly that I wish I had a way to make this better for both of us. Because if there is one thing I can't handle right now, right when she's turned me from steel to glass, it's wondering if my dead brother would be proud of me.

"Do you wanna go to a house party? There's a heated pool."

Confusion washes over her face, and then understanding. We get each other on this, know this specific type of pain, better than either of us could have imagined. "I shouldn't," she says.

"I didn't ask if you should; I asked if you want to."

She doesn't answer right away, likely mulling it over in her head, so I add, "Swimming's good for your shoulder, I bet. And there'll be plenty of beer so you can stop wondering about shit that there's no use wondering about."

She stares at me a minute, her eyes boring into mine, and then she nods twice. "Give me a minute to shower and stuff?"

I smile, relieved, as she heads toward the showers. I don't know if I could have left her here, hurting as bad as she is.

Knowing what that feels like. "I'll be in the lobby waiting. Oh, and June?"

She turns back, her hand stilled on the stack of towels. "Yeah?"

I smile at her, the smile of the cat who got the canary. "There's no hot water left."

CHAPTER SIX

June

I FEEL weird about this whole situation the second I step out into the lobby. It was easy to be vulnerable in the tight bubble of the locker room, with no one else around, but I feel raw and a little embarrassed about the whole thing now that I've pulled myself somewhat together. I'm tempted to sneak past and head out to my car, but Ivy spots me and waves me over with a smile that's hard to resist.

She's sitting with another girl, who looks around our age, Asian American with straight black hair and a huge smile on her face. She practically flies out of her chair to give me a hug. I stand frozen and caught off guard.

"Hi, I'm Mia Sasaki, Ivy's bestie, and I'll be your party host tonight," she says, bouncing up on the balls of her feet. "Ready to go?"

I glance at Ivy, who's watching us with clear amusement in her eyes. "I . . . guess?"

"Excellent!" Mia links her arm with mine and leads me out to the parking lot with the enthusiasm of a freshly unleashed Labrador puppy. Ivy trails behind us a safe distance away, and I wonder if she really wanted me to come or if she needed someone to help defuse this ball of lightning she calls a best friend. "We're taking Ivy's car, because it actually has enough gas to get us there for once." She turns her head and winks at Ivy. "Do you want shotgun? Cuz I can sit in the back if you do."

"Um, no. No, the back is fine," I manage to get out, already desperate for a break from all this peppiness. It's only making me feel worse about my current mood.

Ivy hits the unlock button on her key chain, and we all pile into her old Kia Sorento. Or maybe it's her parents' Kia Sorento, judging by the fact that it has a car seat in the back. Unless maybe she has a kid I don't know about?

I try to squeeze around it, but she stops me and then unhooks it herself to toss into the trunk. "Sorry, I have to get my little brother from day care sometimes; it's just easier if we all have one."

"I thought your brother died," I say, wincing at how that comes out. In the front seat, even Mia goes still, waiting to see what happens next.

Ivy hesitates, and then shuts her trunk. "I have two," she says, and the present tense has me curious, but I don't push it. "My parents didn't want me to grow up as an only after Nicky died."

"Sorry, I shouldn't have—"

"It's fine. Let's get to that party," she says, cutting me off as she slips into the driver's seat.

I want to run, or more accurately I want to sink into the puddle by her rear tire and never resurface, but I don't. I sit with the awkwardness, deciding to get in and get buckled while she ignores me from the front seat. I hope this party really does have beer.

IF RIDING IN the car with Ivy was weird, then hanging out with her at this party is alien levels of strange.

For one, she seems to know, like . . . everyone. Which is annoying. I've never met an ump who had so many friends. Granted, I've also never hung out with an ump outside of a game, but still. I don't know what I thought. I guess that they, like, slunk off to some ump store and were put back on the shelf until the next game. I know, I know, but you don't really think of them as people.

During the course of their small talk in the car, Mia shared with me that she and Ivy live about a half hour away, that Ivy doesn't ref for her school or local club for fear of favoritism, that Mia doesn't know why Ivy is even letting me into her car since she's so by the book about fraternization—which earned her a punch in the arm—and that Ivy wants to go pro and someday officiate the Super Bowl or an MLB game or something, which made Ivy blush from her ears all the way down her neck.

It was unbelievably cute, and I craned forward in the back seat a little to see where it ended, before I caught myself.

On a scale from one to ten, with one being a bad idea and ten being the best idea, trying to see how far an official's blush travels down her body is negative a billion times infinity, aka a colossally bad idea. Even I can recognize that.

Mia rushed off as soon as we got to the party, leaving Ivy and me to kind of stand there awkwardly. After we made it safely inside the house, nearly everyone under the sun greeting her or high-fiving her or rushing to hug her, I waved Ivy off, and now I am perched safely by the keg, content to observe.

I can almost, almost forget what day it is as the alcohol melds with my blood in foamy and delicious ways. I know, I know—underage drinking is bad, double bad when you're an athlete and blah blah blah, but when *your* body is pumped full of cortisone shots, and your mom is dead, and you pitch in a state with no pitch count limits, then you get to tell me no.

Ivy keeps stealing glances at me. On the field, I thrive on people watching me. It fuels me. Here? It's annoying. Maybe a little uncomfortable after my earlier confession. It makes everything seem so much more claustrophobic and raw, so I slip down off the counter I was sitting on and decide to go wander around and mingle to get Ivy's eyes off of me.

At least, that's how I try to make it look. I don't know anyone here except for Ivy and Mia, and I don't really even know Ivy and Mia, to be fair.

But I do know this red Solo cup. I wander around the house,

occasionally getting refills as I do, and when I get bored of the hustle and bustle of kids darting in and out of the house—some dripping wet from cannonballs in the heated pool even though it's not a particularly warm September night—I head upstairs. The first few rooms are taken over by people making out, but I'm delighted to find that the third bedroom contains a cat.

I slip inside and poke around. This looks like the parents' bedroom, judging by the en suite bathroom and the very grown-up comforter on the bed. The cat—a chubby black thing—marches right over, eyes bright and tail straight in the air.

I crouch down, but quickly move to sitting when I realize how off my balance is right now. I lean against the bed for support as the little guy—no, girl—climbs into my lap, purring in full effect. My eyes water on their own accord. My mom freaking loved black cats. She told me once that they get adopted last because they're considered bad luck and don't photograph well, like that's any kind of reason. We even used to have one named Void when I was growing up. Mom had gotten him long before she had me; I think she was still in college. He passed away about a year before Mom, and she was gutted. Dad didn't want to get a new one since Mom was already sick by then. He said he didn't want the germs around, but I think he was just scared to be stuck with something she had loved if she died. Having me around was probably bad enough.

He always promised we would get another one as soon as she got better, and, well . . .

I scratch the cat with one hand and take a swig of beer with the other, losing track of time as I enjoy them both. I'm tired from today, my shoulder is killing me, and I'm not even touching the emotional stuff with my mom right now, so what do I have to lose?

"There you are," Ivy says, the light from the hall making me squint as I try to focus on her. "I was looking for you." I don't know her well enough to tell if her voice is wary or nervous, but if I had to guess, I'd say both. Especially judging by how pinched her mouth looks right now, instead of its usual warm, soft . . . Whoops! Not going there. There is not enough beer in the world to make *that* thought okay.

"Here I am," I say, petting the now-sleeping cat in my lap. "Sorry, I just found this little guy in here and couldn't resist." It's half true at least.

"I think Mia and I want to head out. You ready?" she asks, shifting from foot to foot.

I gesture at the cat in my lap. "I am, but I'm not sure she is." That earns a smile from Ivy at least, which makes me feel relieved. I hadn't realized that I was worried she would be mad at me or something for ditching her at this party she so nicely invited me to.

Really, she was offering me a distraction. I'm not stupid. She probably wouldn't have invited me if we didn't share the *dead family member* thing. But still, her smile is nice and warm, and I can't tear my eyes away. Reluctantly, I place the cuddly pile of fuzzy cat onto the plush carpet beside me and follow Ivy out of the room.

"I'm GOING TO drop Mia off first because of her curfew, and then I'll drive you back to the dome to grab your car," she says, and I grunt in affirmation and then snuggle into the back, content to sleep.

At some point, I vaguely hear Mia get out of the car, with some whispered words exchanged, and then things go dark. Ivy starts driving again, and I smile at the steady whir of the tires on asphalt mixing with the comfortable buzz in my head.

But then it stops.

At first, it's fine. I think maybe it's a red light or a stop sign, but when it stretches on too long, I finally push myself up to sitting, wondering if maybe I fell asleep and we're already at the parking lot. But we are definitely not. From what I can tell, we're pulled over on the side of the road, still in the development where we dropped off Mia.

Ivy sees me sit up and sighs. "You're still drunk."

"I'm not really," I say, but her narrowed eyes make me look away. "Fine, a little."

"How many did you have?"

I consider lying, but then remember how she was watching me. Maybe this is a test. "Four," I say. I'm not proud of it, but I did appreciate the happy, cloudlike feeling it gave me. I wish I had it now. She's ruining it.

"Jesus," she says, shaking her head. "I can't let you drive."

"I'll just sleep in my car for a while. It's fine."

"It's a little cold out tonight."

"I'll turn on the heat if I really need it."

"June, no. Then I'm just gonna be stressing out about whether you're safe or whether you're stupid enough to try to drive away as soon as I leave."

"Why do you care?" I ask, and I don't mean it in a defensive way. I'm just genuinely curious.

"If something happened, I wouldn't be able to forgive myself."

I don't bother pointing out that that only covers one scenario. Me sleeping in my car would be fine. What would ever happen at the parking lot of the sports dome? An overzealous player kicks a ball into my car during an early-morning soccer practice? The parking lot is miles away from the baseball field, and the football teams don't practice on Sundays.

"I'll sleep. I promise."

"I'll just drop you at your house. Can you get a ride to your car tomorrow? How far are you from the fields?"

"No," I say, suddenly feeling very sober.

"No?"

"No, the last place I want to go is home to deal with my father. He gets really emotional on days like this. There's a reason I didn't want to go home today."

"Fine, what about that guy's house?"

"What guy?"

"Your boyfriend or whatever," she says, glancing at me in the mirror.

"I don't date boys," I say, and I don't know why I want her to know that so bad, but I do. Add it to the list of things we *definitely* aren't examining any more today.

"Really?" she asks, turning to look at me, and I don't miss the almost happy lilt to her voice.

"Really. I'm definitely one hundred percent super gay." I snort and drop my head back against the seat.

"Same," Ivy says. "Well, bi, technically, but yeah."

"Wow, so we're in the dead family club *and* the pride club together. Go us." I laugh. I meant it to be funny, and in my alcohol-soaked brain it was, but I can see from the way she turns back around and stares straight ahead that she didn't find it that way. "Sorry," I say. "I'm—"

"You're drunk," she says again. "It's fine. Anyway, can I take you to your not-boyfriend's house?" She pulls her car back onto the road.

"He's not home," I say. "His family went to their cabin for the weekend, and he drove up for the night right after our game." I leave out the fact that I could have gone with him if I'd wanted. That I should have, actually. And probably would have if June hadn't invited me to go get wasted and forget instead.

"Okay, somewhere else, then?"

"I'll just sleep in my car," I huff.

"Fine," she says, but then makes a U-turn and starts heading back in the direction of Mia's house. And what? Is she going to pawn me off on her friend? I don't think so.

"Where are you going?" I ask, sitting up again, very annoyed. "I'm not staying at your random friend's house just because you don't trust me to keep my word. That's a little bit insulting, you know."

"I'm not taking you to Mia's," she says. "I'm taking you to mine."

And yep, that shuts me up. I can hardly be annoyed because I'm too intensely curious about what her house is like, what her yard is like, what her bedroom is like, and . . . Yeah, no, I need to sober up fast.

She pulls into a driveway seconds later, long before my sober thoughts can catch up to my drunk excitement, and oh, this is going to be bad.

"Come on," she says, yanking open my door, and I can't tell if she's annoyed or happy. I can't tell anything at all. I can't tell, and I'm wasted, and my mom is dead, and suddenly it's not just my head that's spinning as I walk up to her porch, it's the whole world. And it's maybe not butterflies in my belly anymore, but too many beers and a little bit of car sickness.

And oh.

Oh god.

I'm going to puke.

CHAPTER SEVEN

Ivy

JUNE IS snoring.

She's snoring in a way that most people would probably find very much *not* cute, but I do. And it's not because I have a thing for snoring—that would be weird—it's just because, I don't know, this probably sounds stalkerish, but it's a side of her I haven't ever seen before.

I've met athlete June, and angry June, and sad June, and drunk June, and unfortunately also gets-sick-in-my-front-bushes June, but despite all that, I've never so much as gotten a glimpse of this girl with her guard down. As she lies in my bed right now, softly snoring with the tiniest hint of drool, her guard is so far down it's nonexistent.

Which, of course, is the second that she jolts awake, catching me staring at her. I turn toward my desk, trying to look like I'm doing homework, which I *was*. Or at least I was *trying to* before her cute snores distracted me.

"Were you watching me?" June asks, and I spin around guiltily. She wipes at the corner of her mouth and looks mortified, but I just shrug.

"I was doing homework, but yeah, I just turned around to check on you or whatever," I say, which is almost half true, if you think about it. "You've been asleep awhile."

June sits up fast, wincing and rubbing her arm as she flings back the covers. I gave her the bed last night, or more like she fell into it and passed out, and I didn't feel like moving her, so I slept in the pullout trundle bed. I don't think it had been used since I was little and having multiple people sleep over—Mia and I usually just fall asleep talking in my bed anyway—so it smelled dusty and felt lumpy, but what can you do? A couple fleece blankets and a pillow from the couch and I was tenuously set for the night.

"What time is it?" she asks, pulling her phone out of her pocket. "Holy shit, it's eleven? My dad is gonna kill me! He's texted like fifty times!" She whirls around my room as if it's her own. She doesn't seem to find whatever she's looking for, and raises and drops her arms in exasperation, looking lost.

"Hey, take a breath," I say.

"Where are my keys? Where's my car?"

"It's at the field. I can take you there as soon as you're ready. Do you not remember last night at all?"

"I have the basics. I was upset, and then you took me to a

party where I got super drunk, and then you brought me back here apparently. So thanks for that. Can we go now?" She bends down to grab her hoodie off the floor, hissing as she pulls her shoulder back.

"Are you okay?"

"I'm fine," she grits out, rubbing just below her neck.

"You're not fine," I say, coming up behind her. "May I?" I put my hand on her shoulder and give it a light squeeze, not wanting to go any further without permission.

"I guess, if you really want to," she says, but the way she leans into my palm tells me she's not quite as noncommittal about things as she's pretending to be. I try to ignore how warm her skin feels under my fingers, how soft. This isn't about me or the stupid butterflies I keep getting around her, no matter how much I might be wishing it was.

Not that I have any right to be wishing that at all.

I rub gently at first, up the side of her neck where the muscles are tense and corded, the unmistakable sign of an untended-to injury somewhere. The other muscles are just working over-time to try to make up for it, and the way they're all knotted up tells me it's something that's probably been going on awhile.

"How long has your shoulder been screwed up?" I ask, applying a little more pressure, but backing off when her eyes squeeze shut against the pain.

"It's not."

"It clearly is. You can't even lift up a sweatshirt without winc-ing, let alone put on Biofreeze yourself. What's your deal?"

"I don't see how *my deal* is any of your business."

"Well, maybe because you owe me?"

"For what?" she asks, spinning around to face me. "This second-rate shoulder rub?" Her words might be rude, but they hold no venom, just confusion.

"No, because I was the one who had to hose things off last night after you puked all over my mom's prize rosebushes."

"I didn't."

"You definitely did."

She walks away and sits back on my bed, running a hand through her hair and blowing out a breath. "Gross. Sorry about that," she says, rubbing her own shoulder now.

I shove my hands in my pockets, still warmed from her skin and missing her. Crisis seemingly averted, I force myself to take my place back at my desk.

"Text your dad. Let him know you're safe and you'll be home in a little while."

"A little while? Why not now?" she asks, narrowing her eyes. "I can get an Uber or something if you don't want to drive me."

"An Uber? Here?" I snort, because finding an Uber in this little town is about as likely as winning the lottery. Twice. In a row. I didn't think there were Ubers where she lived either, but maybe things are different on the other side of the highway.

"I could walk." She crosses her arms, even though it's obviously uncomfortable for her to do so.

"I'm not making you walk. It's just, do you really want to go home right now? If you do, I'll drive you. We can go now. But if you'd rather hang out, get bagels, take a breath . . . I'm not kicking you out. And I don't have any games today to deal with, so I'm all yours if you want." My cheeks heat furiously at that. It sounded better in my head, less like offering myself up on a silver platter. "I mean not *all yours*, like not *yours* yours, just like—"

"I know what you meant," she says, cracking a smile and then standing. "Can I borrow some mouthwash or whatever?"

"Yeah, it's in the bathroom."

"I figured." She laughs. "But where *is* the bathroom?"

"Right, yeah, second door on the left when you step out of here."

The second she's gone, I lean back in my chair and blow out a breath. What am I doing? Why am I trying to get her to keep hanging out? Shouldn't I be glad that she wants to leave? She's not my problem, and I shouldn't even be hanging out with her really. I can't afford to entertain the curiosity I'm feeling about her right now.

I look back at my now-empty bed, and I swear I can still picture her in it. Well, that's not good. I jump up and make it, as fast as I can, just to push any thoughts of her from my head. Of course, that only lasts about thirty more seconds, and then she's back, her hair in a pony, smelling minty fresh.

"Thanks," she says, standing awkwardly in the doorway. Apparently, she's not any more comfortable than I am.

"If you want to go back, I—"

"I think it's my rotator cuff," she blurts out.

"Oh," I say, before I can stop myself or think of anything better.

"Yeah, kind of an important thing to not be screwed up when you're a pitcher."

"What do the doctors say?"

She shrugs her good shoulder and looks away.

"Please tell me you've at least gone to the doctor?"

"Of course I've gone. I've gone to the doctor, the physical therapist, the sports medicine center. I just got a cortisone shot in it last month."

I scrunch my forehead. "You're in this much pain after getting that shot? You should still be golden right now."

"You'd think," she says, and pokes her tongue in the side of her cheek, giving me an annoyed look.

"You can't play like this."

"I've been playing like this." She meets my eyes.

"For how long?" I ask. I try to keep my face neutral—the concern I don't really have any right to be feeling off my face—but some of it must get through, because she frowns.

"It's not your problem," she says, looking away.

She's right, I think, and then, like an absolute dumbass, I add, "It could be."

She snaps her head back to look at me. "What's that supposed to mean?"

"Just that I'm here, if you want to talk," I say. "That's all."

And I know that's not all I meant, if the little whir in my belly is any indication, but what June needs right now is a friend, not someone hopelessly crushing on her. I can do that.

She seems to consider my words, then crosses the room to sit beside me. "My mom left me all these notes." My forehead scrunches in confusion at this seeming non sequitur, but June ignores me and continues. "I think she saw it in a movie or something, or maybe there's some guide to dying young with kids I don't know about. It was all the usual, like 'Open this on the day you get your first period or get married or have kids,' that kind of thing."

"Oh, well, that's really sweet," I say, wondering if my brother would have ever wanted to leave me a note and what it would say. Probably *Keep your head up when you have the ball, dumbass.*

"Yeah, but there's also all this pressure, like what if I don't want to get married, or I don't have kids? Do I never open the letters? Do they just sit there, waiting, my mother's dying wishes unfulfilled, highlighting my unrealized potential?"

"I hadn't really thought about it like that," I say, at a loss for anything else.

"She wrote one for my first college game. And my first pro game."

"That's kind of . . . presumptuous."

June shrugs. "My dad was a minor league player. My mom was on a pro softball team for a while. I think it was just a given that I would follow in those footsteps. She always thought I would take after her in softball, but after . . . you know . . . that plan went out the window. I was supposed to switch in seventh grade, but Dad knew baseball, and I still liked baseball, so I just stayed, and it turned into this whole thing where I was the only girl and had to prove myself ten times over, and kids' sports . . . I don't know how it is with officiating, but on the player side it's so competitive, and so much pressure. It's like unbelievable pressure."

"Do you even enjoy it?"

"Of course, I love it," she says, but then doesn't look so sure.

"Okay, well, you're clearly in pain, and you're talking about pressure and letters and competition and how far you've come, et cetera."

"That *et cetera* is my life."

"It doesn't have to be, though. I mean, you don't have to kill yourself for someone who's already dead."

"What the hell is the matter with you?" June yelps, rearing away, and oh shit, I think I pushed too hard. Said what I was really thinking instead of what she wanted to hear. She looks pissed, and I'm tempted to just say forget it and grab my keys, wash my hands of the whole thing, but something stops me. I remember what it was like to be in her shoes—not at this level, but still—and god knows I can relate to the whole *parents putting pressure on you* thing.

"You know, I thought I was going to be some great soccer player when I was little. The next Ronaldo and all that. My parents were paying out the nose for me to take all these private lessons, and my brother would work with me in the yard for hours nonstop."

"And you still sucked?" she asks, which makes me laugh.

"No, I was awesome, actually, thank you very much."

"What happened, then?"

"My brother died." She looks at me, waiting, and I swallow

hard. "I guess I went the other way from you. You want to live up to your mom's expectations; I wanted to do the opposite of anything my brother was a part of. I needed to be away from it. Every goal I got when he wasn't there . . . I realized I wasn't having fun anymore. I didn't love it. Sure, maybe with some therapy I could have pushed through, but why?"

"Because you were good at it, and something outside of your control shouldn't change your whole life course, like my shoulder or your brother dying or anything else that happens."

"What if I told you I was happier as an official than I ever was as a player?"

"I'd say you're full of it."

I laugh, caught off guard. "Well, you'd be wrong, then, because I am. My brother dying made me reframe my whole worldview, and it spun me, I'm not going to lie. But it turns out it led me to my true love."

She leans a little closer, cocking her eyebrows. "Your true love?"

"Officiating," I say, matching her lean until we're so close I can smell the hint of perfume left on her from last night. "It turns out, there are a lot of things you can become passionate about, if you're willing to look. More than just soccer or baseball or letters or other people's expectations. It doesn't have to be all or nothing if you don't want it to be. There's always a middle ground."

"What do you think I should be passionate about instead?" she asks, and it feels like all the air is sucked out of the room.

"I could think of something, maybe," I say, and I swear I can feel my heartbeat all over my body, a constant thrumming that keeps my eyes locked on hers.

"Just maybe?" she asks, her voice low.

I tip my head, parting my lips. "Definitely," I say, barely above a whisper.

Her eyes search mine, just for a second, and then a small smile ghosts over her lips right before she presses them to mine.

CHAPTER EIGHT

June

I KISSED her.

I kissed her. I kissed her. I kissed her.

I kissed her and then *panicked and rushed out*, realizing too late that she still had to drop me at my car. To say the drive back was awkward would be the understatement of the century, even with Ivy putting on music and letting me pretend to doze off.

Now I'm lying on my bed after getting screamed at by my dad for not coming home last night, and I'm a little bit hungover, and yes, I should probably be thinking about the things she said about my letters or the fact that my shoulder is so jacked up or the idea that there can be some middle ground between being the best or nothing. But I'm not.

Because I can't get over the fact that I KISSED HER.

I kissed an umpire. No, not just an umpire. I kissed IVY. And Ivy definitely kissed me back.

In the history of bad ideas, there has probably not been a worse one, except somehow, I'm not even mad at myself about it. It didn't *feel* like the worst idea. Especially not when she was sitting there saying sweet things and talking about being passionate.

Who even says *passionate* anymore?

And oh my god why did I pretend to fall asleep in her car?! What is wrong with me?

I sigh a sigh for the ages, roll over to grab my phone from where I dropped it on my pillow, and check on Javonte's location. I can't process this alone. I need emergency backup, and luckily, it looks like my backup just got home from his family's cabin.

JAVONTE JOGS OUT to my car with a big bucket of baseballs and an even bigger grin. Sure, I may have lured him out here with the promise of an extra practice—important if we want to qualify for the big college scouting tournament coming up—but one look at me and he can tell something's going on.

"Dom's first," he says, eyeing me suspiciously as he buckles in. It's our favorite pizza place. It's also the place where I'm most likely to spill my guts about anything going on in my life. Am I really that predictable, or does he just know me so well that he can tell by a glance? Either way, I've definitely been figured out. No use fighting it, but still, I have to try.

"We can go to the field if you—" I start, but a look from him cuts me right off.

"Dom's. Quit pretending like you don't have something on your mind. Besides, I'm starving anyway."

"How could you tell?" I ask, backing out of his driveway and heading downtown to Dom's International Pizza House and Chicken Wing Buffet.

"Just a hunch," he says, but when I don't say anything else, he adds, "and I tracked your location last night—don't act like you don't do the same—and I know you were definitely not home. Did you find a girl to hook up with or something? Or were you just hiding from your dad? Who do we even know who lives on the other side of the highway?"

I don't want to get into any specifics, not yet, so I shrug, then turn up the stereo. Javonte studies me for a moment and then decides to let it rest. He knows that he'll get it out of me over pizza; he always does.

Dom's sits squarely in the middle of a run-down strip mall that boasts more potholes than parking spaces. It's sandwiched firmly between a Dollar General and a laundromat that's barely ever used—a blink-and-you-miss-it location undeserving of such Italian greatness.

Technically, it's more of a takeout place than anything else. In fact, the members of our team are pretty much their only regular dine-in guests, and we're probably the only ones who ever hit up the wing bar they're so proud of. It's a cute little place, though, even if they only have two little hard plastic booths on one side of the dining area, and one long table with twelve chairs on the other. The rest of the space is taken up by their kitchen, which does an enviable amount of business seeing as they sincerely do have the best pizza in town.

There's no waitstaff to speak of—the only employees being three brothers who inherited it from their father, the original Dom—so we order at the counter and then slide into one of the bright orange booths while we wait.

Everything smells like a mixture of fresh bread and cheese, clearly the most comforting scent on earth. The paper place mat, which doubles as an ad for the laundromat next door, crinkles happily under my fingers. Javonte gives me a few minutes of silence, as if he's soaking up the atmosphere too, before he pounces.

"Well? Whose house was that last night?"

"Stalker," I say, and flick a straw wrapper at him.

"Uh-huh, like you don't? Is that why I had barely walked in the door before you were texting me today?" He sucks his teeth and shakes his head. "Pretending like you wanted to practice when really you just have secrets to spill."

"Hey, we will practice!" I insist, but then sigh. "But okay, yes, I did have an ulterior motive for stalking you right back."

I take a deep breath as he raises his eyebrows and gestures with his hand like "get on with it."

"I spent the night with Ivy last night."

"Who?" he asks, and right, yeah, I need to back up a little.

"You know that new umpire? The girl?"

He narrows his eyes. "The one you said you hated and didn't know what she was doing and should stick to officiating T-ball? That new girl ump?"

I bite my lip and nod. "That would be the one," I say, messing with my straw before taking a sip of my ice water. "That's whose house I was at."

"June."

"Javonte." We both stare at each other until we can't take it. He breaks first. He always breaks first when it comes to gossip.

"You can't just drop that bomb in my lap and then not elaborate. How? What? Why?"

"Who, when, where?" I laugh, and he flicks a napkin at me.

"No, I'm good on that. Those are the only things that you've answered so far: Ivy, last night, her house. Come on. You dragged me out here; tell me the rest of what's going on."

"I don't know what's going on. That's why I texted you! I'm really weirded out right now about everything, but also . . . I'm not. It's just really confusing, and it's a really messed-up time right now with . . . everything."

Javonte reaches over and puts his hand over mine. "I know it's the anniversary weekend with your mom," he says gently. "Are you okay?"

"No, I'm not. Why do they call it an anniversary anyway? I mean I know *why*, but it just makes it sound like some kind of celebration or something. Like an anniversary party or a wedding anniversary. We should call it something else, like,

'Oh, it's your misery day.' Just . . . I hate it," I say, shredding my napkin. "I hate all of it."

Javonte frowns and gives my hand a squeeze. "I do too," he says. We're quiet for a minute before he adds, "Do you want to tell me what happened last night, or do you just want pizza and practice? I'm not gonna push you, and honestly if Ivy got you through last night, I'm not mad about it. I was worried about you as soon as I left. I'm glad you weren't alone."

"Yeah, no, she was actually great last night."

"Okay . . ."

"I don't know! I kept running into her, right? In the locker room or on the field—"

"Probably because you insist on using the officials' room like a total diva, but go on."

"They have a couch, like an actual nice, clean couch in there! And no small children! It doesn't even smell bad."

"Well, if it doesn't even smell bad." He snorts.

"Anyway, you left," I say, but then pause when his frown deepens. "I'm not blaming you; you asked me to come with you and I know that! I'm just saying I chose to stay behind. I was in the locker room, and then she was in the locker room, and we started talking. I was really emotional, one thing led to another, and all I know is that I threw up in her bushes last night and we kissed this morning. There was mouthwash involved in between those two things, though, don't worry."

"Is that some kind of euphemism?"

"What? No. What would that even mean?"

"I don't know all your hip lesbian slang!" he teases. "That's why I'm asking!"

I shake my head but can't help but laugh. "No, I really threw up in the bushes in front of her house, her mother's prize roses apparently."

"I think I'm going to need you to fill in the whole *one thing led to another* part, because I'm not sure how we go from changing in the locker room to vomiting to making out. I knew you had game, June, but—"

Dom Jr. chooses that exact moment to come over with the piping hot metal pan of pizza. He puts it on a little stand on the edge of the table and looks pleased with himself. "Who's got game? June's got game?" he asks, pulling out a stack of napkins from his apron. "Who woulda thought?"

"Thanks a lot," I say, secretly grateful for the reprieve, but he just pretends to duck, like I'm going to throw my plate at him, and then runs back to the kitchen, laughing. There's a reason we all love to come here, and Dom Jr. is a big part of it. He's known me since my T-ball days, as our team's very first sponsor.

He's known me since I still had a mother.

I blink that thought away. She's never far from my mind right now, but I'm done falling apart for the weekend.

"Anyway," I say, steering us back on track as Javonte grabs a couple slices and drops them on our plates. "I kind of lost it for a minute about my mom, and she told me her brother had also passed, so we kind of realized we were in this big, gay, dead family club."

"She's a lesbian?" he asks, wagging his eyebrows. "Go, June."

"She's bi, she said, yeah. After that, she dragged me to this party that her friend Mia was going to."

"Mia Sasaki?"

"Yeah, how do you know her?"

"She's, like, the best soccer player at her school. Who doesn't know her?"

I narrow my eyes. "You have a crush on a soccer player?" I fake shudder.

"You have a crush on an umpire."

I drop my head back. "Ugh, don't remind me."

"I don't have to remind you because that's literally what we're talking about." He grins.

"Why are you smiling like that?" I ask.

"Because I just got you to admit you have an ump crush," he says. "Now spill."

"Clever." I take a bite of my pizza. I can tell by his face I can't drag this out anymore. "Okay, so we went to the party at some basketball player's house—"

"Which basketball player?"

"I don't know! Focus!" I say, and he laughs.

"Sorry, I just used to play rec over there when I was little." He holds his hands up in surrender. "I was just curious if I knew him."

"Anyway," I say, blowing out an exaggerated sigh, even though I'm not really mad. I love how invested he is in this story. "*As I was saying*, I had too much to drink, and she was really nice about it, apparently, even after I puked in her bushes—stop laughing, it's not funny!—and I guess she slept on the gross little trundle bed because I passed out in her actual bed."

"How did you go from making a drunk fool of yourself to her wanting to kiss you?"

"I kissed her, technically."

"Did she kiss you back?"

"Yeah, after a second, but it could have been instinct."

"How long did it last?"

"I don't know!"

"Well, if it was more than a peck on the lips, then I don't think it was like a shocked instinct thing. If you two made out, then—"

"It was more than a peck, but less than making out."

"Hmm, still unlikely to regret it if she still kissed you back even though she saw you puke."

"For all I know I could be here freaking out about having a crush on her while she's out there freaking out about how wrong it was that a player kissed her."

"I doubt it. She invited *you* to the party, right? There must have been something there."

"It was a pity invite, dead family club and all."

"It could have been," he agrees, scarfing down a bit more pizza and then chewing thoughtfully. "But she also could have just given you an *it'll be okay* speech and gotten on with her day. What I can't figure out is why you kissed her, though. As long as I've known you, which has been basically forever, I've never, ever seen you just hop onto someone's lap and go for it."

"I didn't hop onto her lap." I blush furiously. "We were talking, and I . . . I told her about my mom's letters."

Javonte blows out a breath. "Wow, you guys got deep fast."

"Yeah, she's so annoying, right? But so super easy to talk to. It just kind of slipped out. Then she was asking me about my shoulder and saying that like, basically, I shouldn't be putting my mom's hopes about what I would become over what I want from life—"

Javonte tilts his head. "Is that what you're doing?"

"I don't know!" I say, exasperated. "I didn't think so! But I never really thought about there being any other option before she was like, 'It doesn't have to be all or nothing, there are a lot of things in life you can be passionate about, not everything has to be deep,' blah blah blah. Then I was just like . . . I can't really explain it, but the relief was overwhelming."

"Relief?"

"No, that's not the right word. I don't even know what the right word would be. She just seemed to really care and be really interested in what I was feeling. For no reason. Like she's not a coach trying to get on the map or my dad hoping I get a scholarship or my mom writing these letters—"

"Or friends needing you to make their team look good in front of scouts?" he adds, looking down.

"No, that's . . . No. That's not what I meant."

"It's okay. It's true. We do count on you to get us attention. I guess I never really thought about how much pressure that might be putting on you."

"It's fine. I don't see it like that. I just meant like she had no

85

reason to care about me. She actually had a good reason not to, with how I was acting in the games. Plus, you know umps and players aren't supposed to fraternize. She takes officiating freakishly seriously. It's not like the people doing it for a little cash. It's, like, her dream."

Javonte puts down his slice, eyes wide in horror. "Her *dream* is to be an umpire? She *wants* to be screamed at all day and accused of deciding the game or making a bad call and all that other shit? Like, wants to do that . . . for a job?"

"Right? Weird."

"Really damn weird."

"Yeah, Ivy doesn't make *any* sense. I have no idea why she would want anything to do with me, or to even try to help me, and I super don't know why she would risk getting in trouble in order to be nice to me."

"Obviously she likes you back, dumbass."

"You think?" I ask, hopeful, but then shake my head. "No, we can't. I can't. She definitely can't. This is like . . . I'm sure she's regretting it right now."

"Which part?"

"All of it, especially letting me kiss her." I run my hands through my hair and let out a deep breath. "And probably also the part where I panicked and faked falling asleep on the drive back to my car."

"You didn't," he says, breaking into laughter when I give an embarrassed nod.

"Come on, let's finish," I grumble. "I need to go throw balls. I can't—"

"Don't hide behind practice."

"Sitting here guessing and obsessing isn't helping anything. At least the field makes sense."

"Well, there is one way to make this whole thing with Ivy make sense, or at least to figure out what she's thinking."

"Oh yeah?" I say, rolling my eyes. "What's that?"

"Text her."

"Sure, I'll just text her right now, and say, 'Hey, I'm freaking out because you're so nice and so pretty, and I'm a giant emotional mess who needs constant reassurance because I have both mommy and daddy issues.' I'm sure that would go over super well. Thank you, Javonte, for your excellent dating advice."

"I was thinking more like text her and see if she wants to hang out. You'll at least have an idea of where you two stand if you do."

"Like a date?"

"Like a hangout with the potential for more kissing."

"So . . . a date?"

Javonte shakes his head and pushes my phone closer to my hand as he slides out of the booth. "I'm going to go pay. You, text her."

"Javonte . . ."

"Text her," he groans, heading to the counter.

I tap my fingers, staring down at my phone for a minute, and then I pick it up and scroll to her name.

CHAPTER NINE

Ivy

"WHAT IF she kisses me again?"

"Why are you saying that like it's a bad thing?" Mia laughs, her head hanging off the edge of my bed as she upside-down watches me try on outfit after outfit after outfit. "You said, and I quote, 'That girl's lips are phenom.'"

"I just . . . I don't know! It would be bad! I'm an official! She's a player!" I say, holding up two different pink Nike hoodies.

Mia rolls over and points to the one on the left, the slightly darker of the two. "And yet you're still frantically getting ready for the date."

"It didn't say date," I say, pulling the hoodie over my head and throwing the other one back into the closet. "It said 'hang out.'"

"Then I wouldn't worry about kissing. You hang out with me all the time, and we manage to keep our lips to ourselves," she teases.

I sit down in front of the little mirror on top of my desk, glaring at Mia through the reflection. "You know that's different."

"The only reason it would be different is if you admitted that you're *actually* going on a date."

"Why does it matter?!" I ask, exasperated, as I apply my mascara.

"Because if you'd admit that you agreed to go on a date with her, I think you would also realize that that means you probably *do* want her to kiss you again, which would solve this little freak-out pretty nicely, don't you think?"

I sigh, capping my mascara and reaching for my lip gloss. She's got me there. Kind of. "I shouldn't want to want her to kiss me, though. That's the thing."

"I think you're taking this all way too seriously, Ivy."

"It *is* serious! I've wanted to officiate at this level for years, and this is finally my big shot. This could lead to a lot of doors opening. High school, varsity, college. I'm taking my first steps toward chasing down what I want to do, and now I'm getting sidetracked by a pretty girl who is basically untouchable!"

"Calm down, ESPN," she says, and I roll my eyes. She's been calling me that all day because I told my mom I would consider a sports broadcasting major, just to shut her up. She'd texted me almost a dozen times about how she doesn't want me to apply undeclared because it shows a "lack of focus," and I couldn't take it anymore.

Mia told me to just mute her, but last time I did that I was grounded for a month and had to give up all my games—yeah, Mom wouldn't even let me out to work—so no, thank you.

I still have no clue what to major in, but Mom made it clear today that I'd be better off setting my house on fire than saying that out loud ever again. In fact, my parents might even prefer it.

"My job is important," I say quietly as I finish up my makeup, turning to frantically brushing my hair just to ignore Mia's comment and the way it digs under my skin. I just need someone to believe in me, even if it's not Mom and Dad. Mia comes up behind me and puts her hand on my shoulder, her eyes meeting mine in the mirror.

"I didn't mean your job isn't important, and I especially didn't mean that your dreams aren't important. You have a goddamn picture of that woman from the Super Bowl on your wall." She laughs. "I just meant that going out with June tonight isn't that serious. You're in here melting down over picking the right shade of pink hoodie, afraid you're going to lose your job, freaking over whether or not you have any right to want to kiss her—which you clearly do, by the way—when it could all be for nothing."

I turn to look at her properly, my face screwed up in confusion. How could she possibly think this is nothing?

"Don't look at me like that!" She shakes her head. "I'm just saying! Every experience you've ever had with this girl so far has been some big dramatic thing where she's upset or you're upset or you're both upset. It's been a big game or a dead mom or—" I wince when she says that, and she stops, biting her lip like she said too much, and rightly so.

"I shouldn't have told you about that," I say, feeling like I betrayed June by sharing what wasn't mine to share. She didn't tell me that I *couldn't* tell Mia what had her so upset in the locker room, but I wish now that I hadn't. June shared something with me that was personal, and I blabbed it.

"I'm sorry. I didn't mean to sound insensitive or anything," Mia explains. "I only wanted to point out that these are all big, intense things. I mean, shit, she drank so much she passed out at your house. That's kind of a red flag, Ivy. Don't you think you should slow it down to see if the little things line up too? Get to know each other when it doesn't feel so life-and-death. For all you know, you might not even be compatible! You might get to the restaurant and realize she chews with her mouth open or is rude to the waitstaff or snaps her gum or something, and it's game over!" She squeezes my shoulder. "Stop putting expectations on this 'hangout' about kissing and futures and all that other stuff. Just go! Have fun! See if you even *really* like her before you start melting down about what it all means and where it's all going and what's at risk here. Okay? Please?"

"I hear you, but—" Except before I can even finish that sentence, my phone buzzes beside us. It's her. Of course it's her. "She's here."

"Eww, she's not even coming to the door to get you? Not very gentlemanlike." Mia laughs, but I just roll my eyes.

"I don't care about all that," I say, because I've got a date to go on. Or a hangout to be hung. And maybe even a kiss to be kissed.

WE MAKE IT about fifteen minutes in June's car, in complete silence, with my leg bouncing a mile a minute as I mess with the bracelet on my wrist, before she finally says something.

"Do you not want to go?" she asks, her voice snapping my head from the window. "We don't have to."

"Why would you ask that?" I ask, feigning ignorance.

"Because you look like you're on your way to get two hundred root canals or something. We don't have to do this, you know? If you aren't feeling it, I can turn around."

"I . . ." I sigh. "Just, what is this?"

"What's what?"

"What are we doing?"

"We're hanging out? Going to Dave & Buster's to blow all our money on games and bad food?"

"Just hanging out? As friends?" I ask, feeling more disappointed than I expected.

June's grip tightens on the steering wheel as she glances at me through the corner of her eye. "Is that what you want?" she asks, her voice a little quieter and more hesitant than it was a second ago.

And damn, that's a loaded question.

How did me asking *her* what this is turn into *me* having to decide for us both? A big part of me wants to say no, to put myself well and truly out there. I don't think that violates Mia's suggestion to take things slow, more like . . . sets some expectations for us both. Being forward isn't my forte off the field, though, so instead, I turn it around on June, the way she turned it around on me. "What do you want this to be?"

She sighs, and I bet she's thinking the same thing I just was. Quite the conundrum we've created for ourselves. I expect her to dip and dodge again, for us to keep flipping it back on each other for all eternity, just a constant "No, what do you want?" until this date or hangout or whatever it is ends or we both get so frustrated that we can't stand it anymore.

But she surprises me, as usual. It would probably be more surprising if she didn't.

"I wouldn't have kissed you if I wasn't interested in being more than friends," she says, her fingers tapping nervously on the steering wheel as the car falls into silence once again.

I look out the window, if only to hide the intense grin spreading across my face. But I see her shoulders sag out of the corner of my eye and realize quickly that she must have misinterpreted the action. I turn back, letting her see the smile and soaking up the way her whole body seems to relax when I do.

June drops her arm to the armrest, her hand dangling loosely on the shifter, and I don't know if it's meant to be an invitation, but I take it as one anyway. I scoop up her hand with my own and squeeze it as I settle them both back against my leg. Her answering smile is well worth the risk.

"How set are you on Dave & Buster's?" I ask, and her brow furrows.

"Why? You don't like it?"

"No, I do."

"But . . ."

"But it's loud and bright and not super conducive to talking or kissing, so . . ."

She laughs, big and real. "There's a restaurant in the same mall. It's not, like, really romantic or anything, but I think it might be more along the lines of what you're looking for."

"Perfect."

THE RESTAURANT HAS only a short wait, and before we know it, we're blessed with a U-shaped booth in the back corner that allows us to both slide into the center curve. The heat of her leg against mine through the thin fabric of my leggings sends little jolts of butterflies spiraling around my head, and I wonder if she feels it too. I try to focus on the menu, but June is so warm, so soft, so surprisingly open as she talks to me about her day, that I'm fighting the urge to kiss her before the bread basket is even delivered.

We make quick work of ordering drinks—Fanta and Dr Pepper—and even spring for appetizers, getting both when we can't decide between fried pickles and calamari, along with our entrees: Parmesan-crusted chicken for June and a deluxe Impossible burger for me.

And then it's just us again, and the heat of our skin through the little bit of cotton that separates us.

"So," June says, resting her head on her hand and smirking at me.

"So," I say, repeating her.

"I really like you," she blurts out, looking almost embarrassed to be so forward. "If I'm being honest, I've liked you for a little bit."

"Really?" I ask. "I was pretty sure it was the opposite, or like a begrudging friendship at best, until you kissed me."

"You kissed me back, to be clear."

"Sure, but I never hated you, so that's irrelevant."

"I didn't hate you," June says, and I give her a look. "Okay, fine, I *thought* I hated you for a minute, but I was wrong. And Javonte, that's my best friend, the one you thought was my boyfriend"—she shakes her head at that like it's the most ridiculous thing she's ever heard—"he told me to put it all out there with you tonight. He thinks that I have a problem with not going for what I want, and that's something I need to work on. So this is me, declaring that you're what I want. Anyway . . ." She's suddenly a little awkward as she fumbles with her napkin. "Do with that what you will."

"*Do with that what you will?*" I snort. "Very romantic."

"I never said I was romantic. In fact, I try to be the opposite. I've seen how love can destroy someone. After my mom died, my dad was really messed-up. He still kind of is, but I don't want to talk about that right now."

"No, I get it. I'm not saying it's the same thing, but . . ."

"Yeah." She sighs, a little shaky, and I squeeze her hand.

"If we really try this, it's going to be a nightmare," June says, and my stomach clenches, even though I know she's right. "You're an official. I'm a player. It's against the code of conduct on both sides. It's going to be complicated and messy, and we'll have to keep it quiet at least for fall ball, and maybe even this whole year until we graduate and go our separate ways—"

"Wait, we're going to date our entire senior year and then break up?"

"I guess; that's what most people do, right?"

I snort in disbelief. My annoyance turns into a net, scooping up all the butterflies until there are none left. "Let me get this straight. You're asking me out by telling me what an inconvenience it will be for you *and* also pre-choreographing our breakup?" I scoot a little bit away from her, needing some space, and she pointedly looks down at the now-visible leather of the booth between us.

"Be realistic," she says. "It's not like it's not going to be a huge issue for you too. Plus, I'm just being pragmatic. Most people don't, like, end up with their high school sweethearts forever. It's kind of inevitable that we'll have an end date for this whole thing."

I toss my napkin on the table, suddenly regretting the appetizers and how they'll inevitably draw out this dinner longer than it has to be. "Whatever," I mumble, with a huff. "This was a bad idea."

Mia was right to tell me to take things slow, I realize. I'm not compatible with this girl on a fundamental level. I could never be with someone who was ready to put an expiration date on something that hadn't even properly started yet. I rub my eyes and wish we had brought two separate cars, suddenly feeling very claustrophobic.

"No," she says, reaching for me as I slide farther to the edge of the booth. "Wait, please. This is all coming out wrong. It's not a bad idea. It isn't," she insists. "It's just a little more complicated than I'm used to, and I guess I don't really know what to do with that."

"I can't keep up with you, June, not even on a sentence-by-sentence level. One second, you're declaring that you're into me. Then it's going to be a huge problem. Then, in a real backward way, you categorize me as a high school sweetheart, which actually means something! The fact that you think I could potentially be that for you is . . ." I squeeze my eyes shut for a second and take a breath, willing myself to calm down. "Then you cap it off by saying how we're definitely going to break up by the end of the school year. Why would I fight for that? What's even the point, then?"

"The point is that I like you. You challenge me and call me out on my stuff and have been weirdly there for me, even though I've been a jerk to you. I want to do that for you. I don't want it to be one-sided."

"You don't have to date me out of obligation because I'm nice to you. That's what friends do. Maybe we should be friends and save ourselves the trouble of breaking up. We can't break up if we're never together, right?"

"That's not what I'm saying!" June says, clearly getting frustrated. "That's not what I want!"

The waiter brings the appetizers out and sets them in front of us, and I blow out a breath, thanking her. Suddenly our calamari versus fried pickles debate seems so far away and silly. I wish I could rewind us back to that point and then pause, because since we've been talking, everything has gone off the rails. Maybe Mia is right; maybe I just like her because I like swooping in to save the day. Because this side of her—*pragmatic*, she called it—I don't like one bit.

"Look, you're right," I agree, grabbing a pickle in a desperate attempt to make this dinner end as fast as possible. "It would be a pain. We'd have to sneak around. I'd have to try not to ever officiate your games so there's no accusation of impropriety or anything, which would probably make me look bad to this new league. Also, apparently, instead of surviving the year and then living happily ever after with you, we have to break up. So no, I'm not interested in any of that. The payoff isn't worth the price to me."

"You're saying we basically have to agree to get married some-day or we can't see each other." June snorts. "Come on. We're not even eighteen yet."

"I am," I say, realizing just how little we know about each other.

She rolls her eyes. "Fine, you are. I won't be for another four months. Seriously, though, what are the odds that we're, like, soulmates? It happens, sure, but hardly! I'm not going to bank on us being the exception to the rule. I'm not committing to spend forever with someone when I don't even know their birthday!"

"I'm not saying that!" I say, utterly annoyed now. "I'm saying I don't want to preplan our breakup, or be with someone who does that, when we're barely even on our first date. It feels like shit. It takes the fun out of it!"

"Relationships never last!"

"Not with that attitude they don't!"

She laughs at that, but her face falls when she realizes I'm being serious. "I didn't realize you were such a hopeless romantic, Ivy."

"I'm not. Or I wasn't."

"But?"

"But then you kissed me, and suddenly I . . . I don't know! I want to be! And it's the most infuriating thing I've ever experienced."

She huffs out a laugh, biting her lip. "Have you ever considered that maybe you're making me feel like that too?!"

"You sure have a funny way of showing it." I cross my arms, not buying it.

"This is all coming out wrong," she says again, before dropping her head back.

"I don't know. It feels like you're being pretty clear."

"I'm not, though. I'm being a coward." She thumps her head lightly against the booth and then looks over at me. "It's less scary for me to admit that I like you if it comes with an expiration date. It feels less big that way."

"I don't want it to feel less big." I look away, swallowing hard.

"Kiss me, then."

"What?" I ask, snapping my eyes back to hers.

"Kiss me, right now."

"Why?"

"Screw it." She smiles. "You want it big? Let's make it big, then."

"That's not how—"

"If I can't decide how things work, neither can you. I don't know what's going to happen next week, next month, next year, but I know that I haven't been able to get the thought of your lips out of my head since I left your house, or your kindness, however misguided it was, since the day you handed me Biofreeze." She shrugs. "And now you're sitting here, in that lip gloss, with those same very kissable lips, saying you want us to be something, something big, and . . ." She trails off, slipping her arm around me to tug me back against her.

I look away again. This girl is the most confusing, ridiculous person I've ever met, but then her hand is on my chin, gently turning my face to meet hers, and the honesty, the truth, the want in her eyes knocks my breath away.

"Let's be big," she says simply, leaning in even closer. She waits for me to close the distance, to signal I'm okay with it, but when I do, it's clear she's the one in charge. She kisses me, first like an apology, and then like *more*.

When we finally break apart and she reaches for a fried pickle first, instead of her fight-to-the-death beloved calamari, I know for sure that I'm already gone on this girl, and that scares the shit out of me.

CHAPTER TEN

June

IVY LETS me take her on three more dates.

It's weird and wonderful, and somehow sneaking texts to her in between classes becomes the absolute highlight of my day. My favorite thing of all, well, second to baseball, of course. As time goes by, the team catches on that I'm into someone—even if they don't know who—and they tease me mercilessly. Javonte tries to mostly shut them up and does a great job helping me keep it a secret.

Ethan, our shortstop, offers up dating advice any chance he gets. He's been dating the same girl since ninth grade and is a certifiable super-sappy romantic—the kind who sends his girlfriend those candy canes and valentines during all those goofy student council fundraisers. I think he's just excited to have someone else swooning as much as he is.

Not that I'm swooning. I'm just . . . soaking up the fact that I have someone who likes me for me. Who has no expectations beyond the fact that I'll keep showing up for her, and that I'm not allowed to talk about what happens at the end of the school year. Honestly, I'm not sure I want to think about it either right now.

Meanwhile, Casey and Diggy, our third baseman and out-fielder, respectively, only want to know if I've hooked up with her yet. Which is a conversation that Javonte shuts down immediately, even though I really don't need him to. The truth is, there's nothing to report . . . yet. But maybe someday. Eventually. It wouldn't be the worst. Not that I've really thought about it.

Okay, who am I kidding? I've thought about it. I *am* thinking about it. Like, a lot. Which is wild because I've never wanted to do that with anyone before. Still, I don't need Casey and Diggy to know that. They talk about body counts so casually you would think they were talking about the weather. And I get it, sorta.

Our team is a big deal, and while I'm hesitant to say we have groupies . . . we kind of have groupies. At most schools, it's the football or soccer guys who get all the action, but we don't have a football team, and the soccer team mostly keep to themselves. They're very much "head down, GPA up," and all that. It's the baseball team, specifically those of us who also play on this premier club team, who have all the swagger.

Me not having ever gone all the way with someone isn't for lack of opportunity. There are plenty of girls in tall Nike socks hanging around the fences wanting to talk to me after games. Especially being the only girl baseball player, not just on the team but also in the area, I tend to stand out a lot more, and I'm not exactly quiet that my preference solely lies with girls. It's just that none of them really caught my eye before. At least not enough to make me want to put down the glove and step off the field long enough to make something happen.

Which is why I think I'm feeling a little upside down over the idea that I might want something serious with Ivy. Something *really* serious if I'm being honest with myself. She told me not to plan for our breakup, but I wonder how she'd feel about me planning for our forever.

God, that's cheesy. Like, so cheese. Like, ridiculous quantities of cheese. Who am I?

The best part of all of this is that I'm so distracted by how I'm feeling about Ivy, I've barely registered how my body's feeling lately. The constant aches in my shoulder and elbow fade to the background every time my phone vibrates with a new text from her. That girl's better than cortisone and ibuprofen combined.

It's perfect, almost too perfect.

Which is, of course, why, when I walk into my house after a particularly long practice, I shouldn't be surprised to see my dad angry and red-faced at the dining room table.

Good things never last for me.

"What's up?" I ask cautiously as I set my bag on one of the chairs.

I run through my head, trying to think of what I could have done to piss him off. I took the trash out last night, and I definitely unloaded the dishwasher. Yeah, I took the twenty out of the drawer in the kitchen to surprise Ivy with lunch and

Starbucks, but it's specifically there for me to take when I need cash! And taking my girlfriend—oh Jesus, is that what she is now?—on a date is definitely a *need* these days, so it can't be that.

Dad puts his arms behind his head and leans back in his chair. "There something you want to tell me, girl?" he asks.

Girl. I *hate* when he calls me *girl.* He only uses it when he's mad. Some people use it as a term of affection, but not Clint Smith.

"I don't think so?" I say, the words coming out slowly, like the question they really are. "About what?"

"I hear you're hanging around with some girl on a regular basis."

I crinkle my forehead. "Yeah, but I told you I was when I asked to borrow your car to take her out, because it's nicer. You said yes."

"I didn't just say yes. What else did I say?"

I roll my eyes. "You said yes, but don't get distracted." I sigh. "And I'm not. I'm keeping up with my practices and my schoolwork, not that you even care about that—"

"Homework's not gonna get you into college and pay for you to stay there."

"I'm pretty sure that's the opposite of what most parents say."

"Most parents don't have a baseball prodigy living under their roof," he says, fighting a smile even though he's clearly still mad about something.

I hate how happy it makes me to hear him say that. The way

it makes me preen a little, even though I'm tired, to know that he thinks of me as the best, as a prodigy even. It's just nice to be seen like that. To be seen at all, really.

"Mickey texted me earlier."

Suddenly, that good preening feeling dissipates, and I know exactly where this is going. Mickey is my private coach, a stout Latino man in his forties who actually did play pro for a couple seasons. He's super sought-after in the area, and we have to drive almost ninety minutes—sometimes more, depending on traffic—just to get some time with him.

Which is probably why Dad is so pissed that I rescheduled this week's lesson so I could take Ivy to see some band she was excited about. They played for one night only, a random Wednesday pit stop at a dive bar that doesn't check IDs, on their way back home to the city. It was worth it to see her there, singing and dancing. To hold her hand and spin her around and kiss her. Not being able to kiss her whenever I want makes those stolen kisses about a thousand times sweeter. It makes up for all the sneaking around we have to do at the fields. Like we aren't *really* doing something against the rules, but protecting something special instead.

"I didn't cancel. I just rescheduled, and there wasn't a late fee. He told me it was no problem and to have fun."

"Mickey's not your father. That's not his call. You didn't tell me."

"Are you upset because I moved the schedule around or because you didn't know where I was? Because I have to say that you usually give me a pretty solid free rein, so I don't really get it."

"That's because up until now, the only places you were ever at were school or the ball field or getting dinner with Javonte. There's a major tournament coming up in a few weeks, and you guys need to qualify. Every college coach under the sun is going to be there, and a lot of them are hoping you'll be there too. Have you even checked your recruitment emails? I logged in last night just to see, and you have a ton of responses to write. Get your head in the game, June. You can't coast in the ninth inning; we've worked too hard for this."

"Wow, Dad. It's not like I'm blowing off baseball for real. I've still been practicing constantly. Javonte and I go straight after school and get to work with most of the team. Ask Coach! And I should have never given you the password to my email, because I *am* keeping up with it—at least the ones from the schools I might actually accept an offer from if they send it. Half of those coaches are trying to get me to switch to softball!"

"Dammit, June, you should be replying to any coach that wants to talk to you. It's ridiculous. I don't have a ton of money sitting in the bank, and there's nothing left from the life insurance. You need those coaches to send some money your way."

I'm tempted to point out that maybe he should have saved some of the insurance money for college instead of using it to pay for so many damn private lessons, but I don't. Because the truth is, most of the time, I'm glad he didn't. I'm glad that I had the best opportunities, the best coaches, the best clubs, the best everything. I used to feel so lucky. Sometimes I think I would do anything to get back to that feeling.

"I just don't want you to get distracted, the way—"

"The way Mom did?" I finish for him. "Mom didn't get distracted; she got married. To you, someone she super loved. She could have done worse," I say, going to put my arm around him.

"Not by much," he says, the familiar refrain making some of my frustration with him drain out of me onto the floor.

I know he's just worried, and I know he's still hurting, just in a different way than me.

I lost my mother. He lost his soulmate. It's hard to console each other when we're lost in our own pain. Grief hits everyone differently, and in our family, it turned into obsessive practicing and worrying about the future. In others, who knows? Maybe they hug it out.

I think I look too much like my mom to bring him any comfort, and he's too bitter about losing his happily-ever-after to be anything right now but the best coach I've ever had.

Dad reaches up to give me a backward hug. "I just don't want you to lose sight of what matters when we're so close to the finish line," he says.

"I won't. I'm not," I tell him, letting myself relax against him. Sometimes when I think about how he's the only parent I have, I can't breathe. Such a heavy burden on us both. The only parent. The only child. I hate it.

"Okay, June," he says, patting my arm where it's still circled around him. And I'm too relieved to be June again, instead of *girl*, to worry about whether or not he's right.

IVY'S HEARTBEAT IS a steady thump beneath my ear, her breathing a comforting whoosh that gently pulls me up and down. I'm curled against her, her arms wrapped around me as we lie under the stars in the back of her dad's pickup truck.

When she asked me if I wanted to go to Stars Hollow View, I thought she was kidding. It's equal parts party spot and hookup spot when it's warm out, and while I've been thinking about how far I want this to go, I haven't made up my mind.

But she was so cute, all scandalized at my concern, promising she really just wanted to show me the constellations, scout's honor. And she meant it too, wrapping us up in two giant comforters and pointing to every celestial body she could see. She brought pillows and snacks too, and if I thought maybe this was all a trick to get me to make out with her, or more, that thought was gone the second she started waxing philosophical about how we could still kind of see Hercules, and definitely Saturn, and maybe even the head of Taurus if it wasn't too cloudy up there tonight—but that the Dipper had moved on, or rather we had, orbiting around on this speck of dust as we are. I wonder if she's going to study astronomy in college, but I know that question is off-limits.

We made a new rule; she doesn't ask about my shoulder, and I don't ask her about college—or rather I don't ask her about the pressure her parents are putting on her. I know it eats at her, though, the way her parents don't believe in her, how they want her to live for her brother who never got the chance. If I start thinking about that too hard, it leads me right back to thinking about my mom and her letters, and no, thank you, I'm good on that.

Ivy does seem to notice I'm a little off tonight, though, no matter how much I'm trying to hide it. Not wanting her to think it has anything to do with this epic date she planned for us, I lean up on my good arm and study her face. "Sorry, my dad is kind of upset at me. It's got me in my head a little."

"You want to talk about it?" She glances at me and then goes back to looking off at the stars, like she knows it's easier for me to be honest when she's not looking.

"Not really," I say. "I think it's mostly fine now. He just didn't know what to expect with . . . us."

She smiles, her eyes drifting shut in satisfaction. "He knows about us?"

"Yeah. Well, he knows I'm seeing someone and that they really matter to me."

"They do?" She smirks, even though she has to already know that.

"Just a little," I tease, and she tosses one of the blankets over my head in retaliation. I pull it off, laughing. "Fine, maybe *more* than a little," I admit.

"So what's got him upset, then?"

My laughter dies in my throat as I look down. "He's worried that you're a distraction."

"Am I?" she asks, pushing up to her elbows to look at me thoughtfully.

"No," I say, settling in beside her and pulling her down against me. "Can we not have this conversation right now? I just want to be happy tonight, with you, here."

"Sure," Ivy says, like that's the easiest thing in the world. And maybe, I realize, it *is* easy. Things are always so easy with her. It's nice and strange, and sometimes a little bit hard to trust, or frustrating to keep secret, but it's never hard. Being with her is never hard. It's just . . . good.

I smile down at her, tipping my head so I can sort of see her face.

"What should we talk about, then?" she asks hesitantly, when the silence has stretched out too long.

"Anything," I say, and then add, "You, talk about you. Tell me what you're thinking about when you stare up at those stars."

"I'm making wishes."

"Yeah?" I ask, listening to the steady beat of her heart. I like that someone so solid can believe in wishes. It makes me want to too. "What did you wish for?"

"I can't tell you. It's bad luck." She sighs.

"Give me a hint."

"The future."

"What about the future?" I ask, following her gaze up to the stars over our heads.

Ivy seems to consider her answer for a minute. "You already know that I want to eventually make it all the way up to the NFL. Be the second woman to take the job, or hopefully not. Hopefully a lot of other women get to before me, but I want to be one of them, eventually, so I guess it doesn't hurt to tell you that I was wishing for things along those lines."

"I still think that's such a cool goal," I say, echoing what I said the first time she ever told me.

"Yeah, I feel like I'm finally getting somewhere with it too, now that I'm getting higher-level games. If only my mom wasn't riding me so hard to figure out where to apply to college and what I want to go for, maybe I'd be able to enjoy it more."

"Yeah?" I say, testing the waters. If she's bringing it up now, she must have had another fight with her mom over it. It sounds like neither of us had the best time at home today.

"My mom is really hitting me hard about this. She joined all these *paying for college* groups that I was hoping she would never find. Lately she's been on me constantly about, like, early-action deadlines and essays. You know how I panicked and picked a random major the other day just to shut her up? She's been nonstop sending me information ever since about every school that has it. I finally told her today that I don't want to go for sports broadcasting, and she made me sit down with her and brainstorm other potential career ideas. Sammy was bored out of his mind, and she didn't even notice. It's like all her energy is focused on me and this stupid college application cycle! Every dinner turns into a war zone, and Sammy just has to listen to us fighting all the time. It's not how it's supposed to be! It's not how things were for me when I was little. It's such a fucking raw deal, and I—"

"Why don't you tell your mom to back off?"

"Oh, like I'm sure you told your dad tonight?"

I huff out a breath; she's got me there.

"Exactly, and I mean, I know her heart is in the right place. If

I really wanted to go into sports medicine or sports marketing and management or anything else we discussed tonight as my potential fallback, I do need to start to eventually get serious about applying. I just wish it didn't feel like she was constantly tightening a vise around my head every time she adds something to my to-do list. I'd love to go to community college, and still work for Harry, and see what happens with the ref jobs . . . but sometimes she gets in my head. I start to freak that maybe I'm making a mistake by not taking this college-major thing really seriously."

I prop myself up on my elbow, scrunching my forehead. "Why would you do that, though? If you know you want to be a ref, why would you plan for failure?"

"Says the person who planned our breakup on our first date," Ivy says, and I roll my eyes.

"That's different!"

"How?"

"Because people are messy, unpredictable—"

"So are the type of careers you and I are after."

"Yeah, but if you work hard, and you believe it, and it's what you really want, you'll be fine."

Ivy laughs at me. "Come on, June. You know working in the entertainment industry isn't exactly guaranteed. It's not a meritocracy."

I bristle at the way she refers to my athletic career as being part of the "entertainment industry." It's not like I'm hoping to be an actor or something. I want to play ball, and I have the skills, practice, and work ethic to get there. I'd imagine Ivy could say the same thing about officiating.

"But it's your dream," I say, baffled that she could even have a plan B, let alone one that included years of extra schooling. Being in sports medicine or managing a team or whatever it is she wants to do would be like . . . dream adjacent. It would be ridiculous, I bet. Painful. Horrible.

She laughs at my confusion and rolls me over, carefully tucking herself behind me, making me the little spoon as she trails a hand up and down my side. "It's not always black and white, June," she says softly. "People can have more than one dream. If you still don't realize that, you should consider coming off that diamond a little more."

I sigh, catching her hand and pulling it up to place a gentle kiss on her knuckle as I turn her words over in my head. If my dad ever heard her say that, she would probably be permanently banned from our house. Still, I can't shake that a little tiny piece of me, shoved way down low, is left wondering if maybe there's some truth to what she's saying. I'm chasing this future so hard, I've never stopped to wonder what will happen if I actually catch it.

Or what will happen if I don't.

CHAPTER ELEVEN

Ivy

WE TRY to be subtle. We really do, but somehow, June and I both end up in line at the snack bar at the same time.

Our schedules have been so opposite lately, I've barely seen her all week. But I got called in at the last second to cover a soccer game for a ref who was sick, and she had back-to-back home games this afternoon. The way her eyes widen in surprise and then flick straight to my lips as she smiles makes it hard to stay in line, casually buying Gatorade, like my heart isn't beating in double time. I want to go tackle her in a hug. I want to press those lips she keeps looking at all along her neck, exactly where she likes it. But I can't. I know I can't.

"Hey," I say, trying to be cool as the line moves forward.

"Hey, yourself," she says, sliding in line behind me, and then quietly adds, "You look good in stripes." She stands a little too close to me, and it takes all my willpower not to lean back into her. I bite the inside of my cheek, trying to swallow my smile.

Be cool, Ivy, I tell myself. *You're at work.*

The person in front of me pays, and I go to order, but my foot catches. June's standing on the back of my sneaker—on purpose, no doubt—and my heel pops out. I spin around laughing, forgetting for a second where we are and how bad it would be to acknowledge each other, soaking up the satisfied smirk on her lips.

My face falls when I see the person walking up behind her. Aiden takes his place in line, arching an eyebrow, and panic slices through me. Did he notice? Did he see how casually comfortable June and I are together, when we're supposed to still hate each other? Did he see how happy I was to be near her or how desperate I was to touch her?

"Asshole," I snap, sounding like I mean it. The happiness on June's face gives way to confusion, and I hate that I did that. I spin back around and step to the counter, ordering my Gatorade as I fix my shoe and hoping she realizes what's going on.

Hurt flashes across June's face as I pay and turn to leave. She opens her mouth to say something—apologize, maybe—but I cut her off. "Aiden, I need to talk to you."

June turns her head just slightly as she steps up to the counter, and I see a little glimmer of understanding in her eyes as she does. At least I hope I did. Either way, I'm going to apologize for the way I just spoke to her as soon as we're alone.

"About what?" he asks, crossing his arms.

"The schedule for next week. I want to switch some things around."

"Like how?" he asks, just as June pushes past us and heads to the parking lot, flashing an annoyed look at Aiden as she does. "What's your problem?" he shouts after her, but she doesn't even look back. Good. "Jesus," Aiden grumbles. "Why can't she just play softball like every other girl? Instead, she's gotta steal some poor guy's spot and act like a bitch while she's doing it."

It takes every tiny bit of self-restraint for me not to flip out on him. I clench my fists so tight my nails dig in, and force myself to take a deep breath. Jumping to her defense would be suspicious. Plus, I need a favor, sort of, so all I can do is mumble out a weak "Girls can play baseball too" as he steps forward and orders his curly fries.

He leans against the counter facing me as he waits for them to be reheated. "But why would they want to?"

I open my mouth to protest, but then shut it again. It's better if he thinks I hate her too. "Yeah, about that, actually," I say, swallowing down the sick feeling of betrayal that comes with what I'm about to ask next, even if June and I *did* discuss it. "I can't work with that girl."

Aiden raises his eyebrows. "Why not?"

"If I have to put up with her attitude for another game, I'm gonna flip out. Can you just do me a solid and trade with me?"

Aiden smirks. "What, does she make you a little hot, Ivy?" he asks, and I'm not sure how to take it, so I double down.

"Honestly? She annoys the shit out of me, and I don't want to be around her if I can help it."

"What's in it for me?" he asks as the cashier hands him his fries. "I don't exactly enjoy her company either, you know."

"What do you want?" I ask begrudgingly.

He sits down at one of the high-top tables, narrowing his eyes. "Demonstrated interest."

"What?"

"Demonstrated interest, for the schools I like. They want to see that I'm actually invested. You know, log in with my email, click on virtual tours, shit like that. I have to do everything I can to set myself apart with the way the deck is stacked."

I scrunch up my face, not sure I'm following any of this. "And you want me to . . ."

"Click around for me. I've got a bunch of essays left to write, but I know you suck at school. I can't ask you to draft or proofread for me, obviously. So you can do the grunt work."

"You just want me to click around, pretending to be you?"

"Yeah, it would save me tons of time." He shoves a fry into his mouth, chewing thoughtfully. "Unless you don't want to trade that bad. Then I guess I can find someone else—"

"I'll do it," I say. "Can you take my Saturday games this week?" And god, why can't I escape this college application shit for one fucking second?

"Absolutely, I can." He grins. "I'll text you my logins tonight."

"WAIT, SO YOU'RE not working this weekend at all?" Mia asks the next day, her eyebrows raised in confusion.

"I was scheduled for June's doubleheader Saturday, but I gave it to Aiden."

"And he didn't give up a game for you to do?"

"Nah, he didn't really have anything," I lie.

The truth is, he did, but didn't want to give it up. At least not until he was sure I was upholding my end of the bargain. Which I am. Last night, my mom was over the moon to see me registering for virtual visits and Q&As at several top-twenty colleges. Thankfully, she didn't notice that the email I logged in with wasn't my own.

Mia frowns and stares down at her bag of chips. It's fifth period, which we both have free by design. As seniors we're allowed to spend it in the cafeteria, library, or courtyard—we just can't leave campus or get into any trouble, or they'll stick us right back into a monitored study hall like all the underclassmen. I do *not* miss having to sit silently with nothing but a notebook for company. They don't even allow phones. The monitors don't care if you're eighteen; *no phones in an active class* is school policy, and sadly, monitored study halls count.

"Is Harry still going to put you in the showcase if you keep ditching games?" Mia asks, reaching for more chips. "Or will you finally tell him about June and ask him to stop scheduling you to—"

"Shhh," I hiss out, even though June doesn't even go to this school. Odds are, no one around here would even know who she is, but the baseball kids probably do. And seeing as how I don't know anyone on our sucky team here—like I said, baseball *was* my least favorite sport—I wouldn't recognize them if they were at the next table over. "No," I add. "Harry definitely doesn't know about June, and we need to keep it like that."

"Then how is he letting you off from officiating any of her games? He has to have noticed your dodging."

"He doesn't care. He says as long as I have coverage it's fine. I told him I couldn't do Saturday because I had a college visit, but I could do Sunday. He's giving me a few soccer games so I can get in some hours. And it's not like Aiden isn't *ever* going to give me his games. Just not . . . yet."

"Are those real soccer games or kiddie games that you're getting in the meantime?"

"U10," I say, and when she rolls her eyes, I find myself growing frustrated. "What?"

She sighs. "You already put in your time with those little kids, and you were finally getting high school games. This college showcase was like your sole obsessive focus until you met June, and now it's like she's your whole focus. It's wild. No, it's messed-up, if I'm being honest, not wild. You're so close to shoving your toe in that door. I don't want you to blow it because you like kissing someone."

"You were the one who told me to go for it!"

"Technically, I told you to hang out with her and see if the little things lined up—which was my way of saying take it slow, not turn into a black hole with a mission to absorb every second you can with her."

"Come on. When you dated Benji, I barely heard from you for like two months, so don't even."

"Yeah, but I was *also* in the thick of it with recruiting visits and soccer practice! I barely had a second for Benji, which is why, if you remember, we broke up. I'd like to think I'm in a better place now," she says, fanning her Syracuse University hoodie, the one she got when she verbally committed last month.

"Fine, maybe you were a little bit busy," I say. "But then you should understand!"

"I was busy crushing my goals *while* making out with a hot football player. Your goals—which, might I remind you, are important *breaking boundaries and smashing through glass ceilings and rah-rah womanhood* shit—seem to be falling to the wayside. Giving up games? Really? Throwing away what could be your big break? And it's only been, what, three weeks, a month, since you started seeing her? It doesn't come off like you're taking this as seriously as I know you want to be."

I hate that she's right, and I hate even more that I don't really care. I like being with June. I like being around her. I like making her laugh, and I love how she makes me laugh. Yeah, it's probably just swoony brain chemicals and a dash of endorphins or whatever—what is love but a chemical cocktail designed to make you obsessed? But still.

"I'm just having fun, but I hear you," I finally say.

Mia narrows her eyes like she doesn't quite believe me. "Look, I like June. I think she's a little bit of a mess, but she seems very sweet, and I love how happy she seems to be making you. I just don't want you to get lost in all of this."

"I won't, I promise," I say, nudging her with my shoulder. "Now, can we finish these chips and get out to the courtyard? It's sunny for once, and I want to soak it up."

MIA'S WORDS ARE still heavy in my head when I meet June at her house after she's done with practice. She's tired and sore as usual, and I love the way she melts under my palms as I massage her back and shoulders.

Her dad reluctantly invites me to stay for dinner, and June looks a little nervous when I agree. I've been hanging at her house more and more—it just makes sense since Aiden would be the most likely person to report us, and he lives near me. Her house should be a safe zone for all of this, whatever this is.

Plus, my parents are a lot, and I don't just mean on the college application front. I think they get more excited than even I do when I'm dating someone, even if I've followed June's lead and not exactly explained who she is or how I know her. All they know is that she slept over that night after the party, and now we're together. Honestly, I don't think they care who I date; they just see it as another way to get me off the field. Another potential ally on their quest to get me to apply to a top-tier college. In fact, that was the only question Mom even asked. "And where is she applying?" I lied and said Princeton just to shut her up.

They're too much sometimes. It's like, after Nicky died, they put the full force of parenting two kids solely into me. It's a heavy weight sometimes, and other times it's awesome. It's gotten a little bit better since Sammy was born a couple years ago, his chubby cheeks and belly laughs winning me over instantly and soothing any fears I had of feeling like he was a replacement brother, but still, I'm not about to expect June to deal with that in the middle of her most important ball season. They will have plenty of time to get to know each other over the winter, when the fields are snowed in and June's training schedule is cut in half.

I hope it will be halved anyway.

This shoulder, this elbow of hers? It stresses me out, even though I try not to let it show. Her ache turned to sharp pain about a week ago, and my stomach dropped when she explained that her doctor said she wasn't eligible for another cortisone shot for a few months since she's had so many. She tried to hide it from me, but I knew. It was obvious. Her dad and Javonte have to know too, and I don't understand why they aren't doing anything to help her.

As I sit here at the table—waiting for June's dad to pass me the salad after dishing some out onto his plate—it's taking all my willpower not to mention it, not to question it, really. But I couldn't. I wouldn't do that to June. I never want to be the person who adds to her troubles; I want to be the safe one, the one who helps make them all better.

June's dad—"Call me Clint, not Mr. Smith," he says—passes me the salad and the tongs and sets to work eating with a little grunt that I take to mean, "Well, go on, then."

June smiles at me as I scoop my salad, and then hers, and slide the bowl back to the middle of the table. Clint has a frozen pizza cooking up in the oven right now, the room just starting to fill with the familiar comforting scent of dough and cheese, and I shift in my seat.

"So how did you two meet?" Clint asks. His tone is warm, but the words seem loaded, pointed even.

I look to June, not sure what she told him about me, about us. She squeezes my hand under the table. "I told you, Dad. She works at the field."

Clint chews thoughtfully, pointing at me with his fork as he does. "Right, right, snack bar, Junie said?"

I open my mouth to agree, assuming this is the lie she's going with and just feeling grateful that he didn't recognize me without my ump gear—thank god for face masks behind the plate—but June cuts me off. "Field maintenance, Dad, remember?" she says, giving me a look that says maybe we should have discussed this before dinner.

"Right," he says slowly. Clearly, Clint isn't as happy to swallow the lie as June thought. I don't think he's buying anything we're saying right now, and I'm also not sure that wasn't just a trap I almost walked into. "Do you play a sport, Ivy?"

"I used to, but no, not anymore. I'm more . . . sports adjacent," I say, trying to figure out how to answer him truthfully without actually being truthful. "June says you used to play in the minors. That must have been awesome."

He smiles at me, and it's equal parts nice and I-know-what-you're-doing, but he must decide to go with it because he immediately launches into a heap of stories about just how good the good old days were, back when he used to play on a farm team for the Astros.

I listen with rapt attention, first because they actually are really funny and interesting stories, but also because I can tell that he appreciates it. I wonder how long it's been since he's had an excuse to share them. Some of them seem very well practiced, the timing of his antics just right, and I bet June's mom used to humor him and listen to them all the time. I can almost picture them all laughing around the dinner table. I wonder if this is the first time he's had to dust them off for someone since she passed.

Beside me, June looks a little bored, clearly not having the same experience I am. She looks grateful when the buzzer for the pizza goes off and her dad jumps up, worried that it might burn.

"You good?" she asks quietly so he can't hear.

"Yeah, your dad's really nice. I like hearing his stories."

She looks incredulous. "No, you don't."

"I do!"

"Mm-hmm. If you're trying to win brownie points, I have to warn you, it probably won't work," she teases. "I don't know that this is a getting-to-know-you-better dinner so much as it's a fact-finding mission."

Fact-finding?

Before I can ask her a follow-up question, her dad is back, placing the pizza stone on a little stand and slicing it up. It's all very official looking, and I can't help but notice that both the pizza stone and the floral oven mitts are monogrammed with what I'm assuming are her mom's initials. In a weird way, it makes me miss June's mom. Well, not *miss*, but it makes me wish I had a chance to meet her. I wonder what the dinner would be like if she were still here, what June would be like if she were still here.

I know I would be different if Nicky were still around. I might even still be playing soccer, having no idea that my real life was on the other side of the game. Losing my brother was like a hot knife through my heart, the kind of pain you never heal from. The kind you wish you never felt. I needed my mother more than anyone to get me through it, to hold my hand until I figured out how to exist in a world where Nicky didn't. And she did, bravely. Not letting herself fall apart until she was sure Dad and I were on our way to putting ourselves back together.

As much as I hate what Mom and I have become to each other, I know I would've been lost without her back then. I just wish that—

"You okay?" Clint asks, and I nod, blinking fast at my watering eyes, my vision still snagged on those monograms.

"Sorry, I just got lost in my head for a minute." June looks at me, clearly worried. I smile to reassure her. "I don't know why—something made me think of Nicky, and—"

"Oh," June says, and her dad's face falls just enough to let me know that she must have told him about my brother already, about just how much June and I have in common. I can't decide if that makes me happy or sad. Happy, I think, at first, because they should know about him. Everyone should. But I hate the idea that she might have warned her dad about it, like to stay away from certain topics or something.

"Pizza?" he says, a little too cheerfully, and I accept, ready for this meal to be over.

"I ACTUALLY THINK he might like you," June says, while we're cleaning the kitchen. Her dad has gone off to watch baseball in the basement with a bottle of Diet Coke to relax a little before his shift tonight. Apparently, her mom had a rule that whoever

125

cooks doesn't clean, a tradition that she and her father have carried on, even when there are guests. I don't know if that bagged salad and frozen pizza really count as cooking, but when in Rome.

I glance at June. "You think so?"

"Yeah." She nods. "Super-ideal outcome considering he definitely went into this not wanting to."

"He didn't want to like me?!" I pout, and she laughs and flicks some soapsuds at me.

"He's been freaking out that you're distracting me," she says, and my stomach free-falls to the floor. "I think you won him over tonight, though."

"Mia said something similar about you," I blurt out, even though I probably shouldn't have. The idea that *I'm* the distraction in this scenario has my head spinning a little and my control over my mouth slipping, apparently.

"Oh," she says, going more serious as she plunges another plate into the sink. "Do you feel like that?"

"Do you?" I counter.

"No," she says simply, meeting my eyes.

"Me neither," I say, but I can't help but feel maybe that's not one hundred percent true.

For either of us.

CHAPTER TWELVE

June

IVY TEXTS me during my lunch period that she has news and to meet her at her house after practice.

I beg her to tell me what it is, but she refuses, only teasing that it's good news and she's going to be on standby with pizza from Dom's at 7:00 p.m., which she knows is the soonest I possibly can get away.

Thursdays are my longest days, double practice, back-to-back. First, I have our regular team practice from 3:30 to 5:30—I basically rush straight from last period down to the ball field. Then I only have a fifteen-minute break before my local private coach, Hank, appears. He works me out from 5:45 to 7:00 p.m. solo. He loves to say it's easier because I'm already warmed up from practice, but really it's just more exhausting.

I'm tempted to reschedule his lesson like I did with Mickey, but then I remember how upset my dad got over that, and I decide that I had better not. The whole *better to ask forgiveness than permission* thing doesn't really work with my father. I pushed the limits by rescheduling a lesson once; I can't imagine what would happen if I tried to do it again.

Resigned that I'm not going to get to see Ivy any sooner than tonight, the day creeps by at a glacial pace. I'm not even sure what the teachers were talking about today, and that distraction carries over into practice. My pitches are off, my coaches are shouting at me, my teammates are annoyed, but I'm so fixated on what she wants to tell me.

I let myself daydream a little, ridiculous stuff like maybe she's getting called up to officiate for the majors or got a full ride at one of the colleges her mom is always nagging her to apply to. Maybe her family hit the lottery and they're putting in a pool.

But then my head starts drifting to negative places, like maybe she wants to take a break, or see other people, or end things for good because she's sick of all the sneaking around. I try to shake those thoughts off, though. She said it was good news, and besides, I don't think she would dump me over pizza. Like, pizza from Dom's doesn't sound like dumping food.

I throw another pitch, and it's perfect, but it tweaks my shoulder just enough to remind me the pain is still there, lurking right under all the ice and ibuprofen and cortisone. My coach says, "Finally," and, "More of that," and I push through the pain.

I try to distract myself by falling down a rabbit hole of deciding what exactly *would* constitute a good dumping food. I decide on sushi, for no real reason other than this one time, Javonte got dumped at a Japanese restaurant. His ex said she wanted to do something nice for him to lessen the blow of their breakup, but all it did was make him hate sushi, his formerly favorite food.

No more leftover peanut avocado rolls for me. Thanks a lot, Kiana.

Oh no, I hope that's not what Ivy's doing.

My next pitch is a ball that goes wide, and my coach literally throws his hat in the dirt and asks me, and I quote, "What the hell is the matter with you today?"

Okay, no more daydreaming. I need to focus.

My next three pitches are perfect, even if they make my shoulder scream. I lean into the pain, letting it motivate and guide me. It stems from overuse, right? So if I'm feeling it this much, I must be doing something right, just like I've done everything right a million times before. The more my shoulder burns, the happier my coach seems.

I'm relieved when practice ends, and I rush into the dugout to greedily gulp down half the contents of the oversized water bottle Ivy surprised me with the other day. At least I can have this at the field with me, even if I can't have her.

Ethan jogs up next to me and studies my face. "You okay?" he asks, in a tone I usually only get from Javonte and his parents.

I look at him, confused. "Yeah . . ." I say slowly, and he raises his eyebrows.

"You know, if you ever need a break or to talk or anything, we're all here for you, right?"

Before I can answer, he's getting called away by Coach to answer for some mistake or another, and the moment is ruined. I would be suffering a similar fate if Coach didn't know I had a lesson on field four in less than ten minutes.

I grab my bag and sling it over my good shoulder, pushing thoughts of Ethan's comments and Ivy's news out of my head, the way I've been trained to push everything out for so long. I start walking to the other field more slowly than normally, wanting to savor every second of my little break before I have to push my body to extremes yet again.

"June," Coach calls, his voice gruff. And no, no, no, just let me go. I don't need a lecture. I know I sucked today. As I start walking toward him, though, I realize that he's got everyone else gathered around him too, so I pick up my pace. He's not the type of guy who would gather everyone up just to humiliate me, so it must be something else.

Coach is beaming at everyone around him when I get there, despite having screamed at us for most of the practice. Coaches are weird like that. They'll do whatever it takes to get the performance out of you they need, even if it's not always the best means. Then it's over, and they're someone completely different.

The truth is, sometimes I want to kill Coach, sometimes I want to hug him, but I always want his approval. I'd imagine he feels the same about us, well, on the first two fronts anyway. I doubt he really cares about our approval.

I take another swig of water and set my bag down as he clears his throat.

"I didn't want to share this till we wrapped up today," he says, folding the brim of his hat until it's just right. "But I found out this afternoon we were officially accepted into the Tristate Classic. I thought we probably would be, with our record, but you can never be too sure until the email comes and the check is cashed. It's happening, guys, so get ready."

Everyone whoops and hollers, and several people high-five me, rightly acknowledging the role I played in getting us here. I've already had several coaches reach out and ask if I'll be there; it's not a secret that I'm a draw. So far, I've been telling the colleges that I'll keep them posted about my schedule. I smile because now I'll have not only a reason to email them again—always good during the recruiting process—but also confirmation that they'll all have the opportunity to come see me play. Some of the guys on the team have already had offers made. I've had a lot of interest but no one offering a spot. Hopefully getting our team into the showcase is going to change that.

I don't want to sound too braggy. It's a prestigious showcase no matter how you slice it. We all worked hard to get here, and the coaches will be there scouting tons of players, not just me, but I also know something else . . .

"And you may not have realized"—Coach grins—"this will also mark the first time a female has ever been invited to this showcase."

And yep, just breaking down the barriers over here. Do I love that he just referred to me as a *female?* No. Does he get a pass for being old? Also no.

"First *woman* to ever play there, right, Coach?" I correct.

Coach looks confused. "Isn't that what I just said?"

Javonte puts his arm around me. "You said *female*, technically. Not the same."

"How is it—"

Javonte laughs. "I'll tell you after. Finish your speech."

Coach shakes his head—not in a mean way, in a kind of befuddled way—and then goes back to what he was saying. "Anyway, June will be the first *woman* player to ever participate in the showcase. That's going to get us some more attention than usual, I'm guessing. Coaches want to see what she can do, even if they aren't scouting a pitcher for the upcoming year. That means a lot of extra eyes on us and a lot of extra opportunities for everyone to get scouted. It also means I want to make damn sure we're ready. For the foreseeable future, I'm going to be upping our practices to include Tuesdays. Sunday will remain a rest day, but I'd like you all doing some stretches or yoga or cryotherapy or something. You wanna make it to the big leagues, you gotta train like the big leagues."

Some of the boys groan at the mention of yoga, but I think they all secretly enjoy it. I know I do—the gentle stretches working out tired muscles, the focus on breathing—it quiets my brain and body in a way I don't often get to.

What I don't love, though, is knowing that I'm going to have to practice on Tuesdays now too, a night that's usually reserved for hanging with Ivy. At least it's only for a few weeks.

Looks like she's not the only one who's going to have news tonight.

I SMELL THE pizza the second I walk into the house, noting that besides Ivy's, mine is the only car here. Her parents must be out. I hope they took her little brother too. Not that the kid isn't cute, but I'm not really a babysitting kind of person, and the few times we *have* hung out here, he's mercilessly followed me around. Once he even chased me with a toy dinosaur until I agreed to sit and watch *Bluey* with him. Ivy thought it was *adorable*, though. Getting bonus points from her was the only thing that made it almost worth it.

I'm smiling from the homeyness of the house as I head toward the kitchen, where I can hear Ivy moving around. Even if all the pictures of her older brother hanging up make me sad, it's nice that he's still present. Still here. Dad took down all the pictures that had Mom in them right after she passed. He said it hurt to look at them. I found them later in the basement, carefully wrapped in a sheet, like a burial shroud. I took a couple of my favorites and hung them up in my bedroom, needing proof that she'd existed once even if she didn't anymore. Dad never said anything about me taking them, but he won't look at them when he comes in, and he's always in and out of there as fast as possible, like he can't bear her eyes on him or to see her face.

I wonder if keeping them up all over the house like Ivy's family does is healthier, better, but before my mind can start spinning out too much over that, Ivy is dashing toward me, wrapping me in a hug so tight I can barely breathe.

"You're here! Finally!"

"I'm here," I say, melting against her. I breathe in her warmth, the smell of her shampoo, the feel of her arms tight around me. I shut my eyes, wanting it to last, but before I know it, she's pulling away too soon, staring up at me with a grin.

"Guess what?" she says, her smile infectious as she takes my hand and walks me into the kitchen. The pizza is out on their kitchen table, along with a couple plates. She's even lit a candle, and I realize later than I should that this is our own little date, isn't it?

"What?" I kiss her on the temple and take my place at the table, dishing out a slice for her and then going back for my own.

"Harry told me today that he recommended me for the Tristate Classic, and I got picked. I guess the league has been really happy with my officiating, and Harry thinks I'm ready for an even bigger step up. This is huge. I know the coaches are going to all be there for the players, but this will also be a chance for me to show off what I can handle as an official.

"I'd love to start booking college games, and doing showcases like this is a major leap in the right direction. The more I can build up my résumé, the easier it's going to be to wrench those doors open after I graduate. Can you believe it? I figured it was a long shot as it was, but when you factor in how often I've been swapping games and stuff whenever I'm booked for yours, I wasn't sure if he'd—"

"You thought he would hold that against you?" I ask, a little nagging worry creeping along my spine. "You never said that when we talked about it." I study her face. "I wouldn't have been so on board with it if I thought it was risking your job."

"I wouldn't call it 'risking my job,'" she says. "I just . . . I didn't want there to ever be a question of my judgment, and I wasn't totally sure what my judgment would even be with you anymore." She must see the worry on my face, because she's quick to add, "It's fine! Clearly, it's fine! The league is pulling me up! You know what the best part is?"

"What?"

"The ref schedule is going to be round-robin. I'll get to officiate for every team at least once. If the coaches are happy, they might even book me for other premier leagues around us too. This is a big opportunity."

"Every team? That's wild." I smile, her enthusiasm growing on me . . .

Until I remember my news.

My news that is technically the same as hers, but when you account for how hard she's been working this whole time to make sure we weren't scheduled together, and how excited she is to book this tournament, I almost don't want to tell her.

"What?" she asks, her tone going serious as she studies my face. "Are you upset?"

"No," I say, fumbling with my napkin. "That's great, Ivy. I'm really proud of you."

"But . . ." she says, looking confused and maybe also a little hurt.

"No *but*. Just an *and* . . . I also found out today that I'm going to the Tristate Classic. My team just got the official invite. I have a lot of coaches to email back who were hoping we would make it, so yeah," I say, blowing out a breath. "I guess I'll see you there."

I don't miss the way her face falls, probably running through the same thoughts as me. If she's working with every team, eventually she'll have to do mine. She won't be able to trade. This is going to be a major event for both of us, and it might get hard when my goal is to win, and her goal is to be neutral.

"I was so excited I didn't even think about that," she says, biting her lip. "I mean, of course your team would get in. You're the best." She rubs her hands over her eyes. "Shit."

"It's fine." I grab her hand determinedly. "We're going to make it work. Just because you *haven't* been officiating for us, doesn't mean you can't! No one knows about us; we just need to keep it up a little longer than we thought. It's going to be great," I say, no longer sure if I'm trying to convince her or myself.

"Yeah," she says, looking down at her untouched pizza and then back at me. I can see the nerves in her eyes, the concern, and I hate it. I hate that I've dulled even a little bit of her shine. She was so happy a second ago, and I want that back. I lean over and kiss her, trying to press all of my feelings into her, to say all the words that I can't, to prove just how okay we will be.

She kisses me back, slowly, gently, but pulls away long before I'm ready.

"You should eat," she says, with a little smile that doesn't quite meet her eyes. "You work so hard on the field."

I nod and take a bite, but I don't miss the way her eyes go far away, like she's lost in her thoughts.

CHAPTER THIRTEEN

Ivy

WE KNEW it would happen eventually—the shifting schedules, the avoidance at work; it could never last. Especially not now, with the showcase and its round-robin officiating schedule looming over us. We just didn't expect it to happen only days after we shared our showcase news with each other.

Unfortunately, fate had other ideas.

Aiden texts me Friday night to tell me that he's come down with something that he thinks is the flu. His COVID tests are negative, at least for now, but he won't be able to cover June's game for me this weekend after all. Since he was technically doing me a favor by swapping—and it's not like he *planned* to get sick or anything—I do my best to tamp down any annoyance I feel. I text him back a hopefully cheerful-sounding *get well soon* message and then flop onto my bed.

June had just left my house a few minutes before, and I pull my phone back up to text her the news, holding my breath until she replies. This will be our first time on the same field since we've been together. She was so weird about the tournament. Even though she kept saying it would all be okay, that it would be just like it was before, her voice was off. It felt like she was trying to convince herself that what she was saying was true. A part of me can't help but feel like she's going to be even more awkward or maybe even get mad at me over having this second game now added to the list without warning.

I'm extra relieved when she writes back just a few minutes later.

Just got home. Aww, cute! It will be fun. Good practice for the tourney anyway. 😉

It's the wink that really relaxes me. June is stingy with things like that. She thinks they're cheesy and only should be deployed when the moment really calls for it. A little bit of me is wondering if she's trying to oversell this the way she was on our pizza date, but I do my best not to dwell on it. Still, I need to make sure we're on the same page for tomorrow, so I write: **Should we establish some ground rules now?**

June doesn't reply for a while, and while I know she's probably just taking a shower and getting ready for bed, I can't shake the little panicky feeling that maybe I've offended her somehow without meaning to. Like the implication is that we won't be professional without explicitly outlining it or something. We talked about having to come up with a plan for the tournament, so logically I know that this isn't any different, but her silence is stressing me out.

When she still hasn't replied a half hour later, I try again: **Just nervous, sorry.**

And then I force myself to get ready for bed. It's going to be a long day tomorrow, longer still if I've somehow managed to piss her off by accident, and dwelling on it isn't going to do anything but make time pass slower and more stressfully. I might as well be tucked in while I freak.

My phone buzzes on the bathroom counter as I brush my teeth, and I jump, rushing to pick it up and hoping it's her. It is, thank god. I smile at the little preview window—just seeing her name sets my mind as ease—and then click open her message to read the rest.

Sorry, talking to Dad tonight. Another rough one. He opened one of Mom's letters, and it hit him hard. He's ok now, though, and yeah, tomorrow will be great. But yes, ground rules. I don't know you, you don't know me, till we leave the parking lot . . . After that all bets are off. 😌

Another emoji. I'm *definitely* suspicious now, but my relief overwhelms my concerns. I'm not proud of it, but I one hundred percent hug my phone, all of my stress draining out of me.

I'm not glad her dad is having a rough night, or that he dragged her into it, but I am very glad she wasn't avoiding me for asking to set ground rules. It's weird how much of my good mood is tied to her, to us, now. I don't know what it is about

June. I'm never like this in relationships, but this one just hits different. There's something about it that I don't ever want to lose. Something making it feel more precious. Something that feels a little bit, maybe, if you squint, like . . . love.

OFFICIATING THE FIRST three innings of June's game goes as smooth as butter. I'm behind home plate, fully geared. One glance in the stands and it's clear now that June's dad has figured out that I'm not just his daughter's girlfriend, and that I don't actually work in field maintenance. Or maybe he didn't figure it out and instead June just gave him a heads-up so he wouldn't react. But either way, he gives me a little nod of recognition and goes back to watching her. Any worry I had that he would flip out or make a scene was for nothing, and I find myself actually enjoying the game.

Both teams play good, clean ball. Any calls that are mine are the super-basic kinds—strike, foul, keeping track of the pitch count. Nice, drama-free, obvious calls that everyone agrees with. June's team takes an early lead and are up by two. At least until the start of the fourth, when the opposing team—some travel team from New Jersey with, weirdly, an octopus on their jerseys—hits a home run with two players already on base, and they sneak into the winning position. June is pissed at herself for giving up such a good hit. I can tell she's upset from a mile away. I have to fight the urge to comfort her as she stalks off the field and to the dugout after finally striking out the third player.

I need to be neutral. It's my job to be neutral, but I can't help but root for her, just a little. I remind myself there's a lot of game left, and they can easily come back from this. And then I double-remind myself to be objective even though it's hard. June can't be my girlfriend right now. I can't be maybe in love with her. She is just a player, this is just a game, and there is nothing special or different about any of it.

Javonte walks up to the plate and gives me a shy smile and quick nod that I hope no one else notices. Is it weird to acknowledge an ump? It is, right? Has he ever done that before? Did anyone see it? My brain is so flooded with thoughts about whether everyone is onto us because Javonte smiled at me that I barely realize they're all waiting for me to make a call.

"Uh, ball," I say, hoping I guessed correctly, because I was barely paying attention. Javonte didn't swing, right? And I think it *was* a little off plate. All the New Jersey octopus families are screaming that it was a strike, but the other team always does that, don't they?

Not the *other* team. I'm not on a team. Shit. This pushes me even further into my head. Was it a strike? Am I subconsciously showing favoritism? Are these last few years of hard work and integrity slipping through my fingers because I agreed to take on this game today?

I squat down a little lower, leaning in a little closer to the catcher, praying the ache in my thighs grounds me and drags me back into the game, into objectivity. It doesn't matter that this is Javonte at bat. And it definitely doesn't matter that he's

June's best friend in the entire universe, the only solid thing she's had in her life until me.

The next pitch is a little questionable, but still, it's *technically* in the strike zone.

"Strike!" I say, and the other side of the bleachers stands up to shout at me. Dammit. Why do I care? Obnoxious parents are part of the game. I'm used to this. I've got this.

"What the hell, Ivy? That was definitely a ball," Javonte whispers just loud enough for me to hear. I don't bother replying. I can't. I pretend I don't hear him.

Javonte's bat connects with the next pitch, a pop-up that has him out long before he even makes it to first base. I don't miss his glare as he walks by, as if my call made any difference. *You hit a ball! In! The! Sky!* I want to yell. Of course it was going to be caught. This is the premier league, not the rec league.

I shake my head and crouch down again, feeling annoyed but ready to tackle the next round. The next hitter—Ethan, I think June said once—gets struck out in three pitches, all of them fair. The pitches were good, and he swung at every one. So how come now it's not just the parents who are losing it, but also the bench behind me? I even hear June's voice in the mix. It makes my stomach clench, but I don't turn around.

The third hitter, a tall, gangly white guy with hair bleached so white he looks like something out of a V. E. Schwab book, decides to bunt, and it doesn't end well. The octopuses are off the field before June's team even got anything going.

Javonte takes his place beside me at home plate as June jogs onto the pitching mound. "Thanks for nothing," he says, and I shake my head. Players shit-talk; they always shit-talk. This can't bother me. He isn't her best friend. She isn't my girlfriend. What the hell, brain? Stop giving a damn about anything but calling plays right now.

Still, I can't help but worry over the fact that June's clearly pissed and won't even meet my eyes. I know, objectively, the game isn't going her way, and she had an uncontrollable temper even before the extenuating circumstances of her girlfriend being the one calling her players out—and yet. I bite my lip. Even though I think my calls are good, I can't help but feel like I screwed up. Bad.

June easily strikes the first hitter out. The second makes it to first, but is thankfully held there by Ethan. The third gets walked because of balls, and I hear June's dad shouting about needing a new ump. I know he's not talking about the one in the outfield, and I'm not going to lie, it fucking hurts. I shake my head to clear it, just as an obviously pissed off June throws a wild pitch. It was probably meant for me, subconsciously or not—god, I hope not consciously—but it ends up striking the batter in the hip. An automatic walk.

June throws her glove, and Javonte jogs over along with their coach to talk to her. I stretch my legs and try to ignore the way Javonte keeps shooting me angry looks as he tries to calm her down. I roll my eyes at a particularly obvious one. Yes, she's the star, and yes, she's totally hotheaded, and yes, that was part of what attracted me to her, if I'm being totally honest, but now, on the other side, knowing the person behind the pitcher and knowing that I'm her goddamn girlfriend and not some random untrained asshole off the street, it's a little less endearing than it once was.

Shouldn't she trust my calls more than any other official's? Doesn't she believe in me the way I believe in her? She knows this is my dream, and she knows that I value my integrity above everything. Her outburst stings in a way I wasn't expecting.

By the time everyone gets back to their places and June deigns to grab her glove off the ground and slap the clay off it using her thigh, I'm so heated I can barely stand it. I wish I could throw a baseball right at her face for once.

No. I need to stop fucking around and get my head in the game. I'm a professional. If I let myself melt down, then I'm no better than how she's acting. A sense of calm passes over me as I finally get my brain in check. I'm trained for this. I'm good at this. And I'm done being distracted.

The next player hits a single, but the player running to home gets out. Two outs, bases still loaded. June's glaring at me like I'm her personal nemesis and not the girl she was kissing last night, but I don't care. This is work and work has nothing to do with our relationship.

She strikes the next batter out easily, ending the inning, and heads back to the dugout with a satisfied smirk, like she showed me—and maybe she did. But not what she thinks. She showed me a side of her I didn't like, a side that I thought the ground rules would prevent. Maybe that's on me—I should have predicted this would happen, given where we started. It would probably have been weirder to spectators if she wasn't flipping out on me. Being a hothead is kind of her thing.

Hang on. *Being a hothead is kind of her thing.*

That must be it. She's not really upset, just putting on her usual show for everyone else so no one suspects. It would be unusual if she was suddenly super chill and respectful to the umpire, given her history. This makes perfect sense; I just wish she would have given me a heads-up. Maybe that's what she meant by her text when she said, *I don't know you, you don't know me.* This *is* business as usual, or as close to it as we can get.

My frustration seeps out of me. I bet that satisfied smirk was her indicating she was happy that we were pulling it off, making it look believable. We're good, then. She does trust me. So I need to trust her.

I hang on to that thought, on to that smirk, for the whole rest of the game. Her team still ends up losing by one, never fully recovering from that one inning. But it was a good game, a solid game, and I can't wait to get back to the locker room, and to her.

CHAPTER FOURTEEN

June

"UM, WHAT was your deal out there?" I snap the second Ivy joins me in the officials' locker room. I snuck in through a connecting door in the women's locker room when none of the soccer players were looking, not daring to risk going in the front door. I was just glad the side door was unlocked so I didn't have to knock. I've been sitting here, tapping my foot impatiently, for the last five minutes.

Ivy drops her backpack onto the couch and turns toward me, smiling. "Besides an Oscar-winning performance by both of us?" she asks, and then crosses over to me like she's going to kiss me. Kiss me! As if her bad calls didn't lose us the game—an important game, mind you. One that could affect seeding for the showcase. I press my hand lightly against her chest and move her away. She frowns, obviously confused. "What's wrong?"

"What's wrong? What's wrong is that you cost us the game,

and then came in here acting like I was just going to kiss you and get over it." I'm aware on some level that I sound like a petulant child, but I can't help it. If she hadn't called so many strikes against us—ones that were, in my very experienced opinion, obviously balls—then we would have had a decent shot at making a comeback.

"Excuse me?" she says, crossing her arms as her annoyance ticks up in her voice. "All my calls were fucking good."

And great. I guess the apology I was hoping for isn't coming after all.

"You called strikes that were so far out of the strike zone it wasn't even funny! It's like you were trying to make us lose!"

"Why would I ever do that?"

"I don't know!" I raise and drop my hands in frustration, realizing, too late, the extra strain that puts on my shoulder. "Maybe so people wouldn't suspect us? Maybe out of guilt—"

"I don't feel guilty about us," she says, tilting her head and stepping closer. "Do you?"

I shake my head and look away, but she grabs my hand, and somehow, a smile blooms up from inside me at the feel of her warm, dusty hand in mine. "No," I say, looking back at her, "I don't, but that's beside the point!"

"Remind me. What's the point, then?" she asks, taking another step closer. She's breathing a little heavy, and for the first time I notice all the smudges of dirt around the edges of her face and on her nose, where she must have rubbed with her hand. She's distracting me, and it's working. She flashes me a full-on smile now, looking a little cocky. "You see something you like? Because if you do, you could probably kiss it, you know."

I pout, doing my best not to laugh. "I'm trying to be mad at you."

She tugs me closer against her, her game-warmed skin hot against mine. "Why would you want to do a thing like that?" she asks, and then leans in. Her lips barely brush against mine, and she waits there patiently, giving me the chance to close the deal or pull away. I kiss her; of course I kiss her. How could I ever not? As infuriating as this game was, she's still Ivy and I'm still June and our bodies are still magnets made only for each other.

Her body relaxes against mine, her lips curling up with a hint of a smile when she realizes that I'm kissing her back, making me forget, if only for a moment, the whole damn game. The whole damn everything, except her lips on mine and the way her hair laces between my fingers like it was always meant to be there.

She rests her forehead against mine and sighs, squeezing my hand once more before stepping back. "Okay, now that you're not irrationally angry at me anymore, let's talk."

I cock my eyebrow. "First of all, 'irrationally angry' sounds like what men used to say to send justifiably upset women to sanitariums back in the day, so no, no to that phrasing. Second of all . . . well, I don't have a 'second of all' right now. Did you seriously just kiss me to calm me down?"

She flashes me that cocky smirk again. "That depends. Did it work?"

She's infuriating. Infuriating! But also, damn, it did work.

I decide to be mildly evasive instead of giving her the full satisfaction of admitting it worked, but she can tell. She can definitely tell.

"Don't gloat," I say, and she preens a little. "You want to talk, talk."

"I'm glad you feel better," she says. "I'm gonna go take a shower."

"What?!" I shriek. "I thought we were going to talk!"

"We will. I'll just be in the shower." She winks at me and heads to the shower stall with her bag of toiletries. She slides the curtain shut and starts tossing her clothes over it and into the aisle. "Are you going to tell me why you were pissed?" she asks once the water's started up. I try really hard not to imagine her in there, bubbles cascading over wet skin as she cleans up. "June?"

"Sorry, um," I say, blushing. "What?"

She laughs from behind the curtain. "I asked why you were so upset when I came in here."

"Right, yeah, that." I try to remember anything beyond how badly I want to be one of those bubbles sliding down her body right now. "Um . . ."

Ivy sticks her head out from behind the curtain. "You okay over there?" Her hair is full of shampoo, and she's got a comical expression on her face, like she knows what I'm thinking about. She probably does.

"I'm great," I say, coming back to my senses. "I mean, no, I'm upset because a lot of your calls favored the other team."

"They didn't," she says, disappearing back behind the curtain. A few minutes of awkward silence pass before she adds, "I'm sorry if that's how you feel, but I hope you know that my professionalism and integrity wouldn't allow me to be anything less than fair."

"I disagree," I say, because there's no way I'm letting her have the last word on this. "Well, not about the integrity part. I know you *think* you were being fair. But I think in an effort to be, like, impartial or whatever, you swung too far to the other side. Inadvertently."

"Would you be talking to me about this if I wasn't your girlfriend?" Ivy asks. The water stops, and she steps outside the shower wrapped tightly in a towel.

"What's that supposed to mean?"

"It means maybe we need to go over those boundaries again. If Aiden or Harry or anybody else was the umpire today, would you be seeking them out after the game and asking for a play-by-play of their reasoning or for them to justify their calls?"

"No, but I wouldn't be kissing them either, to be fair."

She sighs. "That's my point! We aren't a player and an umpire off the field, so we need to leave those sides of us out there. It was really hard for me to separate that today. It felt like shit when I thought you were mad at me, and when your dad was calling for a new ump."

"I didn't hear him," I say, mortified. Why would he do that? He didn't realize it was her, did he?

"Yeah, well, between that and Javonte glaring at me and you flipping out, it fucking sucked. I convinced myself that you were doing it all as an act—you're almost expected to be hot-headed out there. The fact that it wasn't an act and you're *still* pressing me on this really bothers me, June."

"I—" I start, not sure what to say. I hadn't really considered what it must have felt like for her on the other side of the plate.

"When we're together, we're Ivy and June, not player and ump. You don't get to critique my calls, and I won't bring up that you threw a wild pitch that almost took out the other team's shortstop."

"I did not!" I yelp in mock horror, trying to lighten the mood. Ivy, to her credit, lets me.

"Okay, agree to disagree." She laughs, walking over to me. "But even if you did, it would have been left out there, on the field. Got it?"

As much as I want to press her for more, as much as I want to get her to see the obvious error of her ways, I know she has a point. It probably *would* be better for us if we left our work life or whatever you want to call it outside of the relationship, healthier maybe even.

"Fine," I say, "but I might need a minute to cool down after games, then. Okay?"

"You're the one who keeps crashing *my* locker room, remember?" she snorts. "Take all the time you need with the peons."

I groan and drop my head back. "You can't seriously expect me to get changed with the middle schoolers."

She kisses me on the tip of my nose. "I am if you need space from me before you can play nice. Today sucked out there, and I'm not doing this again."

Her tone is light, but her words are a definite warning. I watch as Ivy pulls her clothes out of her bag and disappears into the changing room.

This whole *not talking about the game* thing is going to be hard. Harder than I thought when I agreed thirty seconds ago, but I let it go. Deep breaths. Leave it on the field.

Ivy comes out a few minutes later, her hair wet but somehow still looking amazing. She flashes me a smile I can't resist, and I wrap my arms around her from behind while she brushes her hair and puts on some mascara.

"Did you want to shower?" Ivy asks, turning around to face me.

"I didn't bring my stuff. I'll shower at home."

"Okay, I'll meet you there, then?" She zips up her backpack, and I'm so relieved that we're not mad at each other anymore that I grab her hand as we step out into the hall.

It was instinct, that's all. I just wanted to be close to her and reassure myself that everything is fine. I pull away once I realize what I've done. We weren't even going to walk out together, let alone holding hands, but I was so caught up in the conversation that I didn't think.

Panic slices through me when I hear Ivy mumble a quiet "shit" as a vaguely familiar boy walks up to us. I jerk away from her like she burned me and keep walking fast out to the parking lot, trying to play it off like Ivy was just in my way. As the glass door starts to shut behind me, I can just make out Ivy saying, "Hi, Aiden, what are you doing here?"

CHAPTER FIFTEEN

Ivy

"WASN'T THAT the girl you hate?" Aiden asks, shoving some of his messy brown mop out of his eyes. He's casually leaning against the wall, craning his neck to watch June walk out. It makes my skin prickle.

"Aren't you supposed to be sick?" I ask, not bothering to answer. Maybe he didn't see our hands. Maybe somehow the umpire gods have smiled down on me and blocked Aiden's view just long enough for June and me to have remembered ourselves and let go. But then again, if there *were* umpire gods, they probably wouldn't be smiling over the fact that I'm clearly going fully head over heels for a player, which is against every official's code of conduct.

Or maybe they would. Gods are a tricky thing.

"You two looked pretty cozy." He grins.

"And you look pretty healthy for someone who had to call out last minute."

"Fine, maybe it was less the flu and more realizing my application essay was looking a little weak and I needed some extra time to polish it, while also weighing the pros and cons of early decision versus early action."

"God, you sound like my mother." I shudder. "That still doesn't explain why you're here *now*, though."

"I got done what I needed to do, and I came here to talk to Harry to see if he could use me for any of the afternoon games. College tuition isn't going to pay itself, you know, and the Ivies don't really give merit."

I tilt my head, trying to decide if he's lying. But why would he? It's impossible that he knows anything about me and June, not for real, so this must have just been cosmically bad timing.

Good luck on his part, horrendous luck on ours.

"You don't know how good you have it, Ivy," he grumbles. His hair has fallen back in his eyes, and he shoves it back roughly, his frustration apparent.

I raise my eyebrows. "How good I have it?" If he didn't look so goddamn miserable about this whole application process, I would definitely be listing all the reasons that's bullshit.

"Do you know how much pressure is on me to come up with a good hook?" He scoffs. "I need to kiss Harry's ass and get onto that college showcase. Maybe if I can say I'm the youngest umpire to do that, I could add supplementary essays about it and shit. Get some bonus points with some of the colleges beyond all the little clicks you're covering for me."

I swallow hard. So he doesn't know that I already got the spot. And this also means Harry definitely didn't recommend him to ump too. This is awkward. I feel kind of, almost, bad for him.

"You're lucky you have a built-in hook, though, being all gay and a girl and shit." He says *girl* like it's a dirty word. Like it's giving me some unfair advantage over him or something. "Do you know how hard it is for a straight white guy to get anywhere these days?"

And there it is. The reason Aiden and I will never actually be friends. Any concern or empathy I was feeling goes right out the window.

"Compared to who?" I snort, rolling my eyes.

"Compared to anyone who's not. They see high-stat white guys, and they don't care. They want to create a 'diverse' campus. How about you just take the people who are the most qualified, right?" He shakes his head, like somehow we're on the same page, even though he just reduced my life and my sexuality to being *a hook*.

"Uh, I think straight white guys still have plenty of advantages," I say before I can stop myself.

He narrows his eyes. "You wouldn't get it."

I almost take the bait. Almost. "Well, it was nice seeing you, but I have to get home. My parents were expecting me already," I say, not really sure how to end the conversation but wanting it over. Immediately. There's no reason to prolong this. Especially if he didn't see me with—

"Are you meeting up with June after?" he asks me, so casually it almost sounds like he means it. Like he's asking me my weekend plans instead of accusing me of something. Except, how? How does he even know her name?

"June?" I say, trying to play it off like I don't know who he means.

"Yeah, you know, the pitcher girl? Are you hanging out with her later?" There's a glint in his eyes that I don't trust, like he's laid a trap and I've already stepped in it. My stomach free-falls to the floor.

"Why would you ask that?" I bite the inside of my cheek, trying not to react. If he can act casual, then so can I, right? Two can play at this game.

"You guys looked pretty cozy just now, so I thought . . ." He trails off, rubbing his chin. "You know, when I saw you two flirting in line that day, and then you asked me right after to switch games, I got a little curious. I started thinking about what it would mean if I was right and something was going on between you two. It felt like my duty, as an official who also signed the code of conduct, to look into it a little more. And then today I just happen to stop by and catch the two of you coming out of the officials' room."

I notice how he said *catch*, and suddenly my suspicion that he planned this and it wasn't random doesn't seem so off base. Even if the whole essay-polishing excuse was true, I doubt he had to come in *now*, right after the game finished. A quick glance at the schedule, broadcasted 24-7 on one of the TVs hanging in the corner of the dining area, tells me that there aren't any games starting for the next ninety minutes due to

156

a thunderstorm warning in the area. A bunch were also re-scheduled to be safe. There's no way he's picking up extra hours anytime soon. He had to have known that. He must check the app just as often as I do, and the storm alert was posted when I was walking to the shower.

"Catch us?" I ask pointedly. "What do you mean?"

He shrugs but looks down at my hand—the same hand that June was just holding—and then back up at my face. "I don't know, a person could get an idea, I guess."

"Well, they'd be reading into things too much." My lie doesn't even sound convincing to myself.

"Would they?" he asks, tilting his head like a puppy, only one that you actually want to kick. My toes curl in my cleats, the only sign of anger that I'll allow myself. I keep my face passive, almost bored, determined not to give anything else away or accidentally confirm something that's just a suspicion.

He could be fishing, I tell myself, willing myself to calm down. But that smirk on his face tells me he's not. He has proof, and he's going to use it.

I grab his arm and drag him into the officials' locker room. June accidentally left her hairbrush behind on the counter, and my eyes snag on it, a little beacon of light in the middle of this shitstorm she's left me in.

Why did she grab my hand?

A bubble of resentment rises up in my chest because she did this, accidentally or not, and then got to leave while I'm left cleaning up the mess. When she grabbed my hand, she, for all intents and purposes, backed me into this corner. Now I'm at Aiden's mercy, a place I didn't ever want to be.

I let go, and he jerks back like I bit him. "Watch it," he says, rubbing his arm. He follows my gaze to the hairbrush and smiles like he somehow knows it's hers.

I bite my cheek harder.

"Okay, what do you want?" I ask, when I trust my voice not to come out in a shout.

"What do I want?" he asks, pretending to look put out by the question.

I stare at him, unimpressed. "Clearly you came here at this *exact* time hoping to see something, which you might *think* you have, but—"

"No, I know I have." He smirks, and it would be almost cute, if the person it was attached to wasn't so horrible. "The question is, what am I going to do with the information?"

"You don't have any information at all," I say, trying my best to sound indignant.

"Well, I have the fact that I saw you holding hands with a player just now, which is against our code of conduct. I'm pretty sure the players sign one with their club, just like we do, so I'm guessing it's against hers too. Who would've thought, the star ump and the star pitcher? It's almost a cliché."

"No one would ever believe you."

He makes a sort of sucking sound with his teeth and points up to a camera that I never noticed before. It's situated high in the corner of the room, where it's barely visible, and pointed straight over the door. It wouldn't have been able to see June and me actually in the locker room, but it may have heard us if it records sound, and it definitely would have recorded us walking out the door holding hands.

"I wonder what Harry would see on that," Aiden says, following my eyes.

"Is that even legal to have in a locker room?" I ask, horrified.

"Relax," he says. "It just records who comes in and who leaves. You can't see anything else. It was mostly just to catch whoever was stealing towels or whatever. I wonder how often it would show you and that pitcher in here together. I bet it caught her holding your hand today." He scrunches up his forehead. "Plus, there's proof that we switched the game schedule all the time. I'm sure Harry would be curious about that too, considering the hand-holding video. I'd say I just got pretty believable, wouldn't you?"

I huff and cross my arms. "Is there a point to this little villain speech you're doing?" I ask, trying to sound braver than I'm feeling at the moment.

He grins like he knows I'm full of shit. "I'm just saying! I mean, I wouldn't *do* anything with this information. We're friends, right?"

Friends is not the word I'd use, especially not right now, but I'm not about to say that out loud. There was a time, not too, too long ago, that I maybe would have agreed, before he got all competitive and weird and obsessed with college rankings and applications and stuff. I look at him, waiting. I know the other shoe is about to drop, and I'm trying to brace myself as best as I can. This isn't just about me; this is about June now too.

"Friends do each other favors, right?" he asks. "Like switching games?"

"Yes," I say, confused. For a half second, I think maybe he's going to actually be cool about all this. For a half second, I think maybe he's just going to ask me to take his shittier games in exchange for him taking June's or something. Ones where it's hot or raining, or ones known for having parents who are assholes.

"What if the favor is that you give me another game?" he asks, the way one might ask about the weather. He's so calm, I don't see where this is going or how sinister a turn things have taken until he adds, "Like the college showcase."

I feel like I'm going to be sick. Suddenly the room is spinning, and I back up until I find a chair and promptly sit on it. This showcase means everything to me. Everything. I've worked so hard to get here. I can't do this. I can't.

"How do you even know about that?"

"I asked Harry about it yesterday. He said he was all set and that he could only recommend one person. It doesn't take a rocket scientist to know he picked you. You've always been his favorite."

"I'm . . . no," I say, trying to wrap my head around what's happening right now. I mean, shit like this doesn't happen in real life. This is some, like, cinematic bullshit right here, and I want off this ride.

"You know I need a hook, Ivy," he says, like that justifies anything. "Being invited to do that would be amazing. It would also be a good opportunity to chat with college reps who are there, plus some of the older umpires who might be able to hook me up with jobs or recommend me next year after we graduate. You know you're not the only one with dreams, right? I need the money, I need the connections, and I need the essay material."

"So you're blackmailing me?" I all but shriek.

"No." He shakes his head. "No!" he says a second time, a little more urgently. "I'm not blackmailing you at all. I'm just pointing out that we both have things we want right now, and we can help each other out. I want to work the showcase, and you don't want Harry or that girl's coach to find out about you two, right?

"I mean, the timing! Imagine, their star player gets suspended for an ethics violation this late in the recruiting season." He blows out a concerned breath. "We can't let that happen to her or to you. Let's help each other out."

"She wouldn't be in that position if you weren't such a snake," I snipe.

"Come on." He laughs. "We both know Harry gave you that job because it ruffles some feathers to have a girl working the ball games. It gets his program some attention by having you there. You're not that special, Ivy, face it."

"There's no guarantee that Harry would even go for it. What makes you think you'd be next in line even if I did recommend you?"

"If you call out with short notice, he wouldn't have a choice, would he?"

"How would that even work?"

"You call in sick right before the showcase. Tell him you texted me to cover for you, and that I'm already on my way. It would be too late for him to find an alternative, so he'd definitely go with it. Not to mention, I'm the only other person he pulled up with you for this league. I'm good, Ivy. I just need a chance to show it, and the way he's playing favorites, I never get it."

I resent the implication that I've only gotten here because I'm a favorite, or because I'm a woman, but he's got my back against the wall on this one, so I swallow my words, saving my indignant speech for another day.

I can't let June lose this recruiting season. She needs this showcase more than I do. There will be other showcases where I can officiate, someday, probably.

My heart sinks as I realize this whole thing is slipping just out of my reach.

"Can I think about it?" I ask.

"Sure," Aiden says. "But don't take *too* long, or I might have to, you know . . ." He turns his left hand into a puppet and pretends to make it talk.

I look at him in disgust, but he just smiles.

"You have until next weekend's games to decide, or else I'll have no choice but to tell Harry everything."

"Of course you would still have a choice." I sneer.

He leans down closer to where I'm sitting. "No, I don't. If you saw the admission rates where I'm trying to get in, you would get it. I need every edge I can get."

"Am I supposed to pity you?"

"You're supposed to realize that I don't really have anything to lose here."

And with that, he's gone, the locker room door swinging shut behind him.

Shit.

CHAPTER SIXTEEN

June

I'M FULL-ON pacing my room by the time I hear Ivy's car finally pull up outside. Before she even turns the engine off, I'm racing down the driveway to meet her. I'm relieved that Dad went to work early today, so we can have this conversation in peace without him trying to eavesdrop or dump his opinions on us.

When I say he went to work early, I really mean that he took off in a fury. I might have gone off on him a little bit when I got home, for being rude to Ivy about her calls, which led to a DEFCON 1–level argument, with him saying he could not believe that I would risk dating an ump this close to the end of the recruiting period. Hopefully, he'll have calmed down somewhat by the time he gets home, but I can't really worry about that right now, not with Ivy finally here.

"What happened? What did he say?" I ask the second her car door opens.

"Nothing much," she says, giving me a tight smile. "He just wanted to say hi."

"He just wanted to say hi?" I repeat, incredulous. "He didn't see us? Are you sure? Why was he even there if he was supposed to be sick?"

"He wasn't sick. He just stayed home to work on college stuff," she says, walking past me into the house. "Your dad home?"

"No, thank god," I say, following her into the kitchen. I don't know if she's eaten yet, but I'm starving now that the anxiety over what Aiden may or may not have seen is letting up. I pull out the bread and some peanut butter and jelly. "Want one?"

Ivy sits at the island on one of our little stools and watches me work. "Sure," she says, but she sounds distracted, far away somehow.

"Is everything really okay?" I ask, studying her face.

"Why wouldn't it be?"

"I don't know, possibly because Aiden saw something he wasn't supposed to because I'm a jerk who can't resist holding your hand every chance I get?" She smiles at this, and a little bit of the knot unclenches in my chest.

If I can make her smile, it can't be that bad, right?

"He didn't see anything," she says, more firmly this time. "And you're not a jerk."

"Promise?"

"Are you gonna make me a sandwich, woman, or are you just gonna keep overthinking this?" she teases.

"Woman? Woman?!" I say, balling up a slice of bread and pitching it right at her. She laughs, for real this time, at least until she sees me rubbing my shoulder. I shouldn't be throwing anything, not even a fluffy piece of bread, when I'm so sore from today's game. There's not enough Biofreeze in the world to make me feel better right now. All I want is a snack, an ice pack, and my girlfriend snuggled up in my bed with me watching old reruns of *Superstore*.

Ivy teases me about my comfort show being about a big-box store, but I don't care. My mom worked very, very part-time at Target toward the end, once she officially had to let go of her speech therapy practice. They gave her a flexible schedule and understood when she occasionally called out. We would watch *Superstore* together, even Dad, and she would laugh so hard tears would come out, swearing up and down that some of the customers or weird things that happened on the show really were true to retail.

Is it a dorky show? Yes. Does it make me feel like I'm closer to my mother? Also yes. Way more than all those letters, her little list of dreams that read more like demands. I'll take memories and crap TV any day of the week. Especially on days like this when my dad isn't home. He can't watch it for the same reason I can't stop. It reminds him of Mom.

Ivy's warm, gentle hands massage the area around my shoulder and biceps, and I lean back into her, daydreaming about the kind of cozy, sleepy afternoon we can have without my dad around to interrupt or grill me about the game. I usually hate when he works doubles, but lately I've found myself looking forward to it.

The house is somehow less empty with Ivy around, even less lonely than when Dad's home with me.

"Okay," I say when she leans forward to kiss my temple while I slather peanut butter on the bread, careful to fully coat each slice. "I take it back—you can call me *woman*."

She smiles, wrapping her arms around me and resting her chin on my shoulder, observing. "Why do you put peanut butter on both slices?"

"To seal the bread," I say, confused. "Do you not?"

"No, one peanut butter, one jelly, done and done."

I gasp and turn my head to look at her with exaggerated shock. "You make *soggy* sandwiches? No, thank you. I undo my take-back! I'm not your woman. It's like I don't even know you right now."

Ivy swipes a finger in the peanut butter and presses it against my lips, effectively shushing me. I'm just about to protest when she kisses me, a deliciously peanut buttery thing that makes me hungry in an entirely different way.

"I don't know," she says, pulling back to look at me with a satisfied smirk on her face. "It definitely seems like you're still my woman."

WE'RE THREE EPISODES into *Superstore*, our bellies full of sandwiches and Sun Chips, curled up around each other in my bed when she says it. I'm half dozing, the ice pack dulling some of the pain in my shoulder enough to let me finally relax, so I'm sure I've misheard.

"Huh?" I mumble, trying to pull myself from sleep to focus.

Ivy is up on her side, her elbow propping up her head as she looks down at me, her eyes snagging on the tight ice wrap I have around my entire shoulder and arm. I look a little ridiculous, I'm sure, but it's no time to be self-conscious, not with her, and especially not when she's giving me the *this is important, June* look. Maybe I didn't mishear.

"I don't think I want to do the showcase," Ivy repeats, clearly waiting for my reaction.

I push up as best as I can, and she moves to sit cross-legged beside me.

"Of course you're doing the showcase, Ivy," I say. "It's going to look great on your résumé. Not to mention it would make you a shoo-in to get varsity games in the spring. It's a huge deal."

Ivy shrugs, and I stare at her, my mouth popping open in confusion. I feel like I've slipped into an alternate universe, because the Ivy I know would never give an opportunity like this up.

"Wait, what is going on right now?" I ask, super confused.

"I just don't think I want to do it."

"Why?!"

"It's so much pressure! Is it a great opportunity? Yes. But is it worth all this stress? I don't know."

"What stress?"

She shakes her head. "Nothing."

"Ivy, talk to me," I say, running my hand down her arm until she finally meets my eyes. "You know I'm here for you, right?"

She nods but looks away, like she's embarrassed or upset or something. "Yeah, I know."

I gently turn her chin so she's facing me again. I lean forward and place a chaste kiss on her lips, not trying to start anything, just wanting to feel the connection, wanting *her* to feel the connection. I don't know what's going on in her head right now, but I want to make it all better.

She lets out a shaky breath and shrugs again, like she doesn't know what to do with her body. I lie back down against the pillow and gesture for her to do the same. Ivy settles her head against my chest, running her thumb over the small expanse of my skin showing between the hem of my crop top and the waistband of my sweats. I card my fingers gently through her hair, doing my best to stay awake, hoping she'll tell me soon what's wrong.

"Everybody's putting so much pressure on this one showcase, like it's do or die," she says finally.

I consider her words for a minute, deciding how to answer. "Well, for me it sort of is, I think. Most colleges have their pitchers already, and they aren't women. I need to have a good showing here. I'm just crossing everything my shoulder will cooperate."

"It's really bad today?" she asks quietly, like she already knows. How could she not, with this hulking ice wrap?

"Is it ever not?" I ask, not willing to let her distract me. "Hey,"

I say, quietly turning my head to look at her. "If you *really* don't want to do it, that's fine. Who knows? It might even be for the best."

It's a lie, but a pretty one. One I think she wants to hear, maybe even needs to hear.

She glances up at me. "How so?"

"You said it yourself, the stress is getting to you. Plus, we've both been so worried about an ethics violation. This would get rid of that fear completely."

"I'm not quitting reffing completely," she says, her body going stiff.

I've said the wrong thing, or I've said the right thing too convincingly. Either way, I know I've screwed up.

"I didn't mean forever, obviously. I just meant for this showcase. There would be no way for anyone to say I was shown favoritism or anything. Not that anyone really knows besides, like, your best friend and mine. You said Aiden didn't see anything, right?"

"Yeah, I guess," she says, rolling onto her back and tucking her arms behind her head, obviously upset.

"Can I call a time-out right now?" I sit up to look at her, at a loss for how to fix this. "I don't want to fight with you, please? You said you were feeling stressed and didn't want to do it. Why are you so annoyed that I'm trying to find a silver lining?"

"I'm not annoyed," she says, grabbing the Apple Remote and pushing play again. "Let's just watch."

"You're acting pretty upset for someone who isn't annoyed," I say, a knot tightening in my belly.

"I'm fine," she says, smiling urgently, like she wants me to drop it immediately. "What, you don't believe me?"

She pulls her phone out of her pocket and punches out a text to someone. I can't see who, but the determination on her face isn't exactly convincing me that she's in the best headspace.

"What are you doing?"

"I just texted Harry," she says, falling back down beside me. "I told him I couldn't do the showcase and he'd need to fill the slot for me."

"Really?" I raise my eyebrows. "You don't want to sleep on it or . . ."

"No, like you said, silver lining, right? It takes the pressure off me, and lets you focus on the showcase without worrying about any distraction or us fighting over a game or your dad accidentally blowing our cover when he's pissed at my calls. I'm sick of stressing about it anyway. Like you said, this showcase is way more important for you than it is for me. There's only one game left in your regular season, and I'm not scheduled for it, so if I drop this showcase, we made it."

"We made it," I repeat, relief washing over me at the realization that she really did just undo all of our problems in one fell swoop. "We're not even going to have to sneak around soon!"

"Yeah," she says, smiling. It looks forced, but I'm too caught up in what this means to question it.

"Oh my god, that's gonna be amazing! We'll just say it started after the end of the season. We'll wait it out a bit, of course, and then act like we're going on our first date." I suck in a breath, all excited. "You can take me to my fall formal even! Oh my god!"

"Yeah," she says, snuggling in beside me as we both settle back in to watch. "Sounds good."

My mind is swirling with a thousand thoughts about how great it's going to be to finally be out in the open with the person I care about. Just a little while longer, and we're home free. Ivy pulls one of my heavy blankets over us, helping to counteract the ice on my shoulder. She buries her face against my neck as I reach up to play with her hair, feeling lighter.

Her hand squeezes tight on my hip, and she whispers, "It's gonna be good. It will."

I don't realize until I'm too far past the line where dozing turns to sleep that maybe I'm not the one she's trying to convince here. But hey, if she's not ready to be happy, I'll do my best to be happy for the both of us.

CHAPTER SEVENTEEN

Ivy

I LIED to June.

I'm not fine. Not at all.

It's been two days of watching June practically walking on air, and it's getting to me. Okay, fine, maybe I'm overstating things a bit in my bitterness. She's not walking on air, but she's definitely not all that worried about my sudden decision to back out of the showcase—it's almost like she wanted this to happen the whole time.

She doesn't seem to even realize how unlike me something like that is. Me? Walk away from something because it's high pressure? If that's how I felt, then I wouldn't have a shot of making it in the pros. Reffing the NFL? The Super Bowl? Forget all of it if you're the type of person who cracks under pressure.

Maybe June doesn't really know me.

Or maybe this relationship is more one-sided than I thought. I'm always worrying about her—is her dad pushing her too hard, is her shoulder holding up, how is her *mind* holding up, did her dad spring another letter on her, and a hundred thousand other things.

It's why I'm lying here awake at 3:00 a.m. at an impromptu sleepover at Mia's house after an emotional dinner with my parents where they talked about Nicky more than I'm comfortable with. I wanted to scream at them, *Hey, I'm still here. Sammy is still here.* But instead I went to Mia's. And now I'm lying in another bed, at another house, still thinking the same thing—*Hey, I'm still here*—only about my girlfriend instead of my parents. It's getting to be an unfortunate habit. One that's making me rethink a lot of things, like taking back my text to Aiden.

Yeah, that's the other thing I lied about. She thinks I texted Harry to back out and that it's all a done deal now, but I didn't. That's not how the plan works after all. I actually texted Aiden and told him I was agreeing to his terms. For this plan to work, it has to be so last-minute that Harry can't call in anyone else. I have to leave Aiden as the only option just to be safe. It's a shaky plan at best, but it's the only one we've got. There's no guarantee that Aiden would be the automatic second choice.

But really, whether June notices or not, it's not like I really had a choice. What was the alternative? Not give it up and have him ruin both our chances? The fact that both our futures are held in the sweaty palm of an asshole just looking for his college essay hook doesn't really bode well for either of us.

And god, I'm so fucking sick of it. I'm sick of the pressure of college, of my parents riding me nonstop that we need to chase merit or get a better SAT score or write the most perfect college essay, of Aiden and everyone else buying into it. It's bullshit. All of it. Designed just to make you feel like shit or give you bragging rights accordingly.

It's like the only time my parents remember I'm alive is to nag me about it. *Pick a major, pick a college, get a scholarship. Everyone else knows what they want already. What is wrong with you? Why are you wasting this life you have? If Nicky were still here, he wouldn't waste a single second.* Otherwise, they're just busy mourning one child or playing with his replacement.

And Sammy. Poor Sammy. I took him out for ice cream today after day care just to keep him out of the house for a little bit longer, and my mom freaked, full-on freaked about it, because she didn't know where we were for five fucking minutes.

My dad said I should be more sympathetic, but I'm not. The way Mom fixates on him—it isn't healthy. It's like me times a million. She practically wanted to take him to urgent care for a skinned knee last week. How can she seriously expect me to go to a fancy out-of-state college and leave the poor kid to deal with this alone? Even if I wanted to, I wouldn't. It's too much.

Shit, I'm giving myself a headache just thinking about it.

I roll over, trying my best to focus on the idea of taking June to the fall formal instead. I'm desperate to push out any thoughts of what I'm giving up, or how little June notices, or how I have to sacrifice *my* dream for everyone else's. I've never felt so much like a worm on the hook as I do right now, and I hate it.

"You good?" Mia's sleepy voice cuts through the silence.

I lie still, not wanting to let on that I'm awake. If I'm lucky she'll think all this tossing and turning is happening in my sleep. I just need to turn the noise down in my head, all of it. I squeeze my eyes shut, but Mia climbs over her pillows and drags my shoulder down so I'm flat on my back.

The impulse to smile is overwhelming, my body's urge to blow up my spot, and I try to focus on my breathing, slow and steady, the way I think a sleeping person's would be. Of course, Mia's quiet scoff has me opening one eye with a frown.

"You've always been the worst fake sleeper, Ivy," she says. "I don't know why you even try. Do you get away with this with June?" She laughs.

I sigh, telegraphing my feelings a little too loudly, because the truth of the matter is that lately, I feel like June wouldn't notice *anything*. If she didn't notice my obvious lie about why I wanted to back out, I doubt she'd have an opinion on if I was actually asleep. In fact, I could probably be rolled over blinking in her face, and she'd still be like *Nah, I think she's out* if she wanted to believe it.

"Okay, spill," Mia says. "Is this about your parents bringing up so much Nicky stuff today? Because—"

I groan. I can't help it. Can I just not talk about him for one goddamn minute? "No," I say, then instantly feel guilty about it. If I don't talk about him, then who will? Who am I to begrudge my parents talking about him? Who am I to get annoyed that Mia just brought him up again? I'm selfish. Maybe as bad as June. Maybe June isn't even that selfish. Maybe it's

176

just me being a massive asshole. I pound my head against the pillow a few times, wishing I could pound the thoughts right out of me. "Sorry," I mumble, throwing my hand over my eyes.

"What's up?" she asks, and even though she sounds casual about it, I can tell there's a solid undercurrent of worry on the edge of her voice.

"Nothing, just go back to sleep."

"Not until we talk about whatever has you tossing and turning in my bed at three o'clock in the morning on a school night." She smiles. "Is it June, then?"

I look away rather than answer and just catch her nodding out of the corner of my eye.

"Okay, so it's definitely June," Mia says.

"Aiden found out about us."

"Oh my god," she says, and any sleep that was left in her voice is now most assuredly gone. "Did he tell Harry?"

"No . . . not yet at least."

"Shit."

"It gets worse," I say.

"How?"

I tell her everything, the words spilling out of me like they'd been bound up, just waiting for anyone to ask, anyone to care. I tell her about backing out of the showcase. I tell her about the pressure I'm under. But unlike with June, I tell her the total truth about how Aiden is blackmailing me, how he forced me to give up the tournament, and our whole plan to let him have it by canceling late. I tell her how important this tournament is for June's recruiting process, my fear of an ethics violation, and how that could be a major black mark on both our records—especially mine, when I'm supposed to be guided by rules. Rules are the whole *point*. I'm like the hall monitor of sports.

Mia sits in stunned silence while I talk, aside from an occasional "wow" and "seriously?"

"What does June think about this plan?" she asks when I finish.

"She doesn't really know."

Mia raises her eyebrows. "How could she not know?"

"I didn't tell her," I mumble, looking away.

"You lost me," she says, leaning over until she meets my eyes.

"I told her that we got lucky and Aiden didn't see us. She thinks I just gave up the tournament because of the stress and pressure of it all."

"Okay, but obviously you would never do that. Officiating under pressure is, like, your whole thing."

She lets out a growl when I explain that's part of what's keeping me up tonight, thinking about how June didn't even seem to notice how upset I was, or how unlike me it was. How she seemed almost relieved we could put this behind us.

"Why couldn't you just tell her and figure it out together?" Mia asks, sounding frustrated.

I sigh. "Because I'm trying to protect her."

"What about protecting you?!"

I shake my head. "You don't understand what she's going through right now. She needs to impress those scouts. It's all tied to stuff with her mom and dad. Plus, she's doing something really important. There are like *five* women total playing baseball in college right now, and she's trying to change that."

"You're trying to change things too!" Mia says, her voice a mixture of pleading and annoyance.

"I'll have other chances," I say, swallowing hard because I need that to be true.

"If you really believe that, then why are you so upset?" Mia asks, and she's got me there.

I shrug, wiping at my eyes. "I didn't expect to feel so resentful. I made this decision, on my own, so how can I blame her? I need to just focus on things like the fall formal and getting to go public—all the stuff that we were excited about. But I . . . I . . ." I take a deep breath, bracing for her to tell me I'm an idiot, or to flip out about June, but she doesn't. She just looks at me calmly and blows out a long heavy sigh of her own.

"Okay," she says, switching gears. "So you haven't told Harry yet that you aren't coming?"

"Is that really all you took from this?" I ask, pulling the covers over my head. I'm being dramatic, yes, but I think this situation *calls* for being dramatic.

She slips her hand over the blanket and tugs it down just enough that our eyes can meet. "No, but it's the first step in fixing things."

"How do you figure?"

"Well, technically, you're still in. You haven't thrown anything away."

"Yeah, but I can't take it back. I'm not going to risk Aiden telling everyone and messing up the end of June's recruiting period. There would be this question hanging over her, like was she really that good or was she dating an ump? You know?"

"She knew what she was getting into when she got together with you. You both made that choice knowing what was at stake. It's on her that she grabbed your hand in the first place."

"I know, but that was an accident."

"Maybe it was. I don't know. But that doesn't matter anymore. All that matters is where you go from here."

"Where do I go from here?"

"Wherever you want to. You're not trapped. You don't have to let Aiden decide or give him the satisfaction of taking your place. If you want to work this showcase, then don't let him take it away from you. At least talk to Harry and explain the situation. Maybe he'll still pull you, but at least it will be on your terms. And if you don't want to do the tourney, because you're so burned out from being the perfect daughter, the perfect student, and the perfect official, while doing it backward and in high heels because you're a woman, that's okay too. But if that's the case, like you said, stop blaming June and get excited about the formal."

"It's not that simple," I say.

"I didn't say it was simple. I said it was under your control what happens. That part *is* simple."

"I don't know."

"Where does it stop, though?"

"What?" I grumble, rolling to my side.

"Where does it stop? Who's to say Aiden won't keep black-mailing you for other stuff? It's a slippery slope you're on. Not to mention . . ." She trails off, and I half roll over to look at her.

"Not to mention what?"

"Nothing," she says. "I don't want to cause any drama. I *like* June, a lot. In some universe, I think she's good for you. You've been really happy and disgustingly cute together whenever I've seen you. Minus the whole getting shit-faced at the party thing, but who among us, you know?"

Now I fully roll over to face her. "Okay, with the caveat that you like her and don't want to cause drama and don't want to be the person who shit-talks someone's partner, what are you thinking?"

"Are you sure you want to know? Or is this the thing where you say you want to know but then it blows up in my face?"

"I want to know. I promise. My head is so fucked-up over this. Help me think straight. I'm begging you."

"I don't think you're capable of thinking straight when it comes to a pretty girl," she teases, but one look at my face has her going serious again. I'm so worried about what she's going to say, I don't have time for jokes. "It just sucks that you're so worried about June's accomplishments and June's hopes and how much *she* needs the showcase for recruiting, that you're pretending like your dreams don't even matter, when it's clearly killing you."

"I'm not."

"You are, and that's why you're getting so resentful. You shouldn't put yourself second and she shouldn't let you!"

I sigh. That's what I've been worried about the whole time.

"I don't think June is a bad person, or that she doesn't care about you or anything like that. I think her dad has taught her that she *has* to be the main character. Meanwhile your parents have taught you that you're a supporting character at best." Mia holds up her hand when I start to make excuses. "I know your brother getting sick meant he needed all that attention. I'm not blaming them. But I think it's carried over into other parts of your life. I want you to really think about your role in that, and if it's enough for you."

Damn.

Her words hit me right in the chest, and I want to cry or scream or do anything else but sit here and listen to her drop these truth bombs on me.

"Yeah," I say, because I can't form another word. Thinking about this hurts too much. I turn away, pulling the blankets over my head again, wishing I was asleep.

Mia rubs my back a few times, soothing circles like my mom used to do, when she could bear to parent me. Tears burn hot in my eyes, and Mia doesn't stop. She just stays there, close by, in case I need her.

CHAPTER EIGHTEEN

June

IT FEELS like my body is on fire, the pain searing up my back and radiating out, up my neck, and down my arm, but I don't stop throwing the ball. I'm in a private lesson with Hank, although we might as well be in a joint lesson with my father. He's hovering by the fence, recording my throws so he can re-watch them in slo-mo. He insists on adding to all of Hank's feedback, barking at me about posture and form.

I'm tired, and cold from the drizzle of rain that kicked up in the last half hour. Javonte went home straight after team practice, so I don't even have anyone to help soften the blow or get some of the heat off me. Dad pays extra for this time to be solo, almost ninety dollars an hour. I know he makes good money with the shift differential and can spend it however he chooses, but all I can think about is how bad I want to go home and wrap myself in ice and blankets and Ivy.

If she's even around today.

Things have been weird the last few days. It's like I can feel her pulling away even though she swears everything is fine. I keep focusing on the fall formal—if we can just get to the fall formal—but this tiny thread of doubt keeps popping up that maybe she doesn't even want that. Last night, my dad went to work early again, and I asked her to come over and keep me company for dinner and to hang out. She said she had homework. Homework. The girl has been doing homework on my bed since we got together. Since when did it become a reason for her to skip out on one of our parent-free nights together?

Now that my dad knows she's an ump, not a groundskeeper, he's been nagging me nonstop about what a massive mistake I'm making associating with her. *Associating*, like she's some random kid at school and not the single greatest thing in my life. He doesn't seem to realize that she's the only thing really keeping me going lately. If he did, maybe he wouldn't be pushing me to end the relationship. But I'm not letting him get to me. I'm not letting him take that from me.

But Ivy . . . Ivy is so distant, and I don't know what to do. I know her mom is on her case about college. I wonder if she's being told the same thing as me about us being together. The more she pulls away, the tighter I try to hold on, and I think I'm just making it worse, but I can't help it. The last night Ivy was able to sleep over was the best sleep I ever had. She rubbed a little of the ache out of my shoulder, tucked herself around me, and told me everything would be fine, and I could almost believe it. Almost.

Still, I keep that memory in my head, focusing hard on it, as I force my arm to wind up and release again. The ache is worse today than it's ever been, making even my bad pain days seem minor, but I try not to let on. I heard Hank and my dad discussing "compensating for the mechanics" as I walked by earlier, as if my body could just figure it out on its own. Their definition of compensation is just muscling through the pain, and we all know that.

In the offseason, I can rest.

Well, I'll still have private training and hours of practice and the occasional scrimmage, but I won't have multiple games a week. I'll have a little bit of downtime. And a lot of time for Ivy. I'm going to sleep for days. I can't wait.

My father has scheduled a billion *final* college visits for those blissful few winter months, still desperate to get me, if not recruited, then at least a walk-on spot somewhere. It's hard on him that I haven't even verbally committed anywhere yet. Every time I ask, "Coach, what's the next step in the recruiting process?" they brush me off with promises that they'll come see me play, or they tell me to keep sending them highlights, while most of the guys on my team have gotten invitations for formal visits and offers with unusually long decision periods.

Javonte and Ethan both had formal visit requests the day the D1 contact period opened, when college coaches were first allowed to actively talk to players. I had crickets minus a few softball coaches and an email from a scam trainer claiming he could guarantee me a spot on the USA Baseball Women's National Team if I worked with him. Yeah, right, that's not how it works. Any *actual* baseball coach I'm in contact with, I've had to drag kicking and screaming into my inbox.

I know that, on one hand, I'm better than most of the boys who have already signed their commitments. I deserve these offers—and any money that comes along with them, whether they call it a baseball scholarship or disguise it as merit. But, on the other hand, sometimes I catch myself thinking about what Ivy said about there being a middle ground, about how it doesn't have to be all or nothing. I don't have to play D1, or D anything at all. I don't have to take on an entire college industry determined to keep girls out. I don't have to do any of it. I could rest, rehab my arm, maybe even remember why I loved the game so much to begin with.

But if I don't, I won't be able to open those letters from my mother. The ones Dad pinned to my bulletin board this summer, when he expected the offers to start rolling in: WHEN YOU GET RECRUITED and WHEN YOU PLAY YOUR FIRST COLLEGE GAME. Two separate letters because she was *so sure* I was going to make it. The thought of disappointing her churns inside of me, turning my stomach to acid. I grab another ball from the bucket, and I throw it as hard as I can. My dad, standing off to the side with Coach's speed gun, lets out a yip of excitement, and I feel warm all over.

There's not much that makes my dad smile since my mom passed away, but when I pitch well, it's a safe bet. I throw another, and glance in his direction to see the smile grow bigger, the worry lines falling from his face, his exhaustion rapidly replaced by excitement.

Forget middle ground. I will pitch until my arm falls off if I have to, just to keep his smile there.

It dawns on me then that maybe I'm not the only one in this family worried about disappointing Mom. Maybe he's feeling just as much pressure as I am to get this right. And don't I owe him that at least? Some fathers wouldn't step up to the plate when it came time to be a single father, but my dad did. I should feel lucky. I should feel—

I execute the next pitch perfectly, but a jolt of fresh stinging pain screams from my shoulder and careens all the way up the side of my neck. It's a stunning kind of pain, and I find myself sitting down on the mound without even realizing it, my legs forcing me to stop on pure instinct alone, as my head starts to spin.

Dad and Coach both come running over, clearly freaked out. "June?" Dad calls, the speed gun still at his side. "June?!" The terror in his voice snaps me back to attention, reminding me too much of those last few seconds with my mother.

"I'm okay," I say, pushing back up to standing with my good arm and brushing off the back of my Nike leggings, now stained a dusty reddish brown from the clay. "I'm okay," I say again, meeting his eyes.

"Let me see your shoulder," Coach says, interrupting the moment. He turns me around roughly so my back is to him and pulls the edge of my tank top strap out of the way. I feel caught, more exposed than I should feel with someone who I've worked with for so long. There's nothing weird about it; he's tended to dozens of injuries for me, taped me, iced me. There's very little dignity or need for privacy when it comes to someone who's pushed you to an elite level over the last decade plus. He's probably seen my shoulder more than I have at this point.

Somehow, his eyes on my skin feel different this time, more like an accusation. He manipulates the joint, gently now, raising and lowering my arm, as he watches for twitches and grimaces. He doesn't have to wait long.

"June," Hank says, disappointment in his voice.

"She's all right," Dad says, tossing a few stray balls back into the bucket.

"She's not," Hank says. My tank top strap snaps back into place as he lowers my arm and comes around to face me fully. "I thought the cortisone shot was helping."

"It is," I lie. Well, half lie, because it was helping. Sort of. For about three minutes. "It's just being stubborn today. I'll kick it in the offseason. Don't worry."

"See?" Dad says.

Hank crosses his arms, looking between me and my father. "She can screw up her shoulder forever playing like this. You shouldn't be encouraging her. I'm cutting it short today. Go ice and rest. I'll reschedule next week's lesson too, and you need to tell her team to put her on a pitch count."

"Now hang on, Hank," my dad says, clearly getting upset. "Is this really necessary? She said she's fine, and we're already paid up!"

"You can see that she's not!" Hank says, raising his voice. "She needs rehab for it!"

I rub my shoulder, not sure what else to do. I feel like a

failure, like I'm letting everyone down, and suddenly I want my mom. I wish she were here, telling me everything will be okay, instead of my dad, arguing that I'm not doing enough. Only I know, whether I pitch a perfect inning or blow it all and never step on this mound again, it doesn't matter. She's gone, just a pile of letters in a hatbox now. Maybe Dad should have burned them.

Maybe then we would both be free, instead of whatever this is—this constant desperation to make her happy, to pretend she's still here watching over us. That she's someone we can still disappoint or please instead of just a body in the ground that I can't get to. That I can't feel.

I'm going to throw up.

They don't even notice how bad I'm spiraling. They're still fighting around me, fighting over me, and I need it to stop. I need it to be quiet. I need my head to stop spinning for two seconds so I can get a grip on all these thoughts in my head.

"I'm fine!" I say, eventually, trying to shout, trying to sound brave in the face of the two men I respect most having a screaming match, debating whether or not I'm good enough, and finding me lacking. I'm not good enough for Hank to keep coaching me or for my dad to stop going in to work early, or for my dead mother and her freaking letters. I'm falling apart, and I'm scared I'm going to lose it in a real visceral way if I don't get off this field right now. "I'm fine," I try again, this time a little louder, finding my voice, but still I'm being ignored.

"If she keeps practicing on a messed-up arm—"

"She doesn't have a messed-up arm—"

"She needs a break, Clint. A real one!"

"The college showcase is in—"

"Who the hell cares about the—"

"This is her dream!"

"Is it, Clint? Or is it yours?"

I don't want to hear the answer to that. I try to tune them out, but they just keep going, cutting each other off, their words spinning through my head. I'm only able to catch small snippets here and there. It's overwhelming. I can't breathe, and everything is spinning, and I want them to stop talking about me like I'm not here, like I don't exist, like I'm just a life-support system for a pitching arm with no thoughts and opinions of her own.

I take a few steps back, pretending like I'm going to scoop up some balls, but bending over seems like a bad idea when your breath is coming in useless pants and your body is screaming *Run, help, you're in danger* on this bright, sunny day.

What is happening to me?

The shouting doesn't help. It's bad, all of it, and I want my mom and I want Ivy and only one of them still exists.

I march past Hank and Dad, but neither of them notices, too caught up in debating whether I should or shouldn't be pitching, whether I'm valid or not, insecure or not, whether I deserve a spot or not.

I dig for my phone, throwing wrappers and seeds everywhere as I search for it in my bag. My stick of deodorant goes flying, clattering to the ground loudly, but they still don't notice. I am invisible. Every part of me is invisible. I am reduced to an arm, a means to move a ball. Just some light physics in the shape of a girl.

I don't even feel real. I'm an idea, a thing, a—

And then I feel it, the cool glass of my phone, grounding me as I drop to the bench inside the dugout. The splinters in the wood poke into my scalp as I rest my head against the rough wall behind me, dragging me back to this moment as much as the ringing in my ear does when I push send.

We never call, just text and FaceTime, so I hope Ivy understands that it's urgent this time, that I need her, that this isn't just me complaining that she didn't come to my house last night, annoying her with my neediness.

Her voice mail picks up, and I leave a message, just a squeaked-out, pathetic "hi" before I hang up. I didn't know what else to say. *Hey, can you come get me? My grown-ups are fighting?* When did I get so pathetic?

My phone buzzes in my hand, just as the tears start to build: an incoming call from Ivy.

"June, are you okay?" Her voice floods my brain as soon as I pick up. She doesn't even wait for me to say hello.

"I'm fine," I say, and then I sob for real by accident. I just can't hold it in anymore.

"Are you at the practice field?" she asks. "I'll be right there."

Then she disconnects, and I sit and I wait, because finally someone is coming, someone who cares about just me, who sees me as more than just a means to an end. Everything will be okay now, if I could just remember to breathe.

If I could just remember to breathe.

CHAPTER NINETEEN

Ivy

EVERYTHING MIA said to me about my dreams and not sacrificing myself goes flying out the window as I drive to get June. I operated fully on instinct as I ran to my car, her tiny "hi" left on my voice mail alerting me that she was in some serious trouble, emotional or otherwise. We don't call each other, and we definitely don't leave voice mails. I didn't even know my voice mail was set up.

Her insistence that she was fine when I knew she wasn't had me charging off immediately. Is it Aiden? Does she finally know that I gave up the showcase to protect her? Is that why she sounds so upset? She's at her private lesson, and I know for a fact that Aiden is reffing the 7:00 p.m. game on the same field tonight—given that it's 6:45, the timing would track if he wanted to get there early and fuck with her head.

Fury spikes in my body as I push the gas pedal down a little bit more, racing to get to the field and not caring that I'm doing exactly what Mia said, putting June first, again. I was at an SAT prep class when she called, one I really needed to get my score into what my mom calls "chasing merit range," but it didn't matter.

Because sometimes you have to put other people first. You really do.

I pull into the parking lot a little too fast, making a bunch of annoyed parents glare at me as I throw my car into park and scan the growing game-day crowds for June. We've been keeping things quiet still, not meeting in public or talking to each other in places like this as the season finally winds down, but today, today is clearly an emergency.

I'm about to run out to the field when I see her rushing toward my car, dragging her backpack behind her with her good arm. Fuck, she only does that when she's really hurting and can't even bear the weight on her at all. I know that bag cost a lot of money. There's no way she would risk it getting torn up otherwise.

I glance up the hill toward the ball field where she was just practicing and realize that her dad and trainer seem to be angrily arguing with each other as the incoming coaches try to force them off the field so their teams can warm up.

I scan the parking lot quick and realize that I don't even see Aiden's car here yet.

My brain catches up to my heart, and a tiny thread of annoyance laces itself through all my knight-in-shining-armor tendencies. If this is even more pitching drama, I'm going to scream. No, I'm going to scream *and then leave* before I say something I really regret.

"Hey," she says, throwing her bag into my back seat and dropping into the passenger seat. Her cheeks are very obviously tear-streaked, little rivulets staining the edges of her dusty cheeks. It's so fucking sad and pathetic and somehow cute that I lean over and brush them away. It smears the dirt on the side of her face, but she doesn't seem to mind as she leans into my touch.

It's dangerous for us to be doing this here, but I'm lost at the sight of her. Confused, worried, and more than a little annoyed, I just want all the bad shit to go away for one single second.

She lets out a long breath, her eyes not so much closing as being squeezed shut, her entire body so tense she's trembling beside me.

"Come on," I say, lacing my fingers in between hers, any thoughts of anger and resentment dissolving at the sight of her so upset. "Let's get out of here."

WE DRIVE FOR a while, neither of us speaking, letting the music play on between us. She never lets go of my hand, her fingers staying tense and hard between mine, like they're holding on for dear life. It worries me more than ever.

I pull off by one of the downtown locks, parking in a dirt patch where a bridge used to be, a hundred years ago, so we can watch the muddy water of the Mohawk River slip by. I let go of her hand, popping open the center console and fishing through it for a minute until I find both the Tylenol and the ibuprofen.

June told me once that if you combine them, it gives you as much pain relief as the prescription stuff or something, and since then, I've gone out of my way to make sure to always keep them stocked for her. She holds out her palm, and I tap two of each into it, and then hide them away like we're doing something wrong.

She dry-swallows them, always unsettling, and goes back to staring at the water, like she wishes she could float away with the stray sticks and leaves in it.

"Are we going to talk about what happened?" I ask, shifting in my seat to face her. "You sounded really upset on the phone, and just the fact that you called—"

"Sometimes I feel like I don't even exist anymore."

"What?" My face scrunches up in confusion. "What do you mean? How could you feel like that? You're, like, *the* player."

She shakes her head like I just don't get it, and I'm trying. I really am. "Never mind," she says.

"No, I want to understand what you mean, June. You can't just say something like that and—"

"It's just . . . I got busted today."

"What?" I jolt up, thinking Aiden must have been there after all. The worry mingles with unexpected relief at the thought of our secret being out. "I can—"

Explain, is how I would have finished it, if she hadn't cut me off.

"My dad and Hank," she clarifies.

"Your dad and Hank?" I repeat, not really sure where she's going with this.

"Yeah, Hank caught on that my shoulder was bothering me more than I was saying. He called practice early."

"Oh, well, that's good," I say. "I'm glad somebody finally has some common sense about what you're going through. You shouldn't have to keep—"

"It's not his decision. I'm not like you. I can't just walk away from this tournament and what it means," she snaps, and okay, that shuts me right up. "Sorry," she adds after another couple seconds, but I don't think she really means it. Honestly, part of me doesn't even care if she means it or not.

When I thought this was about Aiden, that was one thing, but I don't have it in me to listen to her complain when she has it so good. Especially not when she rubs it in my face that I don't get to go to the tournament anymore. Maybe that's not fair, since she doesn't even know the truth, but it's how I feel anyway. She still has her dreams; she still has the showcase.

I try to tamp those thoughts down as quickly as they pop up, though, a constant whack-a-mole of bitterness and jealousy. The truth is, June needs me right now. Everything I'm feeling needs to be put on hold. Fuck what Mia said and any sense that it might have made, because when a friend needs you, when your girlfriend needs you, you show up. Right?

She slides her hand back in mine and shifts in her seat to face me. "Seriously, I'm sorry," she says, her good hand running soothing circles over the top of mine. "Hank cut practice early and then canceled the lesson next week too, and then Dad flipped out. Hank was saying I need to rest my arm, Dad was saying I was fine, and nobody was listening to me at all. They were just talking about me like I wasn't even there. I tried to tell them that I was okay, you know. I was trying to back up what Dad was saying and get Hank to back off, but neither of them listened. They both just kept shouting over each other and over me."

"But you're not fine, June."

She waves me away, like that's just semantics or a sidenote to the real issue, which was that she felt like she wasn't heard. Annoyance bubbles up inside me again, mutating itself into renewed anger. Because of course this is about how June doesn't get noticed for once; it can never be about how much June herself doesn't see. Like me. Like everything about me. I pull my hand back and cross my arms, needing a minute, but she just keeps going on and on about how they yelled over her.

"But then I started to get freaked out," she says, "because I couldn't breathe. It felt like all the air got sucked out of the sky, and I couldn't catch my breath. I got dizzy and hot, and I walked over to the dugout, thinking I was having a heart attack, which is when I called you."

"It sounds like a panic attack," I say, not as gently as I could, but not letting on how frustrated I'm feeling.

I can empathize. I've had panic attacks before, especially in those months following Nicky's death, when it felt like everything was different and upside down. I thought I could die too at any moment, like there was cancer hiding in me the way it had hidden in him. I think I made my mom take me to the doctor once a week in the beginning just to hear them say that I wasn't sick too.

That's something else that June doesn't know about. She doesn't know my sad little moments the way I know hers. She's never bothered to even ask. It's like it never occurs to her that maybe—

"Are you even listening to me, Ivy?" she asks, her voice going hard.

"Yeah," I lie, nodding my head to seem extra convincing.

"Then what did I just say?" And oh, that is one of my biggest pet peeves, and she knows it. Fuck being quizzed, even if I am lying.

"You were talking about your arm and your dad and your coach and blah blah blah," I say.

I'm being rude. I'm being an asshole—I know I am—but I can't take it. I can't sit here and listen to her complain about how hard her life is. And it is; I know it is. I know there's no competition for who got the worst deal or whatever, but Jesus Fucking Christ, does it always have to be about her? Mia's words echo in my head, and I cannot take this for another second.

"Did you seriously just say *blah blah blah* when I was telling you how I thought I was dying?"

"I know you weren't dying," I snap, even though I know that doesn't help anything.

She looks so hurt that I want to stop. I want to hold her and kiss her and make it all better, but also, I want her to feel how shitty I feel. The ugliest part of me wants to make her hurt the way I'm hurting. I swallow hard, wishing I could swallow it down, turn my anger into something less, something more digestible and easier to handle. I wish I was easier to handle.

"What the fuck?" June says, and rightly so. It registers, somewhere, that this is probably the first time I've ever heard her swear. I almost smile, happy that I've at least rubbed off on her a little, but I don't.

"I'm sorry," I say, and I actually mean it. I want to be there for her. I do. What is wrong with me? "I'm just having a really bad day myself," I add, pulling myself together. I care about her so much, and this is important.

"You're kind of being a bad girlfriend right now," she says, obviously hurt, dropping back against the door.

It turns out that was the exact wrong thing to say. All the frustration that's been bubbling up inside me boils over into white-hot anger. "I'm the bad girlfriend?" I practically shout. "Me? The one who just dropped everything to rush to the field and rescue you from, what? Your super-evil coach who wants you to rest your injury? Wow, what a horrible person. I'm so glad I left my much-needed test prep for that. Do you know how much trouble I'm going to be in with my mom for that?"

"God, it's not like you even care about the SAT! You didn't want to take the test anyway!"

"That's beside the point. I was doing something for *me*, and I had to leave it because *you* are too stubborn to realize your coach is right about you needing rest!"

"You know it's not about that," she says. "It's about them not even hearing me! It's about feeling like I only exist to throw balls for people. It's about—"

"What about me?"

"Sorry I bothered you in my time of need. I didn't ask you to leave your precious test prep or whatever." She rolls her eyes. "I won't do it again."

"It's always your time of need, June!"

She huffs out a breath, glaring at me. "Why are you being so mean?!"

"If you think I'm so mean and such a bad girlfriend, why do you even want to be with me?"

"Maybe I don't," she yells back automatically, without even hitting pause.

I exhale harshly, like all the air just got punched out of me, my mouth falling open in shock. Her words, a thousand scalding arrows, dig into my heart until I suffocate on them. After everything I've done for her? Everything I've given up for her? She—

"Wait, Ivy," she says. "I didn't mean—"

"Don't talk to me right now," I say, buckling back up and reversing out of the spot. "Don't say another word."

"Ivy!"

"Please," I say, holding up one of my hands to stop her. "I'm taking you home because I'm not a big enough jerk to leave you stranded here, but then I need you out of my fucking car, got it?"

"I didn't mean—"

"No," I say, pulling out onto the road and heading toward her house. "I don't think there's any coming back from that."

She gasps, actually gasps, and then starts crying.

If I didn't feel like shit before, I do now. I pull over on the side of the road and slip my car back into park. I don't know what to do. I don't even know what I *want* to do.

"Ivy, please, I can't handle this," she says.

I squeeze my eyes shut, utterly lost. All I know is that I don't ever want my resentment to outweigh how much she means to me and, thanks to this conversation, we're reaching that tipping point even faster. Maybe if we just took a beat, a little bit of time to blow off steam without hurting each other . . .

"Look, clearly you're under a lot of pressure, and you're very upset," I say, turning in my seat to face her. "I know you probably didn't mean what you just said, but it was really messed-up."

"I'm sorry," she says, grabbing my hand.

"I know," I say quietly. "I believe you, but maybe . . . maybe we should take a time-out, just for a little while."

"A time-out?" She sniffles. "What does that even mean?"

"It means I'm buried in college prep stuff and family stuff, and you're up to your ears in practice for this showcase." I try hard not to sound jealous of that. "Maybe we just take a minute to focus on our own stuff."

"You *want* me to focus more on baseball now?" she asks, sounding incredulous.

"No, but you're going to either way. It doesn't matter what I want," I say, realizing only after they're out how true those words really feel. I rub my hands over my eyes, pushing away the tears. "Shit," I whisper, not even sure if I want this break I'm begging for. I just want us to be happy. I want us to be good. I want *June* to be good.

She sighs and wipes at her nose, staring out the window, probably leaving me to come up with what to say next. But I think, the truth is, I don't want her to let me take the lead on this. I want her to fight back. To fight for us. To just once prove that I'm a priority here too.

I want us to talk this through together, figure out my feelings and hers. Maybe I'd even tell her about Aiden. I want us to be there for each other *while* taking care of ourselves too, and I think she wants the same. We can fix this. We can. It's only a little over a week until the showcase, and who knows? Maybe when the SAT is done, my mom will ease up a little bit. June and I can hang on that long. We have to.

I'm just about to take it back, to tell her I'm wrong, and I'm sorry too, when she says something else first.

"We *should* take a break." Her voice is cold, and she doesn't even look at me, choosing instead to stare out the window as she rips my heart in half.

"I . . . what?" I ask, hurt and panic rising up inside me. "Wait, I didn't mean like a real—"

"I have too much going on, and so do you. It was stupid to think it would work out. It'll be easier on both of us if we don't have to worry about getting caught or making enough time for each other. I need to focus on what I'm doing, and it's not fair to keep relying on you. We'll see where we land in the postseason," she says, her tone final. "Once I'm done with all the team visits Dad has lined up and stuff."

"That's, like, months from now."

"Is that not long enough?" she asks, and it sounds sincere.

Months? She wants months? Months feels like an eternity. Months puts us past the fall formal.

Wait, am I being dumped? Is that what this is?

"June—"

"I get it. You don't have to explain. I know I'm a lot. We're good. No hurt feelings, right? We tried. We're just . . . It's fine."

"I . . . yeah," I say, putting the car back into drive, too stunned to say anything else as I try to understand what she's saying. That this is a good idea, that this is the *right* plan. That we need to put ourselves first and not be worrying about anything or anyone else.

Maybe that's true. Maybe it is.

But then why does it feel so bad?

CHAPTER TWENTY

June

I'm sorry.

I miss you.

I didn't mean what I said.

I think I love you.

I definitely love you.

I want us to be okay.

Can we talk?

Every night, just before I fall asleep, I type up a text message that I wish I could send to Ivy and then delete it. It makes me feel better somehow. Like my entire relationship didn't blow up on one of the shittiest days in recent memory.

I'll be fine, though.

That's the thing about having a dead mom. You already know what the worst day of your life is. It's happened. And you're still breathing. You don't know how, but you are.

When my mom first died, somebody told me about this old metaphor about grief. It's like you're a little box and grief is this giant ball rolling around inside of you. It's always there, but as it shrinks, it knocks up against you less. Or, at least, something like that. It doesn't hurt any less, but the time between the ball bumping up against you starts to stretch.

I remind myself of this the first few days without Ivy. That, right now, my feelings for her are just a giant ball filling me up entirely.

Sometimes I imagine pitching it away, like I could wad up all this loneliness and brokenheartedness and turn it into some massive curveball. Unstoppable. Use my pain for good or whatever.

But then I start to just feel stupid.

That's another thing about having a dead mom. The sliding scale moves. Things like getting dumped rate a lot lower when you've had the nasty experience of having your ties to the person who created you severed. I don't know. Maybe I'm just being dramatic, or maybe I feel guilty.

Or maybe it's that I'm currently sitting in front of my mother's grave on the last freak warm day of autumn we're going to get. At least if you believe the forecasters.

I don't come here often. Not like Dad, who visits every week, bringing her a Sunday-morning iced coffee like he did when she was alive. He sits out here and drinks one with her, even though he hates iced coffee. He used to tease her about how iced coffee was *not* meant to be a year-round drink, and now he consumes it like clockwork.

I realize too late that I should have brought something personal and meaningful. Instead, I brought generic flowers. The $9.99 ones, like I couldn't even spring for roses or something pricey. I mess with the bouquet—mums, I think they're called—anyway. I fluff them out in the little holder thing Dad had built into the marble and then lean back on my blanket to study my work.

My eyes snag on the words carved onto the headstone. First name, last name, date of birth and death, followed swiftly by WIFE, MOTHER, SISTER, DAUGHTER, SOFTBALL PLAYER.

I run my hands over the words *softball player*—it was supposed to be a cute, cheeky addition to make us smile, but now it just makes me sad—and then drop them into my lap, turning to lean against her marker the way I used to lean against her.

When I was little, she would give me life advice while braiding my hair. She resumed that habit during the last year or two of her life, like she was trying to plait all of her parenting into my strands, tuck it in so I'd have it forever. I try to remember the sensation, but I can't, no matter how tight I squeeze my eyes shut.

I've forgotten what my mother's hands feel like.

Grief hits me, a bolt of lightning, knocking the air out of me as I curl up beside her, feeling only sun-warmed grass where there should be a whole other person.

"I don't know what I'm doing," I choke out, tearing up some of the blades and letting them blow away in the wind. "My girlfriend and I just broke up for basically no reason. I guess I thought she would be better off without me. She probably is. I mean, I'm constantly letting everyone down all the time, even you. You left me all these stupid freaking notes! Why did you leave me so many notes, Mom? You made so many plans for me, and now I have to . . . I have to just live up to them all." I wipe my snot on the sleeve of my hoodie and shake my head. "What am I supposed to do? All I know is baseball. I'm not even sure who I am off the mound anymore. If you're here, if you have any, like, motherly wisdom to share, can you give me a sign or something?"

I wait for anything to happen, a rainbow or a breeze that smells like her or anything else to let me know she hears me. Of course, nothing does. I wipe my eyes. This is a waste of time. I don't even know why I came here.

It wasn't like she was really going to talk back. It wasn't like I was going to be hit with an epiphany or something. She's not here no matter how many iced-coffee dates my dad has, and I'm more sure of that than I've ever been in my life. She's gone. She's marble and grass and flowers and butterflies and probably the occasional freaking worm.

Yet I'm still sitting here, on my own, trying to live up to the expectations of her ghost so that someday, maybe, I can continue the proud tradition of having my sport tattooed onto my gravestone. Like it's the most important thing about me. Like it was the most important thing about her.

I want to scream.

But mostly, I want my mom.

She would know how to fix a broken heart, or she would just hold me through it. Because if she were still alive, this would be the worst I had ever felt, like it was *supposed* to be. I could cry and be gutted and carry on about the end of my relationship, and it would be normal, expected even. I wouldn't feel so goddamn guilty instead. Except no, she took that away from me, didn't she?

I can't even experience a breakup, a veritable rite of passage for people my age—first love, first loss—because my first loss wasn't a romantic relationship. My first loss was my whole world. And everything will pale in comparison to it until the day I die.

It isn't fair. It isn't fucking fair.

I drop my head into my hands, wishing the dirt would swallow me.

I let myself fall apart for a good fifteen minutes before I decide I can't keep doing this. I can't worry about this. If my mom isn't here to pull me back together, I'll just have to do it myself.

Besides, I'm going to be late for practice.

"Heyyyy," Javonte says, drawing the word out as we walk back to his car.

So much for taking time off. Now I'm doubling up. Because here's the thing I realized, sitting in front of my mom's grave wishing I had a girlfriend: If someone is going to carve *baseball* into my headstone, it's going to be the biggest word, the first word, the boldest word that matters the most. Because baseball, I can control. Baseball makes sense.

"What's up?" I ask as we throw both of our bags into the trunk.

"Me and the guys . . ." He trails off when he sees my unimpressed face. Nothing good ever comes from a sentence that starts with *me and the guys*. None.

"Don't tell me," I say, forcing a smile. "You were comparing Richard pics again?"

"No." He laughs. "Although I would like a rematch. There's no way Ethan's is—"

I slam the trunk closed, wincing at the pressure that radiates through my arm from the movement. "Let's not finish that sentence," I deadpan, walking around to the passenger side.

Javonte takes his place in the driver's seat, turning on the car and the heat. It gets cold once the sun sets, and we've been practicing for two hours already. I hold my frozen fingers up in front of the vent, chasing the little bit of warmth that dribbles out while we wait for the car to warm up.

Isn't that the story of my life?

"Actually, uh," he says, looking nervous, "me and the guys are, well, we're worried about you."

"Worried about me?" I practically cackle. "The guys are not worried about me. Not as long as my fastball stays above seventy-five miles per hour."

"That's not true," he says as he pulls out of the parking lot.

"Fine, tell them not to worry, then," I say, settling my head against the cold window and wishing the seat warmer would hurry up for once. I wish it wasn't a twenty-minute drive to my house, since he's made it so awkward.

"I can't, because *I'm* also worried. You look like you haven't slept in days. You can't even throw the ball without it hurting anymore. Are you even eating? You haven't been over for dinner in days. You look like a ghost, and—"

"And the showcase is in a week, and you need me at my prime. Got it," I say, dropping my head back against the seat. "I have it under control. I'm not going to mess this up for us. I know the scouts are coming to see the whole team, but I definitely get that I'm the novelty act that's going to get you guys an extra look. Don't worry."

Javonte slams on the brakes and then pulls over to the side of the road. "You think that's how we see you?"

"What?"

"You really think after all these years we just see you as our pitcher? Come the fuck on, June. You're my best friend—"

"Fine, maybe not you, but the other guys. They could give a shit."

"That's not true."

"It feels like it."

"Then that's really screwed up, and they all suck for that," he says, his hands tightening on the steering wheel. "I know with the showcase coming up we've been . . . singularly focused, but we're a team, and when one of us is hurting, all of us are. We have your back, June, so you can cut the hardass act. You don't win games alone, and you don't have to go through whatever you're going through alone either."

"Ivy and I broke up," I blurt out, before I can stop myself. I didn't want him to know before because I thought it would make him worry unnecessarily about how it would impact my performance, and I don't want him to know now because it feels really freaking pathetic.

"Oh no, June," he says, looking almost as gutted as I feel somehow. "I know how much you cared about her."

"Yeah, well, it turns out that doesn't matter when you call someone a bad girlfriend and they decide to just . . . run with that." I'm not being fair, and I know it. The break was just as much my idea as it was hers, probably even more so, but Javonte doesn't have to know that.

"You called her a—"

"I don't want to talk about this, okay?"

"When Maddie and I broke up, talking to you and Ethan really helped. It's okay to cry and be upset. And it's okay to—"

"No, it really isn't." I let out a sad laugh.

"June."

I look at him, unshed tears pooling in my eyes. "If I didn't fall apart over my mother, I can't fall apart over a girl. A girl I dated for, like, ten minutes. It shouldn't hurt this bad?" That last line comes out like it's a question, not a statement, and he pulls me into a tight hug.

"You can fall apart whenever you want, Junie," he says, and the sound of my mom's nickname for me coming from someone else's lips unleashes the floodgates inside of me.

Before I know it, I am full-on sobbing against Javonte's chest, the center console and shifter digging uncomfortably into me as I cling to him.

"Shhh," he says, running a soothing hand over my back, gently ghosting over the muscles he knows always hurt the most. "Let it out. It's okay."

And no one has ever said that to me before.

No one has ever told me to let it out. Everyone always expects me to be strong, *needs* me to be strong, in my dad's case. Suddenly I don't know if I'm crying over Ivy, or my mom, or myself.

I cry until I can't breathe, until I've used up all of his tissues and three scratchy napkins. And then, eyes bloodshot and nose raw, I sit back in my seat.

"Wow, I needed that."

"I bet," he says. "June, if you need to take some time—"

"I don't," I say, looking at him earnestly so he knows that I mean it. "The showcase is the only thing keeping me going right now."

"You ever stop to wonder if that's how it should be?"

"A hundred million times lately," I say, letting out a shaky smile. "But right now, I need it. I need one thing that's mine. That I'm good at. That I can control."

"What about your arm?"

"That's why god made anti-inflammatories." I laugh, but he frowns, pinning me with his eyes. "Look, I'll take a break after the showcase," I say.

"Promise?" he asks, holding up his pinkie the way he did when we were little.

"Promise."

And if I'm crossing my fingers on my other hand, he doesn't have to know.

CHAPTER TWENTY-ONE

Ivy

I WISH I didn't have to walk past the baseball field to get to the main building that houses Harry's office, but I do. I try not to glance at the scoreboard, but I do. I also *definitely* try not to watch the way June stands proud on the mound, throwing pitch after pitch, commanding a lead in her final fall season game, but I do.

Aiden stands behind the catcher and gives me a two-finger salute as I walk by. I force myself to swallow down all the nasty words I want to shout at him. I glance at June to see if she notices me too, but, of course, she doesn't. She's so focused on herself, her game. Nothing exists for her outside the mound, whether she's actually on it or not.

I know it's technically my fault we broke up. She said something hurtful, and I said we probably couldn't come back from it. In that moment I just felt so overwhelmed. When I said I needed a time-out, I was thinking, like, a week, and then reset. The second she agreed with me? When she started talking months instead of days? I realized I wasn't done. I didn't want to be done at all, actually.

What's happened happened, though, right? Nothing I can do about it now.

I make it up to Harry's office, doing my best to wipe off the kicked-puppy expression that I've had on my face since seeing June again. Harry is sitting behind his giant desk, his hair peeking out from his hat in soft white tufts. He has an almost grandfatherly look to him when he's not getting down to business, and the smile he greets me with has me feeling extra shitty. I almost confess right then that I'm going to call out on the big showcase, but then the glint in his eyes turns to full-on glee, and I can't.

I can't let him down after everything he's done for me, at least not now, to his face. Harry created a safe place for me when my house was chaos. He helped me find direction when I didn't have any. When my brother's death derailed my life so spectacularly, somehow, he was the only one who noticed and helped me get things back on track.

"You texted me to come in?" I ask, guilt clawing up my spine.

"Yeah." He shuffles some papers around on his desk. "I noticed that a couple of your certifications were coming due very soon."

"Is that an issue?" I ask, relief coursing through me at the idea that maybe that will make me ineligible for the showcase. Wouldn't that be the perfect solution to let all of us off the hook? It might even fix some of my resentment. I mean, if I *can't* even do it, I have nothing to be resentful for, and if I don't have anything to be resentful for, then maybe June and I could—

"Oh no, not at all," Harry says reassuringly, completely misreading how I feel. "I just wanted you to come and clock in for a couple hours to get them all done. You get the standard rate, not the game rate, for training, same as when you pick up hours at the snack bar or anything extra like that, but I figured we should just knock them all out here so we're set for the showcase."

He gestures to the empty desk beside him, which sometimes houses his assistants but usually is just a catchall for old schedules and plans. He's cleaned it off so carefully that it makes my heart ache. He really wants the best for me, always, and I'm basically stabbing him in the back. I feel awful.

"Harry," I say, "I have to tell you something."

The truth dances on the tip of my tongue. *I dated a player. I broke the ethics contract. I need to remove myself from the showcase. I'm being blackmailed, maybe forever. I'm in love with a girl who can't see past her fastball. June is killing herself to make everyone happy. Every kid here is drowning, screaming silently, and none of the adults hear it except for maybe you. I don't even know if I want to go to college or what I want to major in if I do. I don't even know anything. I'm only eighteen. How am I supposed to handle all this?*

But I can't say any of that, not really. Instead, I look back up at him, his eyes shining as he waits patiently, like they were the time I showed up at his office crying after Nicky died. I had wanted someone to take care of me and couldn't think of anyone but my old soccer coach turned facilities and ref manager. Because I wanted, no, *needed* to be somewhere where I was the only one crying. Where I was the one getting comforted instead of my weeping mother or my stoic father, who only broke down in the garage, with his records up loud, like crying over your dead kid was some kind of embarrassment instead of a new family activity.

"Ivy?" he says, when I've been silent for too long. "Is everything okay?"

No. "Yes." I pull my hair up into a ponytail, losing my nerve. "I was just wondering if you could write me a recommendation for my college application." I lied. I don't even know why I said it, but the way he beams tells me that was the right thing to say. That I've made him proud.

Outside his window, June is striking someone out. She looks perfectly fine. Better rested than usual even. The score is a veritable blowout—7–0, June's team. Business as usual, like losing me was barely a blip on her radar.

If she can focus on her future, I guess I should do the same.

But that means getting serious about figuring out next steps. Maybe even wrapping up those early-action applications Mom keeps pushing on me. Losing this showcase does ruin the essays I've been writing about working toward it, but oh well. Maybe it's fine. Being a woman umpire is still "a hook," as Aiden says—enough to please my parents and maybe get the schools to throw merit money at me.

Funerals are expensive, after all, and Nicky's was huge. I

heard whispers at the dining table that it drained the money they had set aside for his college and some of mine. Go big or go home, right? Mom was out of work for so long taking care of him too; it's no wonder if they pillaged the 529s to pay the mortgage.

"Of course I'll write you one," Harry says. "Now go re-up those certifications so I have something to brag about."

I ignore the sinking feeling and click start on the virtual course. I'm sure the recertification will look good on my résumé, even if I won't use it again till spring. You don't need this high of a certification for reffing minor indoor soccer games, and I'm sure that's all I'll be assigned after blowing off the showcase.

MIA DRAGS MY comforter off me and throws it on the floor. A rude awakening for sure, and I'm just glad that I'm wearing sweats for once. I roll over and hug my pillow against the cold morning air she's forcing on me.

"How did you even get in here?" I growl into my pillow.

"Your dad let me in," she says. "I knocked. You know, because I had to show up in person because *someone* fell off the grid, ditched school for two days, and hasn't been returning any of my texts or FaceTimes."

"Whoever it is, they sound like a real asshole," I mumble, shutting my eyes again.

Mia rips the pillow from under my head and tosses it across the room. I sigh and roll over, finally meeting her eyes.

"I've let you wallow long enough," she says. "It's time to get your life back."

"It's been, like, a week."

"Yeah, and they say it takes a week for every month you've been together to get over someone, and you were together, like, barely over a month, so you're done."

"Who says?"

"People," she says, exasperated, as she goes to my closet and starts throwing clothes on the bed—black leggings, a pink Nike hoodie, high white socks. Then she shuffles through the bright orange shoeboxes lining my room and pulls out my pristine blazers.

Typical sports girl uniform.

"What time is it?" I ask.

"Seven."

"No," I say, grabbing an old stuffed animal and pulling it over my eyes.

"Yes. You're going to school, and you're going to get back on the horse. The horse being your life. Not an actual horse."

I cock open an eye.

"Go shower. You have fifteen minutes to wash the sad stink off yourself, and then I want you in my car."

"I can drive myself."

She crosses her arms. "Mm-hmm, because you've been so reliable about that this whole week."

"Fine," I grumble, heading toward the bathroom. "But only because you're annoying."

"Persistent," she corrects. "Not annoying."

"Same thing," I complain.

I HAVE TO hand it to Mia, she really does pull out all the stops to give me a good day and to remind me that there's life on the other side of losing the first girlfriend you ever really cared about.

She starts by running us through the best coffee shop in town and getting me my favorite iced coffee with a shot of vanilla. When I open my locker, a single red balloon pops out and floats up. I look at her, confused, and she shrugs. "I was going for more like 'surprise!' mixed with 'welcome back'—I know it's giving Pennywise vibes, but the dollar store was out of everything but red. It's the thought that counts, though, right?" she asks, and I burst out laughing.

God, I'm so lucky to have a best friend like Mia.

For the rest of the day, every class we have together is filled with something funny. She takes full advantage of the student council's singing telegram fundraiser, and I'm serenaded with a song in three different periods, each one telling me good luck or congrats or to have a happy birthday, even though none of those really apply.

The varsity soccer coach cancels practice, so at the end of the day, Mia comes with me to swing by the day care to pick up Sammy. We go to the park we used to play at when we were little and push him on the swings for a while. It's where we always came before we learned how to drive, and god, I miss the simplicity of just being here, of just sitting on a swing and feeling the cool breeze whipping in my hair.

My little brother erupts into giggles when I give him an extra-big push, and his laughter is contagious. This, *this*, is partly why I want to stay local so bad. When I was growing up, I was Nicky's shadow, just like Sammy's mine. If I leave? If I turn into someone he just sees on school breaks and holidays? No. I don't want that, not for him *or* for me.

I catch Mia looking at me, but I just flash her a smile and go back to watching Sammy. He makes living look so easy sometimes. He doesn't know what it's like to have a dead brother, not really, but then again, he also doesn't know what it's like to have a happy mom.

I frown and give him another giant push, trying not to think too much about that and just enjoy the moment, the sunshine, his giggles, the warm air, and the cool breeze.

"You deserve to be happy too," Mia says finally, when Sammy ditches us to play in the sandbox with some kids his own age. We take over the bigger swings as we watch him, toeing designs in the dirt while we twist around, both of us content to spin instead of swing. "You know that, right?"

"Yeah," I say, even though I'm not all the way convinced.

"Senior year isn't forever, you know?"

"What does that mean?"

"I mean that this whole showcase thing, and this college drama with your mom—especially this early-action pressure—none of it's going to matter in ten years. It's just a blip; everything is just a blip."

"Not everything," I correct her, because sometimes she doesn't realize that some moments are life-altering. She doesn't get it the way that June gets it. Some things, like Nicky dying, or June's mom, you don't ever really come back from—you just go on a bit different, changed, a little less you than you were.

Mia is more like Sammy, an accidental bystander to unimaginable grief. They won't ever understand how it feels unless it happens to them, and I pray to every god that will listen that it never does.

"Yeah," she says, as if she knows I'm thinking about Nicky. "Not everything. But a lot of things." She swings sideways, clanking her swing against mine like one of those little perpetual motion machines.

I look at her and see the worry in her eyes, the faint circles like she hasn't been sleeping any better than I have been. "Hey," I say quietly. "Thank you."

She smiles at that, smacking into me again and sending me jolting sideways. It shocks some laughter out of me, and it feels good. I let myself smash back into her, the way we used to when we were little and our parents weren't looking, and Mia smiles, clearly relieved and pleased about this turn of events.

Somewhere, in the back of my mind, I wonder if June could be a blip, but I don't think so. I think she'll just be another thing I don't come back from whole—something else to move on from, another little piece of me broken off. Not as big as Nicky, but still, a chip, a crack, a sign that I loved something and then lost it.

CHAPTER TWENTY-TWO

June

I'M FLIPPING the paper back and forth in my hand, the words I scribbled out glaring up at me before I shove them into an envelope and tear the liner off the flap to seal it. I don't bother writing a name on the outside. Just a number.

Seven.

This is the seventh letter I've written to Ivy, having graduated from typing and deleting text messages days ago. I stare at the envelope and then shove it in the drawer with the other six, before leaning back in my desk chair to stare at the ceiling.

It's possible I've come full circle. We all eventually turn into our mothers, right? And that's all my mother left me, just a pile of letters and the reassurance that my happiness wasn't tied to her physical presence. Maybe not, but it was a hell of a lot better when she was here.

The big difference is I'll never let Ivy see these letters. They're just for me, like I wish my mom had kept her letters just for her. I stare at her two latest ones: WHEN YOU GET RECRUITED and WHEN YOU HAVE YOUR FIRST COLLEGE GAME, still pinned to my bulletin board, right where my dad left them.

He always does that. Once, I asked for them all, just so I could know what I was dealing with, and he said Mom told him they were supposed to be a secret, a little stockpile of motherly wisdom to dole out like candy. He just pins them to the bulletin board that hangs over my desk, like silent bombs ready to detonate grief and frustration all over everything around them.

I have to imagine that, when she wrote them, my mom thought they would be a welcome thing. Something sentimental and precious that my dad and I would eagerly open together, maybe even while talking and laughing—*remembering*.

Some of them are like that, or they were in the beginning, but as the months ticked on and the letters kept coming, it became clear that the letters hurt Dad. Just the sign of her handwriting would send him spiraling, so I started taking them away, opening them myself when no one was around, to spare him the trouble. It went from this kind of remembrance—this reminder that if there's an afterlife, she's happily in it and loving me from afar, and if there's not, then at least she did her best to impart what wisdom she could—to a kind of forced march, a meditation on mortality. Her fears slipping in between her hopes, no matter how inadvertently.

It wasn't long before I started to dread them too. I'd be having a good day and then, boom, an envelope would be waiting for me with no warning, supposedly timed for whatever life experience he thought I might be having: WHEN YOU GO ON YOUR FIRST DATE, WHEN YOU GET YOUR FIRST PERIOD, WHEN THEY CANCEL SUPERSTORE. A reminder that I have a dead mom, but time didn't stop, and neither did her hopes and expectations.

That's why I'm not texting Ivy.

That's why these letters, seven and counting, are just for me. They're going to sit in my drawer quietly, where they won't hurt her. Aside from the fact that it's pathetic, I don't want to be the person who ruins her good day with my bad memory. Oh, you're happy and fine? Here's a reminder you have an ex-girlfriend and she's *not* happy and fine at all.

Maybe I'm lying to myself, though. Maybe it's pride keeping them locked up in the drawer, or even embarrassment.

I saw her the other day. I was pitching; it was a shutout even. I nearly ripped my arm off doing it too, but she just kept walking right by the field like I didn't even exist. I almost blew the whole game watching her walk by. Threw a wild pitch that turned into a ball, then a hit and a steal. It was pure luck that I struck out the next three batters.

I lost all focus, because I'm so lovesick, I couldn't stop staring at my ex, who literally didn't even notice me.

Pathetic. I'm still not over that.

I'm not over her either, but that's beside the point.

I glance at Mom's letters on my bulletin board. I wonder if she wrote one about a breakup. I bet she did. I kinda want to see what she put in it, but to do that, I would have to explain to my dad not just that I'm pretty sure I was actually in love with

Ivy, but also that it's over. No thanks. He hasn't noticed, singularly focused on this showcase as he is.

I wonder if he should have noticed.

Or if I should be as single-minded as he is.

Javonte was worried enough to stage a pseudo intervention last week, but my dad hasn't so much as hinted that he's picked up on my red-rimmed eyes or Ivy's lack of visits. The charitable side of me says that maybe thinking about love and loss just opens up his feelings about Mom. Like maybe he's worried it would dissolve all the stitches he's put in to hold himself together, the bandages woven with my pitching stats and his late-night factory work.

It seems like we're both desperately lonely now.

I unpin the letters and pull them close, tracing my fingers over my mother's beautiful, looping handwriting—WHEN YOU GET RECRUITED.

That one's been haunting me since the contact period started. If everything goes well at the showcase, I might even be able to open it up this weekend.

If they see that I'm just as good or better than any boy.

If my arm holds up.

If my mind holds up.

If my heart holds up.

It's funny, I think, as I list through them all, how separate each thing feels. Is this how everyone lives, just compartmentalizing things so they can survive? My heart is for Ivy. My arm for my dad. My mind on my mother.

Nothing for me.

Nothing for me.

I SHIFT ON the exam table, the paper crinkling beneath me as my doctor, who isn't a hack but *is* acting like one today by sneaking me another cortisone shot before the recommended time, finishes examining my arm.

"You've got grit, kid," the doctor says as he shoves a needle into my shoulder joint multiple times.

Grit. The word haunts me.

Even my coach wrote, *Her grit and determination are prominent both on and off the field* in the pitch letter he sent out to all the colleges he felt were worthy of coming to see me play at the showcase.

They all say it like it's an asset, something to be proud of. I guess I never paid much attention to it. Maybe grit is something you only care about when you don't have it. For me it's just called living.

I mean, is my arm screwed up? Yes. Are we all hurt on the team at this point in the season? Also yes. Javonte can't go a day without icing his hip. Ethan has been nursing a high ankle sprain all year. Owen messed up his wrist when he flipped over a fence by accident trying to catch a fly ball.

As much as I love how Ivy was so willing to fill my head with thoughts of other possibilities, other ways to love the sport, I know that at the end of the day, she doesn't understand.

We aren't just a bunch of kids playing a game. We're warriors. A little army. We're also a family. When I lost my mom, Javonte and the guys were the first ones at my house and the last ones to leave. It was them, and their families, who created a meal train for me and Dad so we didn't have to cook for almost two months. (Good thing, because there was *definitely* a learning curve to my dad taking over kitchen duties.) It was them and their families who made sure I had rides to school and practice, that I didn't miss the dentist appointment Mom scheduled for me two weeks before she passed, that I always had someone around to talk to.

Ivy might be stressed about the amount of pressure on her to get into college, or to make it someday as a pro official, but I have pressure on me for myself *and all these guys*. It's not lost on me that the novelty of a woman pitcher in a field dominated by men—is *dominated* the right word when there's hardly anyone else?—is part of what's getting us extra attention. With great power comes great responsibility and all that. While I might have daydreamed, a little, about finding that middle ground she talked about all the time, I'd be screwing up the team if I ever did.

I need to bring my A game, especially this weekend, which means no more sad-sack June, lying around missing Mom or Ivy.

No more writing letters.

The second the doctor has the needle out of my skin, I'm racing to the field.

I TOE MY sneaker into the mound, winding up and letting the ball rapid-release straight into Javonte's glove. A perfect strike. He whoops and throws his glove in the air, racing out to wrap me in a hug.

"You're back, June!" he calls, swinging me around.

The cortisone shot is already working its magic, and I feel better than I have in a long time. Well, that and the shiny new Toradol prescription Doc gave me. With any luck, I can keep the pain at bay until this week's showcase, the official end of the fall ball season.

All I know is that, right now, the sun is shining, my best friend is hugging me, and it feels like maybe, just maybe, I can let myself believe things will all work out.

Who knows? Maybe I can even get Ivy back after this season ends. If I could just—

"Come on now, back to work," Dad calls from the other side of the fence, but at least he's smiling.

Javonte puts me down, and I give my dad a thumbs-up before I reach into the bucket for another ball. I throw a few more, warming up, before Owen takes his place at the plate. He wanted to get in some extra hits, and since Javonte and I were coming here to try out my shoulder anyway, it only made sense.

He only gets a hit on one, a soft bunt that I immediately catch. If there was someone to catch the ball at first, he would be out long before he got there. I grin. This is already going better than I expected. The pain turned down from a sharp, stinging thing to a quiet hum in the background.

I couldn't think with all that noise, but now I can finally see clearly. *This* is all that matters.

"She's back," Javonte says, stretching out his legs.

"Yeah, yeah, great play," Owen says, trotting back to home base. "I'm very happy for you, June, but now could you pitch like you're human again so I have a prayer of clipping one?"

From off field, my dad laughs, eating it up, and the sound warms me from head to toe. This is what's important. This field. These boys. My dad. My future. All that worry about whether this is healthy, all that worry about if I'm overdoing it and if it's too much for me physically and mentally, fades under the cool autumn sun and the hazy clouds drifting across the sky.

The thing is, even if I *am* just a life-support system for my pitching arm, I'm a damn good one.

Ivy can wait, and hopefully she will, because I've got college coaches to impress and letters to open, and for the first time in a long time, I feel like maybe I've got this.

CHAPTER TWENTY-THREE

Ivy

MIA DRAGS me out to another party at Devon's to try to cheer me up, but then promptly ditches me when he comes by and asks her to get in the hot tub with him. Okay, *ditches* is a strong word. She actually asks me repeatedly if I'm okay with her going, then begs me to third-wheel and join them. No thanks. Neither of us have bathing suits, and the idea of spending the rest of the night in damp underwear isn't exactly appealing.

I'm relieved when she finally gives up, leaving me to my red Solo cup filled with room-temperature soda that I'm pretending is beer, because I'm also the designated driver for the night, and I know how much my drunk friends like to peer-pressure you into having "just one." It's less annoying for all of us when I utilize the red Solo decoy.

As soon as Mia takes off, I decide it's time to wander. The first floor is full of people, not quite typical teen-movie full, but full enough that every couch, chair, and ottoman is taken, and a smattering of people are sitting on the floor. Hardly anyone talks to me, aside from the occasional wave or "Where you been, Ivy?" which isn't exactly surprising because I don't talk to them much lately. I've been so busy with early-action applications and my own drama that all my friends aside from Mia have really fallen by the wayside. A month ago, it was all smiles; now it's like people forgot I existed or are just suddenly remembering that they're too busy to care. It's possible I didn't have to worry about peer pressure after all.

"Flowers" by Miley Cyrus comes on, the Sonos speakers blasting the ultimate fine-after-a-breakup anthem so loud the floors shake. I know I should be soaking it up, but for some reason it just makes me feel shittier. I *can* buy myself flowers, sure, but I don't fucking want to. It doesn't matter that technically June and I mutually parted ways, because really—and my heart twists just thinking about it—I know I got dumped.

I walk into the kitchen to get away from all the couples on the couch, and the cheerleader ironically singing the song *to* her boyfriend, only to find Kaylee and Miles, my respective crushes from last year, making out with each other. Each other. Like some cosmic fucking joke.

I groan, but they don't even pause to come up for a breath, so I pretend like I was here for a refill anyway. I pour some more lukewarm Coke into my cup and laugh when the next track is another breakup song. What. The. Hell?

Lucky for me, Mia's crush lives in a massive colonial, and having clearly exhausted my patience with the upstairs party, I make my way over to the carpeted stairs that lead to the finished basement. I brace myself to find more people making out, or worse, maybe even a decadent cloud of pot smoke or something, but am surprised to just see a couple guys who look vaguely familiar playing *Call of Duty*. They're gathered around a television on a bunch of beanbag chairs looking extremely intense.

None of them fully look up at me when I walk in, although one boy casts a sideways glance and does a double take before getting screamed at that he needs to pay attention by what I'm assuming is his battle buddy, because they're "in the weeds."

It's fine. I didn't come down here to be noticed or acknowledged; I came down here to hide until Mia and her chlorinated underwear are ready to go home. I drag an unused beanbag over to the corner, nestling in between two walls of wood paneling, and decide to doomscroll. I'm miserable, and I'm definitely radiating that misery, so what else is there to do, really?

I've lost June, and the showcase, and every possible open door that comes along with it. It almost seems pointless to even try to turn the rest of this year around. I let my head fall back against the wall, sinking deeper into the beanbag until I'm practically lying down, and then kick my legs out straight in front of me.

I scroll mindlessly through my socials. It's too tempting to go on Snap, where we still haven't deleted each other and she'll know if I see something of hers. I've been avoiding Snap like the plague, although I guess given how our country fared during COVID, maybe that's not really an accurate saying anymore.

TikTok is too depressing these days, my algorithm picking up that I'm a sad sack and forcing my FYP to alternate between videos of affirmations and videos of people crying. So that leaves what? Email? Who even uses that anymore outside of school? I open my old account, just for something to do, and am met with only Bath & Body Works spam from when I was fourteen and signed up for their email list to get a coupon. Jesus, that's bleak. I'm so bored I'm about to download a solitaire app, when I remember Insta exists.

I don't really use it; I think I have three pictures of a sunset on it and a post of me in my umpire gear on the field. That one was supposed to be ironic, but somehow took a hard left and ended up embarrassingly sincere thanks to my caption.

At least it's something to stare at.

I make it exactly five more minutes before I find myself searching for June's Insta. I was never on enough for us to ever become mutuals, but I know hers is public and updated all the time. She told me once it was a great recruiting tool, and as I scroll through, it's clear that she's filled it up with reel after reel of her pitching, along with other cute, quality PR moments like all the guys hugging her after a win, interspersed with her sticking out her tongue or making peace signs or whatever after a successful inning. It's a totally manufactured version of her, clearly meant to provoke the coaches' nostalgia for their

233

own high school days. She comes off as not just the perfect pitcher, but the kind of girl you want on your team, and maybe even the kind you want to date.

June told me once that recruiting isn't really about how good you are at the sport, or how hard you work, or even how much you deserve it over others. That's some of it, sure, but mostly it's about marketing yourself. Making yourself stand out from the crowd, playing the social media game just right so the coaches worry they'll be missing out on something if they *don't* sign you.

I told her that's what I'm trying to do too, or rather that's what my parents expect me to do with these college apps— make myself look shiny and interesting and unrejectable. She says it's different, and I mostly believe her. But also . . . it's not *that* different. Like, my dream to ref is rarer than hers, even if she doesn't see it.

Think about it—there are about 1,700 active players in the NFL, and there are only 121 officials for the entire sport. Sure, there are only around 700 MLB players, but the ump situation is even worse—seventy-six. Seventy-six full-time umpires in the entire MLB.

That's something June never quite got. We're both gunning for elite-level positions. They just look different.

Someone kicks my foot, and I look up, startled to see Javonte standing in front of me. Right. I suddenly realize why the boys playing *Call of Duty* looked a little familiar. They're from June's team. Perfect. Just what I needed tonight.

Javonte looks at my phone with an *I told you so* expression that has me dropping it facedown on the floor in an instant.

"Can I help you?" I huff, because I'm really not in the mood for any June-related bullshit tonight.

"If you're so miserable without her, why don't you just text her?" he asks, like that's the natural flow of the conversation.

"Who?" I ask, as if I don't know.

"June." He shakes his head and points to my phone. "You're stalking my best friend's Insta like you're either ready to re-cruit her or you're as goddamn lovesick over the breakup as she is." I narrow my eyes, but he just smirks. "Oh, wait, are we sup-posed to be doing this, like, *pretend we don't know each other* thing? Because I don't do bullshit like that."

I roll my eyes. "I obviously know who you are, Javonte. I never forget a catcher who doesn't make my life hell. Now I would really like it if you kept up that trend off the field too."

He licks his lips and drops down beside me. "Sorry, can't," he says. "It's my best-friend duty to annoy you until I figure some-thing out. Mainly, why are you hell-bent on breaking June's heart when it's obvious that it's breaking yours just as bad?"

"It's not," I protest.

He drapes his long arms over his knees and leans his head back to look at me out of the corner of his eye. "You're hiding in the basement at a party."

"So are you," I point out, and that makes him laugh. His wide smile is contagious, and it's easy to see why people flock to him. "Why are you even here?"

"I used to play basketball with the kid who lives here. We reconnected after you dragged June to his last party, so thanks for that. And for the record, I'm not hiding. I'm playing a game with my team, who collectively decided to stay sober until after the showcase. I just happen to suck at *Call of Duty* enough that they kicked me off for the next round."

I swallow hard. "Is the whole team here?" I scan the room. It's so difficult to make out faces in the dim glow of the TV that I can't be sure.

"Pretty much," he says, and my stomach continues its free-fall to hell.

Hope and dread tangle together as I take a deep breath and brace myself to ask, "Is June here somewhere too, then?"

"Do you want her to be here?" he asks, turning to study my face. I don't know what he sees there. Panic? Desperation? An assortment of both? Thankfully, he doesn't torture me long. "She's not. She doesn't do anything anymore except work out, practice, and sit at home pretending she's not crying over you when she definitely is."

I scrunch up my face. "I didn't get the impression she gave a shit that we broke up, so . . ."

"So . . ." he says, imitating me, "that just tells me you're really bad at reading people."

"I saw her at your last game. She didn't look upset. She looked like she was out for blood."

"Would that be the same game that I had to drive her home from, crying, because you walked by and didn't look at her? Damn, Ivy, I figured by now you would've realized that she's

236

got a good poker face in public. Just like the shit she hides about her pitching arm . . ." He trails off, like he doesn't want to venture any farther down that path. "She misses you. She's pretty lost without you, even if she'd kill me if she knew I said that."

I snort. "She was pretty lost *with* me too."

That earns me a raised eyebrow. "Can I ask you something?"

"You just did," I say, and roll my eyes, thinking about how Nicky used to say that all the time. God, I wish he were here. He would probably have the best relationship advice of anyone.

"Why did you two break up when you both still obviously care about each other?" Javonte asks, pulling me from my thoughts.

I shrug. "That's not really your place."

"No, it's not, and you don't have to answer. I probably wouldn't. But she's so tight-lipped about it. Maybe if I knew, I could figure out how to help her get through this. Not that it's your responsibility. I'm just saying." He grabs my phone, holding it up to my face to unlock it so he can scroll through June's Insta. I should stop him, but I'm too busy focusing on what he just said.

"Do you think she really misses me? Or does she just miss having someone around to make her feel better all the time?" I ask before I can catch myself, because it hurts a little to imagine Javonte as the one taking care of her now.

"Oh," he says. "Ohhhhh. Got it."

I scrunch up my forehead. "What exactly do you think you *got*?"

"She did that thing she does when she's stressed, didn't she?"

I give him a blank look. "Is she ever not stressed?"

"Nah, not anymore," he agrees, scratching his eyebrow with his thumb in the way all cute boys do. Seriously, is there a manual? And then he looks back at me. "The more worried June gets about something, the more she focuses inward. Makes it all about her. It can feel . . ."

"Shitty?" I offer.

"Lonely," he settles on. "Like what about me, right? And that's super valid. Like, if she wasn't my best friend, I would probably high-five you for having enough self-respect to ditch her ass for that."

"I didn't actually 'ditch her ass,'" I say. "We technically ditched each other, but hers was more final. I said a time-out, meaning like a few days, and she said a break, as in several months."

"Hmmm." Javonte nods, like it suddenly all makes sense. "So she went full dark, then. I don't blame you. When she gets in a black-hole mood, it's hard to deal with."

"Why do I feel like there's a *but* coming?"

"But she's so freaking in love with you, Ivy. That's her defense mechanism; that's all that is. Tunnel vision because her dad makes her, because living up to her mom's letters is the end goal. If she doesn't, she thinks it will all fall apart."

"What will?"

"She's propped up her whole life with tiny little matchsticks, and if a strong enough wind comes, they're going to all blow down. I think she was worried you were that wind—I know you were talking about finding a middle ground and shit that really spun her—but you're not. You are *not* the wind, Ivy."

"Oh yeah?" I ask. "Then what am I?"

"I don't know. I've been up since four a.m., and this metaphor is stretched about as thin as it can get. I'm fried from all the extra practices June is forcing on us. All I know is you're definitely something good, if you want to be, and I think she could be good for you too, if you two can just talk.

"She wasn't always this way, you know. Before her mom died, she was talented and dedicated, sure, but since everything happened, she's been obsessed. It's what's getting her through. Does that mean she can treat you like shit or that you owe her another chance?" He taps his finger on my phone screen and then closes it, handing it back to me. "That's up to you to decide. Like my mom always says, there's no girlfriend worth losing yourself for. I just think, and maybe I'm off base here, but I feel like if you care about her as much as she cares about you, there's gotta be a way for you two to find that middle ground you're so fond of. But what do I know? My longest relationship was three months, and that was in ninth grade."

"Yeah," I say, mulling over his words. He gets up, patting my leg as his buddies announce that he's up. I can tell he's a little torn about leaving me here in this corner, but I wave him off. I've got a lot of things to think about, and I'd rather do it alone.

CHAPTER TWENTY-FOUR

June

NO MATTER how much I cried, prayed, and begged the universe, god, and the ghost of my mother for one good goddamn day, none of them answered.

This morning has been a slog. I woke up nauseated from the painkillers. I moved wrong brushing my hair, and that sent an intense shooting pain up my shoulder and neck that now makes it hurt just to breathe. Getting dressed wasn't any easier. And when I opened my drawer to find a hair tie, I was face-to-face with all those stupid letters I wrote Ivy.

The urge to call her was nearly overwhelming, but I smashed it down. A part of me is still hoping to see her out there on the field today for the showcase. Like she changed her mind and decided the pressure was worth it, that I was worth it. But I can't fall down that rabbit hole.

Today is important. This showcase is bigger than me and my pain. This is the culmination of my parents' hopes and dreams;

this is the culmination of so much hard work, not just by me, but the whole team. Most teams don't even get this chance, and most women never will either. I have broken barriers. I have become the first girl to ever be invited to this tournament. The other day, a little girl stopped me on the practice field and asked for my autograph. Her mom said I give her hope and they've been going to all my games. It really hit home I'm doing things that hardly anyone else has. I'm playing at a level no one else can, at least not locally.

I'm an inspiration.

I'm making dreams come true.

So what if I can't breathe?

My pain is a small price to pay for the happiness it brings my family, and my team, and all the little girls coming to watch today. I see them and all the cute little DMs from their parents' socials, where they follow my recruiting account. Not to mention all the DMs from coaches leading up to this. I'll be opening my mom's letters soon; I can feel it.

I lie back on my bed, trying to focus on calming my mind, and trying to remember how to breathe without moving my body at all. I grab my phone with my good hand and scroll through Insta to make sure I haven't missed any messages from any of the coaches coming today.

And that's when I see it.

A notification that Ivy liked one of my posts.

It wasn't even a recent one. With my recruiting schedule, I update my Instagram almost every day with new reels. She had to scroll to find this one, which means she was probably watching them, all of them. Which means maybe she still misses me . . . unless she was hate-watching.

I frown. She was probably hate-watching. I close the app and drag myself out of bed, not ready to face the day, but having absolutely no other choice.

Javonte picks me up extra early before the showcase. We decided to go a couple hours early to shake off any nerves we might be feeling. He can tell something is up as soon as I get in the car, but he waits until we're almost there to ask me about it.

"Ivy liked one of my posts on Insta last night."

"You should call her," he says, sounding weirdly unsurprised, as we pull into the parking lot, like this *isn't* the most important showcase of both of our lives today. Like this Insta drama matters at all, like the butterfly tornado in my heart is worth talking about. It's not, not right now anyway.

"We should probably just focus on the game." I sigh. "Forget I brought it up." He parks and turns in his seat, hitting the lock button every time I try to unlock my door to get out, until I'm annoyed. "What are you doing, Javonte?!"

"June, look at me."

I ignore him.

"Look at me!" he says again, and I turn to stare at him, indignant. The motion jerks my neck too hard, though, and sends a fresh spasm of pain radiating into the joint of my arm. I do my best to cover it up, but I can tell by his face he caught it.

"I'm fine," I lie, instinctively.

"You think I don't know your arm is extra screwed-up right

now?" he asks. "Because I do. Just like I know you're acting like you don't give a shit about Ivy, when you really do. I've been friends with you long enough to know how much pain you're in—inside and out. You don't have to hide from me. It's insulting that you even try."

I roll my eyes and lean back against my seat. "I really don't want to talk about this right now. Are you going to let me out or do I have to call Coach?"

"Why are you being like this?"

"Probably because everything is riding on my performance today, and you tricked me into coming early to have some heart-to-heart or something, and I don't want it. You can act like we're the same, but we aren't. It's different. *I'm* different."

"Your pain isn't unique, Junie," he says softly, and those words hit me like a machete to the brain.

"What does that even mean?"

"I mean everybody is struggling, okay? Everybody has something that's hurting them emotionally, physically, whatever, and your main character syndrome is seriously messing up your life lately."

I snort. I can't help it. "Main character syndrome? Main character syndrome?!" I screech. "If I was the main character, wouldn't I have some agency here? Wouldn't I at least get a say in things?" I cry, the tears coming in earnest. "I don't have any control, Javonte. None! My entire life is predetermined by a secret freaking box of letters that my dad won't even let me see. I don't know how many there are or when another one might come and show me that I'm not following the plan, not living up to their hopes and dreams, that I'm an absolute disappointment."

"That's not true. You are *not* a disappointment, and you do get a say. You should get a say! That's what I'm trying to tell you. You don't have to keep doing this."

"Doing what?"

He waves his hands around the field. "Any of it! You don't have to live in your mother's shadow, you don't have to play when you're in this much pain, and you really don't have to end things with Ivy so you can stay focused on this stupid game!"

I look at him then, really look at him. He sounds so much like Ivy that time she said I didn't have to kill myself for a ghost.

I wish they were right. I wish any of that were true.

"Baseball is all I have," I say, but he shakes his head. Before he can interrupt me again, I clarify. "I can't control the letters or when they come. I can't control cancer killing my mom. I can't control my dad or how he's happy when I win and depressed when I lose. I can't control Ivy wanting more of me when I'm just so tired. I'm so tired, Javonte.

"And she deserves more. I thought if I could just get us to the fall formal, it would be okay. Isn't that stupid? I told myself I could keep her that long, that we could make it." My voice wavers. "She didn't stick around. No one sticks around."

"June—"

I hold my hand up to get him to stop talking. "I ran her off, okay? Don't blame her for that. I'm at fault here. I hurt her, badly, and after, when she said she needed a break, I ran with it. I could see it hurt her, and she was trying to take it back, but I ran with it anyway, because she deserves better. She deserves better than a traumatized ball-throwing ice pack for a girl-friend. So can we just fucking drop it?" I say, not even caring that I swore. Again. If ever a moment called for it, it's this one.

"June," he says more sternly. "This is not the way."

"I'm gonna go warm up, and I hope you'll help me, but if not, I'll see you on the other side of the mound when the game starts."

THE SWEAT STINGS against my windburned skin and I'm bone-weary, but I'm still standing thanks to another dose of Toradol right before the first game. It's our turn to hit, and I'm melded into the corner of the dugout, where none of the recruiters can see me, using the walls to help apply pressure and keep the ice on my screaming shoulder. To them I'm just refreshing myself, maybe grabbing some water, not dry heaving and trying not to cry while my coach pretends not to notice. If this is how bad it is on pain meds, I can't imagine what it's going to be like to-night when they wear off.

That trip to the cemetery stirred up a lot of stuff, and I catch myself trying to remember the way my mom used to comfort me whenever I was hurt. The afterlife has tried to turn her into an idea, instead of a person, but if I try really hard, I can still remember that when she was flesh and blood, she was love personified.

If she were here right now, she would put her hand on my forehead and tell me to go rest. Tell me to burn her letters up and pretend they never existed. That Javonte was right. That Ivy was right. That my dad will be okay.

But she's dead. So she doesn't, and I'm stuck here, wedged in the corner, trying to hold it all together.

The truth is, I could tell something was off by the end of the first inning, but I could tell that something was very badly wrong by the end of the second. The pain, which used to be a jolt if I moved a certain way, accompanied by a not-so-dull constant ache, has suddenly transformed into the kind of pain that makes you tremble even when you're trying not to. That makes your stomach flip-flop and occasionally purge itself.

I'm relying largely on muscle memory at this point, forcing my body to ignore the signals screaming at me to stop. I have to keep going. Every time I glance over at the recruiters and coaches, they're looking at me or scribbling on their clipboards. The panic that they're writing that I'm not good enough, or that my teammates aren't, is mixing with the adrenaline in my bloodstream to keep me upright.

After the fifth inning, I jog off like a champ and promptly throw up in a now-dumped-out ball bucket. My coach gives me a look that could almost be sympathetic . . . if we didn't have a game to win and half the colleges on the East Coast here to see us do it. I brush him off, telling everyone it's probably food poisoning from sushi I had last night, but I'm not sure anyone buys it.

Javonte sits down near me, carefully blocking the view of anybody who tries to see in. He pulls my legs into his lap as I let my head drop back against the wall, the pain making me sweat in an embarrassing way.

"I think something's really wrong this time, Junie," he says, rubbing soothing circles around my cramped-up calves.

"Yeah." I nod. "But I've got this, don't worry. And then we'll rest."

"And then we'll rest," he repeats, gripping my leg a little more firmly, like he's going to hold me to it.

I shut my eyes as the coolness of the ice seeps into my shoulder, numbing me a little and replacing the tremors with chills. There are no easy games on the schedule, but this one should have been the easiest. I wasn't expecting the other team to go this hard, and as they strike out our third consecutive player, I reluctantly pull my legs back under me and stand up, a little shaky. I know deep down I'm not playing well today, not compared with how I usually play, but I'm still playing better than just about any other pitcher out here.

I'm a failure by my own standards, but a success by everyone else's. Coach squeezes my good shoulder. Tells me I'm brave for going out there with a stomach bug, even though he's very suspiciously avoiding touching my bad shoulder and always has a bag of ice waiting for me when I come off the mound. We both know in another life I would be pulled.

But I'm not in another life; I'm in this one. And in this one, I have an ex-girlfriend and a dead mom plus an entire team counting on me to make them look good. I take a deep breath and jog out, right as the outfield umpire jogs in to home plate.

The other ump's legs probably got tired of squatting, so they're trading for the rest of the game, I guess.

I wish Ivy was one of them. I keep staring at the umpires like magically one of them will turn into her.

As the outfield ump walks by, he gestures toward the scoreboard, where 4–4 is listed in bright red numbers. We're tied in the bottom of the sixth, something no one expected. "It's not so easy without your girlfriend calling plays in your favor, is it?" He smiles, and my whole body goes rigid.

"What are you talking about?" I ask, pain and fury bubbling up inside me, painting my vision as red as the scoreboard.

He doesn't answer me. He just continues on to home plate and leaves me standing there confused and pissed off. It lights a fire inside me that I can barely contain. *I'll show him,* I think. *I'm not a cheater, and neither is Ivy.*

When the batter signals that he's ready, I unleash a fast pitch the likes of which have yet to be seen in this game.

"Strike one," the snake in the umpire gear yells, holding up his finger.

And this could work, I realize, letting the anger coat the pain until it's all I feel.

This I understand. This I can do.

It's not till later, much later, when everything is screwed up beyond belief, that I realize he shouldn't have known. Couldn't have known. Unless . . .

CHAPTER TWENTY-FIVE

Ivy

I'M SITTING in the bleachers with my hood up, praying that Harry isn't around to see me. I wasn't going to come, especially not after calling out sick, but Mia said she couldn't take my pacing anymore. It's not like they broadcast high school baseball showcases on ESPN or MLB Network, and I was dying to know what was happening. She practically forced me into her car and drove me here.

"Come on, sad sack," she had said. "You know you'll regret not being there."

I thought it would be hard to see Aiden out on that field, but it wasn't as bad as it could have been. I think I've made peace with the fact that I'm not officiating this one. There are a million paths to the majors, and officiating showcases at this level is just one of them.

Besides, it's just one tournament, I remind myself. There will be many more. Today, I'm here as a brokenhearted spectator, a lovesick fool, and a number one cheerleader. Watching June on that mound is the real hard part—so much harder than seeing someone else officiate. Knowing I won't be the one taking her home after the game eats me up. Sometimes I hate how much I miss her, but either way, I want to see her succeed. I want today to go well for her.

And who knows? Maybe after things calm down, I can talk to her about trying again. Maybe the fall formal isn't totally out of the picture yet.

I scan the crowd again for Harry. As far as he knows, I'm home sick in bed—definitely not huddled up in a hoodie, hiding out in a crowd of the opposing team's fans. That was the deal I made with Mia; we had to sit with the away team's families. I didn't want to risk running into June's dad or having her see me.

Being here is flying close enough to the sun.

When June comes out for the third inning, I can immediately tell that something is wrong. She looks clammy and pale, with a sheen of sweat on her that doesn't seem to be from exertion alone. It's a cool day, and none of the other players have it. June moves stiffly to the mound with a slight tremble in her step that makes my stomach clench.

I turn to tell Mia that something is really screwed-up, but then remember she's disappeared to get us drinks and popcorn. This game should be an easy one for them, and my anxiety rises when I glance at the score—they're up by one in what should have been a blowout, and that lead disappears in the fourth inning when the opposing team ties it up.

"The lines were so freaking long," Mia says, finally dropping beside me. She passes me a soda and then tilts the bag of popcorn toward me, some kernels falling onto my lap. I brush them away and shake my head. She follows my line of sight to June. "You good, Ivy?"

"Something's wrong," I say, leaning forward to see better.

"The score's weird, but don't worry, I'm sure she'll pull off the win. As much as I hate to say nice things when I'm pissed at her on your behalf, June's a beast. She's going to come through."

A couple of the parents around us shoot us nasty glances, obviously cheering on their own kids and not wanting to hear us wax poetic about how they're definitely going to lose. I try to keep up the façade, to go with what Mia is saying, but I can't shake the idea that something is really messed-up here, and not in a karmic *she's finally sad she lost me* way, but in a *is there an ambulance on standby* way.

Mia nudges me. "Look, she's going into the dugout. She'll get a break at least, and if something really is wrong, I'm sure her coach will pull her."

That makes one of us who's sure about that.

I glance back at the scoreboard, tracing the 4–4 with my eyes. The wall of recruiters and coaches around the pen are all laughing and joking with each other, occasionally marking down notes, and my stomach sinks at the thought that this underperformance is one of their only experiences with her.

They're going to think this is all she is, that she's choking on the big play. Something is wrong, but I'm positive it isn't that. June doesn't choke, ever, and she doesn't have off days, not when it counts.

I twist myself in my seat, trying to see into the dugout. June has headed inside, and any hope I had of getting a feel for what's going on is lost when Javonte walks over and fully blocks the view of her. Weird.

Normally, June sits right in the center, assessing the other pitcher, watching the way the team moves in the outfield, looking for holes and weaknesses. Her sitting in the corner is nearly as unlike her as the score. My heart twists painfully in my chest as I see Javonte sit down and pull her legs into his lap, massaging her calves. They cramp up sometimes, but only when she's dehydrated or overtraining.

I wonder which one this is. Probably both, knowing her.

"Mia," I say, grabbing her hand from nerves. "I think something might be really, really wrong. I'm freaking out a little bit."

"I think you're just anxious for her." She smiles, trying to keep it light. "I'm sure her coach or her dad or someone would stop it if it was really bad."

"I'm not. She said once she felt like they only saw her as a life-support system for her pitching arm. That doesn't really give me a lot of confidence in their judgment."

"Will you two stop talking?" the gruff dad sitting in front of us asks, his big arms crossed.

"Or what?" Mia asks, which seems to confuse the man. He narrows his eyes, but then waves his hand at us, as if to imply we're not worth it as he turns back around. "Thought so." She smirks, taking a sip from her giant Diet Coke.

She got me Fanta, my favorite, and in any other circumstances, spending the day watching a game with my best friend and my favorite drink and perfect sports park popcorn would be the ideal situation, although I probably wouldn't pick baseball. But even all that can't help me escape the existential dread building up inside me over the idea that June is obviously hurting and no one but me seems to care.

The inning ends too soon with three consecutive outs, the score still tied as June makes her way out to the mound. She passes Aiden as he's jogging in from the outfield to take over the home plate position. I don't know what he says to her, but her body goes taut, like a finely tuned piano wire. I can tell the moment she snaps inside, determined to go hard.

Aiden takes his place behind the catcher, and even from here, I can see that his smile is more of a sneer. She winds up and unleashes a wicked fastball. I would be thrilled to see it if I wasn't so worried. She strikes the first player out with ease, but every time she throws the ball, she wipes her eyes. I tell myself it's fine, it's just dirt, but I know it's not.

I want to run out to the field. I want to stop it. I want to hug her and tell her it's okay. That she doesn't have stand here and perform in tears just because every adult in her life expects her to. I want to do a million things, but I can't. All I can do is sit and watch as it all comes crashing down.

CHAPTER TWENTY-SIX

June

I CAN'T stop thinking about what that ump said.

The implication that my girlfriend—*ex-girlfriend*, I remind myself—somehow rigged the games for me—games that Aiden mostly officiated himself!—doesn't make any sense.

Did he just say that to throw me? Does it even matter if he did?

I should thank him, the anger and competitiveness kicking my gameplay up a gear. My fast pitch keeps coming, and I almost start to dissociate, my body on autopilot as I strike, strike, strike the other team. If Aiden was trying to shake me, it didn't work.

Javonte tries to talk to me again as we jog in, letting our batters do their jobs as I ice my arm. Aiden's words roil inside me. I brush him off, though. I need to stay in the zone now that I've finally found it. I need to stay outside of myself—outside of what Javonte thinks or anyone else. The truth is, there's no escaping what I am or whose shadows I'm living in, and I'm not about to listen to someone who thinks I can. Even if he is right about me loving Ivy.

When did it become love? I wonder. Was it after she left? That thought slices through me, dragging me back to earth like a popped balloon. No. No, I need to keep my head in the game, where it belongs.

Coach uses an ACE bandage to wrap the ice pack in place, and I shove myself back into the corner, trying to breathe through the shock of white-hot pain mixing with the freezing-blue cold of the ice. I'm a mixture of sensations, inside and out, and none of them are good.

We get a hit, and then another. Owen steals third when Ethan makes it to first. One more hit and we get a run, and I can relax a little. I need to win this game. I need the college scouts to see us win. And I need to open the letter from my mother. I can't take it anymore, the way it leers at me from my bulletin board.

If there's an afterlife, does it have baseball?

Javonte watches me warily—no more holding my legs, no more massaging away the muscle spasms as my entire body conspires against itself.

Aiden calls a third out. Dammit.

We left our hitters on base, no score, and suddenly Coach is ripping off the ice pack and helping me to my feet. I jog out to the mound, carefully avoiding eye contact with the ump, only this time, Javonte follows me.

He holds his catcher's mitt over his mouth as he talks to me, makes it look like we're strategizing or something, even though we're not. "Junie, are you okay? No shit?"

I nod, bouncing the ball in my hand a couple times and trying to get back to the rage I felt in the last inning. I need to focus. I need to focus on the letters, on the coaches, on proving myself.

"June," he says again, and my eyes flash to his. Whatever he sees there must be fine, or at least frighten him, because he shakes his head and walks away, crouching down to signal the first pitch. He calls a curveball, and I shake my head. He calls it a second time, and I fight the urge to flip him off, shaking my head again a little harder. Frustrated, he gives me the sign for the fastball and shifts into position when I nod.

I fire off a pitch, and he catches, and then another and another. It's going so well that I don't notice at first.

Until I do.

Somewhere deep inside me, the painful tugging turns into a harsh and bitter burn—a tearing sensation that blurs my eyes with fresh tears. I've struck out two players already; I just need to hold on for one more. I wipe my eyes and throw a wild pitch that Aiden instantly calls a ball. Before I can even complain about it, I have the weirdest, sharpest, most dizzying sensation electrifying my entire body. My entire brain goes silent in shock, and somewhere far away I hear someone calling my name.

I turn my head and lift my arm just enough for the razor-sharp pain to lance fully through me. I stumble back, tripping over the plate and falling into the dirt. A few blades of grass prickle my skin. Around me, people are shouting, but I'm staring up at the clouds, which seem like they go on forever and ever.

I wonder if my mother is up there looking down at me. I wonder if I made her proud, if I made everyone proud. If I won the show, if everybody saw what they wanted to, what they needed to. I stare up, not moving, barely breathing, letting the ground hold me up. I'm so tired. I'm so tired, and everything hurts.

I might just lie here in the dirt forever, I think, watching the clouds drift by. Everything hurts so much that maybe nothing does, my body working overtime to dump adrenaline and other chemicals into my bloodstream in a useless attempt to keep me from passing out from the pain. A tiny voice in my head is telling me to get up, but a louder, better voice, one I like so much more, is telling me to just watch the clouds.

Mom.

A tear forms and falls from the corner of my eye, trailing into the dirt. It feels like years, long peaceful years, short painful ones, before people gather around me.

I just want to sleep.

Javonte comes first, kneeling beside me and calling my name, and I'm not the only one crying now. I smile to let him know I'm okay, but worry it comes out as more of a grimace. Coach is next, and then the entire team is surrounding me, blocking the crowd's view like true friends.

But it's okay. It's okay.

I blink again, tired, so tired, and maybe I'll just let my eyes stay shut.

Someone passes me a water bottle, tipping it into my mouth, but I don't cooperate. I'm not thirsty. I'm exhausted. Broken. Useless?

"Can you walk, June?" Coach's voice is hard, firm. "We need to get you up. What happened out here?"

"Her goddamn shoulder, that's what," Javonte shouts, hot, angry tears falling down from his cheeks to mine. "I told you, June. I knew it."

I stare up at the clouds, at my mom, for another second, and then the boys scoop me up to sitting. I smack away the water bottle that Ethan keeps trying to shove into my mouth—he's probably just looking for something to do. The pain is worse sitting up than lying down, like gravity is trying to rip my arm right out of its socket.

I try to lie back down, but Javonte wraps his arm around me, lifting me up bridal style to carry me off the field as Coach stabilizes my arm. The crowd is clapping. I feel like I'm dying, and they're clapping.

Even the umpire, the same one who was a shithead to me, looks worried as I'm carried to the dugout—which is how I know I really must look awful. He calls a time-out to warm up the next pitcher, which we don't even have. One of our third basemen can throw semi-decently, I guess, and with only one person to strike out and a couple more innings, hopefully they can limp along.

I want to win, though. I want to win.

"Just let me ice for the time-out, and I'll go back out there," I mumble, pressing my head into Javonte's chest as my eyes slip shut again.

"June," Javonte says, setting me down in the dugout and trying to examine my injuries. "You need a hospital."

"I've already got Nathan on the field," Coach says gently. "You're done. You need to be done." I push against Javonte to stand up, but Coach presses me back down. "You're done," he says again more firmly. "Javonte, get back out there. Nathan needs you right now. You're calling the plays until I get back. Owen, help me get her to her dad."

"No," I say. "At least let me stay."

"You need an ER, kid, not to sit here," Coach says.

I shake my head. "I'm not leaving until the game is over."

"I'll forfeit, then," Ethan says.

"Me too," Owen calls, already pulling off his glove.

"I'll walk if you don't go to the hospital, June," Javonte says, looking me dead in the eye. "I'll fucking walk."

"No! You guys can't. The scouts, the—"

"I don't even know if I want to play ball in college anymore," Javonte says. "That's what I've been trying to tell you! None of this matters to me, especially not more than you."

"Go out there, please. You have to go."

The whole team stares at me. "None of us leave this dugout until you're in the car on your way to a doctor," Coach says, and my eyes go wide.

If we forfeit, that's it. This is our last tourney, the final chance the guys have in front of the college coaches before it's decision time on both sides.

I take a deep breath and nod. "Can somebody . . . can somebody get my dad?" I choke out through the pain. "Have him pull around the car."

"Coach, let me stay with her," Javonte says. "Let Owen catch; he reads Nathan better anyway. I'll get her in the car, and I'll be right back, I promise."

Coach studies him for a minute and then nods. "Fine. Hurry up."

CHAPTER TWENTY-SEVEN

Ivy

"WHY IS she lying there? Why is she just lying there?!" I ask, grabbing Mia's hand in a death grip. I start to run down, forgetting for a minute that I'm supposed to be hiding, not even caring that Harry's already jogging onto the field, his field, but Mia pulls me back.

"You can't," she says, her grip not loosening even when I try to shake her off. "She's okay; she's just hurt or something."

Mia says it simply, as if being okay and being hurt are remotely the same thing. June is hurt, June isn't getting up, she is *not* okay, and all I can do is watch.

All she probably wants me to do is watch anyway, if I'm being honest. I am the ex after all. Only I want to be down there in a way that almost scares me in its intensity. It's not over for me, we're not over, but I need her to be okay to tell her that.

I squeeze Mia's hand and pray for June to stand up. More

people gather around her, her entire team coming to form a wall around her, blocking her from view. Good, they should.

"Such a shame," the dad sitting in front of us says. "That your friend?"

I nod, numbly, and keep watching.

"She was a big deal for a while," he continues on, like that's all over now. I almost wish that was true, as horrible as it sounds. I wish this would be a wake-up call for her, but if there's one thing I know about June, it's to never count her out. This will never end unless it's on her terms.

June gets up, finally, or rather Javonte carries her off to the dugout. My heart pounds in disbelief. She needs a doctor; she doesn't need one of Harry's athletic trainers wrapping her in ice and sending her on her way. I will tackle her myself if she tries to go back out on the field.

The only thing keeping me stuck to the bleachers—besides Mia's iron grip—is that one of the other people on her team, the third baseman, I think, seems to be warming up as a pitcher on the side of the field. If they sub her out, she can't go back in.

Knowing her, she's fighting it tooth and nail . . . unless she's too hurt to even do that.

"I need to go talk to her," I say. There's a little window on the side of the dugout, and while nobody really uses it, I can probably shove it open to talk to her, or at least to get Javonte's attention so he can tell me what the hell is going on.

"Ivy, wait," Mia says, never dropping my hand. "Give her a second."

"I gave her all the seconds while she was lying on the field. I can't sit here knowing she's right over there, hurting. Please, let me go."

Mia looks at me with something close to pity in her eyes. "Are you sure you're the one she wants to see right now?"

Her words stun me, sounding more like an accusation than she hopefully meant them to. The truth is, I don't know the answer to that. A fresh round of worry kicks up inside me.

It was hard enough to see her hurt when we were together, and then easy enough to pretend it wasn't still happening when we were broken up. This? This is the worst-case scenario all around.

"I . . ." I look at Mia, lost. "I don't know what to do right now."

"Do you wanna go?" she asks as I stare at the dugout. I can just make out shouting, no doubt June saying that she doesn't need to be pulled. That has to be a good sign, but her arm . . . her arm was hanging at a weird angle, a fucked-up, get-a-doctor angle, and . . .

I shake my head. "I don't want to go until I know she's all right."

"Do you want *me* to go try to talk to someone? Maybe I could talk to that catcher you told me about, best friend to best friend?"

"No." I bite the skin on the side of my thumb, a nervous habit that I thought I'd abandoned a long time ago. My eyes never waver from the dugout.

I let out a massive sigh when Javonte starts gathering up her stuff—including the sparkly purple water bottle I bought her when we were still together. If she's still using that water bottle, then she must not completely hate me, right? Maybe she even misses me?

Somewhere in the back of my mind, I know that there could be a million reasons why that perfect sparkly bottle made it into that dugout, but as I stare at it, watching Javonte open it and pass it to Coach, who passes it to someone I can only assume is June, it feels like a sign.

I need it to be a sign, and before Mia can stop me, I'm racing down the bleachers. This is probably a bad idea. I know it. We broke up and haven't talked since, and me being here might make everything worse . . . but it might not.

And fuck Harry if he sees me and doesn't understand, or gets mad that I called out, or doesn't trust me enough to know I would never fix a game for my girlfriend. I can't worry about this small field, in this small town, when something as big as June's future *and June's future with me* are on the line.

The crowd is restless as I push through it, everybody using the injury time-out as an excuse to mill about, heading to the bathroom or refilling their popcorn and sodas. Mia is right behind me, yelling, "Wait, Ivy, wait," but I can't.

Because I feel like a part of me was lying in that dirt right along with June. I don't care about temporary time-outs or monthslong breaks. I don't care about how angry I've been feeling about how we fell apart, and I don't want to remember how we almost had the fall formal and then threw it all away. We were stupid. We were so stupid.

Why the hell are there so many people here, slowing me down?

When I break through finally, I'm already too late. June's dad is pulling away from the curb, hopefully to get her to the hospital. June's lying in the back seat, her knees barely visible through the glass.

My shoulders slump at the sight of them driving away. She doesn't know I was here. She doesn't know I tried to get to her. She doesn't know that I lied when I agreed to take time apart. I never wanted that, and I want it even less now.

I spin toward Mia. "What do I do? Do I call her? What do I do?" I'm shouting, panic clear on my face, and Mia wraps me in a hug.

"It's okay. She's going to be okay."

"You don't know that!"

"I do. They wouldn't let her dad drive her if it was really bad. The trainer would have called an ambulance or something. I'm sure it's her shoulder or her elbow or whatever it is that pitchers hurt. If it was life-threatening, there would have been an ambulance. She's going to be okay, Ivy. Breathe."

"She won't be if she can't play. You don't understand. I need to go. I need to figure out what to do. I have to— Do you have my keys?" I ask, remembering that she stashed them in her crossbody for me.

"I'm not giving you the keys when you're this upset," Mia says. I reach for her bag, but she spins it behind her. "I will, however, take you wherever you want to go, your home or hers, even though I think it's a bad idea to just show up."

"I don't even know where to go," I say, taking a step toward the parking lot, needing to be anywhere but here now that she's gone. I barely make it three steps when a strong hand grabs my arm and I startle.

It's Javonte, standing there looking just as upset as I am. "Ivy," he says, trying to force out a small smile. "Sorry, I didn't mean to scare you."

"How is she? What happened?"

He huffs out a big breath through his nose, looking absolutely miserable. "Her shoulder. Torn rotator cuff, if I had to guess. Probably messed up her biceps too, and who knows what else. It looked bad. She was in a lot of pain when I helped her to her dad's car, but she was able to walk herself there, with some help."

"Is she going to be okay?"

He shrugs, looking lost. "I don't know what this means for pitching. It's not life-threatening or anything, but . . ."

"But to her it might feel like it is," I finish for him, and he grimaces with a nod. "Where is she going? I want to be there. I want to see her."

"Her dad's taking her to the emergency room. Coach thinks she might need surgery right away, but who knows? She'll probably just sit there for hours and then get referred to an orthopedic surgeon or something. You don't have to go."

"I want to go."

"They're not gonna let you in to see her, Ivy, especially not if they're taking her to surgery," Mia says gently, and Javonte hums in agreement.

"Here, give me your phone," he says. I unlock it and hand it to him. He punches something in and then hands it back. "Okay, I put my number in there. Text me so I have yours. I have to get back, but I'll give you updates as I get them."

"Does the game even matter right now?" I ask before I can stop myself.

"Not really," he says, his eyes watering, "but she made me promise I would finish it, and I'm not breaking that."

I laugh bitterly. "Of course she did."

"Look, the sooner I get back there, the sooner we're done," he says. "Text me, okay?"

"I . . . I guess," I say, feeling helpless.

"I'll make sure she gets home safe," Mia says, pulling out my keys and putting her arm around me.

Javonte gives her a look I don't get, and she nods. It feels like they're having some kind of secret conversation with their eyes that only the best friends of disasters can. Before I know it, he's heading back to the game, and Mia is leading me off to the parking lot to go wait at my house.

I text Javonte as soon as I get in the car, and then, fuck it, I text June too. I ask her how she is and tell her to update me as soon as she can. I tell her that I miss her.

The day turns to night, and neither of them respond.

I try not to think too hard about what that might mean.

CHAPTER TWENTY-EIGHT

June

DAD DOESN'T talk as we drive to the hospital.

It's a short trip, barely fifteen minutes, but it feels like an eternity when I'm still fighting to stay awake. It's like, now that I've finally stopped moving for a second, all of the exhaustion of the last few weeks—last few years, really—is catching up to me all at once.

Dad parks outside of the ER and leads me inside, where I sit in a rough, scratchy chair as he checks me in and talks to a nurse. Being upright makes the pain on the left side of my body scream even more, and I go back to the light shallow breaths that hurt just a little bit less.

They take me back right away—or at least I think they are—but it turns out they're only taking me to a little room to be triaged. They take my temperature and blood pressure and stuff, ask me if I've had COVID and if I've recently traveled out of the country—no and no—and then instead of giving me a room, they send us right back out to those scratchy chairs. Pointless.

I should have just stayed at the game.

At least there I'd have ice and a dugout and friends who talk to me and distract me from the pain, instead of my dad, who is just sitting there tight-lipped and jaw-clenched.

I let him down. I know it.

That's all I think about every time I look at him. It doesn't help that every time we make eye contact, he quickly looks away to study his phone or a chart on the wall. At first, I thought I was imagining it, but I'm very much not. I drop my head back and shut my eyes, trying to give in to the sleep that suddenly feels like it's slipping out of reach thanks to the business of this hospital. It doesn't work. Of course, it doesn't.

At the very least, I wish I hadn't forgotten my phone in the car, but given how my dad is acting, I'm definitely not going to bother asking him to get it. I wish I knew what he was thinking—like if he's really mad or just kind of mad, if this is a screwup we can come back from, or something that changes everything forever. I know how much this showcase meant to him. I know how much my getting recruited meant to him too.

There were so many scouts there. So many coaches watching. I wonder how Nathan is pitching without me there to handle it, and if we're going to win or lose. What the scouts thought of their star prospect lying in the dirt and crying up at the clouds because her arm hurt and she missed her mom and she missed her girlfriend and she missed the man her dad used to be

269

before everything bad happened. Back when he was goofy and funny and a little bit irresponsible. Before he was determined to mold her not just into the best she could be, but into a better, younger, cooler replica of what he wished *he* had been.

I'm pretty sure that I embarrassed us both.

I sniffle and wipe my eyes, trying to be discreet. Dad must hear me because he passes me a tissue without a word, going back to looking at his phone with the intensity that only someone avoiding someone else can do. I take the tissue gratefully but silently, dabbing at my eyes with a shaky breath before I go back to staring at the ceiling. And together, we wait.

By the time they call my name, hours later, when it's already dark outside, I'm practically crawling out of my skin from the hurt. There's a heavy sheen on my pale skin, my stomach gone sour from anxiety and getting sick earlier, and my face is drawn up in exhaustion and pain. I haven't eaten all day either, and I'm not sure what's making me woozier.

I sound like a crybaby. I feel like a crybaby. I mean, I've dealt with pain before. I'm good at pain. But whatever is happening to me now isn't that. This is next-level, full-body misery, and it overwhelms me at a cellular level.

Dad makes no move to get up, probably thinking I'm too old for him to join me, or that I might like my privacy. But a part of me worries that maybe he just doesn't want to be back there, doesn't want to hear what's wrong with me. Wants to pretend for a little while longer that I didn't screw up the whole plan.

I stand up to follow the nurse, and am tempted to let him

stay there, but I'm scared, and everything hurts, and if I can't have my mom, then . . .

"Please come?" I ask quietly, plaintively, shakily.

Dad looks surprised, but quickly stands up, shoving his phone in his pocket. "Yeah, of course. If you want me to."

"I do," I say, even though it kills me to acknowledge my weakness twice in such a short period of time. I want my dad; I *need* my dad. I'm not his little thoroughbred right now, or his star pitcher, or his protégée. I'm just a kid who wants a hug.

Even without saying the rest of it out loud, he must read it on my face, because his expression goes from confused to this weird, sort of soft-seeming realization. He comes up beside me, wraps his arm around me, and then together we head back, away from the scratchy chairs and into the overwhelming vastness of the local emergency department.

IT TAKES A long time to see the doctor, and longer still for all the tests, but I'm in a bed, and I've been given some IV pain relief that almost lets me think, dialing it down from about a million to a much more comfortable eight on a scale of one to ten. But it makes me loopy, so there's a definite trade-off.

They do an MRI. Some bloodwork. An X-ray. It's all very methodical, a nurse occasionally checking in to tell me that they're ordering more tests or that a doctor will be in shortly. Dad sits silently beside me through it all. The only time he says anything is when my stomach grumbles become too loud to ignore and he asks the nurse if I can have some Jell-O or if he can run to the vending machine. He explains I haven't eaten since breakfast. I don't bother correcting him that it's been even longer than that.

Sadly, the nurse says I can't, because they aren't sure if surgery is on the table for today or if I'll need to come back for it. Her words hit me—she didn't say *if* surgery was needed, she said if I would need it today or if I'd have to come back, like it's a foregone conclusion.

Anxiety spikes up inside me. Surgery in my senior year isn't good, plus rehab time? I'm screwed.

My dad pats my hand gently, like he can tell I'm freaking out, and I fight the urge to cry. The nurse gives me a tight smile, as if she may have said too much—we're still waiting for the doctor, after all—and then heads out, pulling the curtain closed behind her.

Dad goes back to his phone, and I go back to staring at the ceiling, terrified of what this all means.

"I'm sorry," I say a little while later, the words scraping up my throat painfully.

"For what?" He sets his phone down and angles his chair toward me, a pinched look on his face.

"I messed it all up. I let you and Mom down. I was supposed to be the best, and I—"

"Shit, June," he says, shaking his head. "What have we done?"

I look at him, confused. Dad rarely swears and even more rarely swears in front of me. But at me? That's something I never thought would happen. He must be more upset than I thought.

"I'm sorry," I offer again, tears welling up, even though I'm trying to fight them. "I wanted to be good, and I tried, I really tried. And now I don't know what's wrong with me or what I'm supposed to be doing. I didn't mean for this to happen. I swear I just wanted to push through for you."

"Push through for— Junie, what? You're in the hospital hurt, and you're worried about me? Do you think I'm angry with you? I've been sitting here this whole time trying to figure out how to apologize to *you*."

My eyebrows shoot to the ceiling, or at least I think they do. "To me? For what?"

"Because this is completely my fault."

"I don't remember you running onto the field and tearing my rotator cuff." I snort.

"No, but I pushed you so hard." His voice cracks, and he looks away. "Way too hard."

"Dad?" I grab his hand with my good one, like he's the one who needs the reassurance, even though I'm the one in the hospital bed.

His eyes get all red and wet, and he somehow looks even more exhausted and worried than he did just a few minutes ago. I've been reading him all wrong. He isn't mad, he's upset, and those are two very, very different things.

I let out a shaky breath. "It's fine. It's okay. It's—"

"It's not fine," he says through gritted teeth. "You're sitting here needing surgery, and it's not fine! Hank tried to tell me I needed to slow you down. He tried to tell me that you weren't doing well, and I ignored him. I ignored all of it. I was so focused on getting you to the right school so you could play for the right minors, and then get to the majors. I was trying to make sure that everybody knew you were Steph's daughter. I just wanted you to take the world by storm the way she never got to . . ." He breaks down then, resting his head on the side of my bed and squeezing my hand. "I'm sorry, Junie. I'm sorry. You didn't deserve to have all that put on you. Your mom would be furious with me right now. I'm the one letting her *and* you down. I lost sight of things, but it's not going to happen again."

My heart shatters and is glued back together all in the span of his speech. Dad is hurting just as much as I am, missing Mom just as much as I am, and instead of turning to each other, we turned away. We both focused on the only thing we could control: the ball.

I do my best to give him a one-armed hug, and he gives me a weepy smile. "We're going to get through this, okay?" he says. "I'm gonna find a way to make this right, yeah?"

I look at him and nod, overwhelmed, and then I rest against my pillow and let my eyes drift shut. His hand never lets go of mine.

I WAKE UP two hours later to find that my father hasn't moved.

"Still waiting for the on-call ortho," he says, giving my hand another squeeze.

I nod, still sluggish but a little less so, and reach for the TV remote while we wait.

"Hey, Junie?" he asks after a beat. "I've been thinking about something else tonight while you were sleeping. I hope you don't mind me asking, but what happened with you and Ivy? If I'm being honest, I owe you an apology for that too. I could tell something was off when she stopped coming around, but . . . a part of me was relieved. I told myself you made the right call, and I let myself believe it too. No more distractions or worrying about an ethics violation. That shouldn't have mattered, though. I could see she meant a lot to you. I should have checked in.

"I don't want to bring anything up for you if you don't want to talk about it, but I'm here if you want to, and I'm sorry I wasn't before. I'm so sorry, Junie."

"It's a long story." I sigh, shutting my eyes and keeping them that way. I want to tell him. I do. I don't want this distance between us, but it hurts to think about her, and it hurts that she's not here—even though she probably doesn't even know what happened.

"I have time," Dad says. "If you want. Or I could . . . I could pull up *Superstore* on my phone?"

My eyes snap open at that. Mom's show.

"*Superstore* sounds good," I say, but as he smiles at me and fumbles to get his phone out of his pocket, I realize I want him to know me. Not just baseball me, but all of me, good and bad, starting with what I did to Ivy. "We decided to take a break so I could focus on this showcase, but then feelings got hurt and it kind of started to feel a little more permanent," I say, but I know I'm not being completely honest.

275

He nods and keeps downloading the Hulu app, like he knows it's easier to talk to him about this when he's not looking.

"No, that's not totally true." I sigh. "We got in a fight, and I just . . . I went nuclear and I regret it. Bad. A part of me just wanted a break from worrying about someone finding out about us, but a bigger part of me was freaked out by how much she meant to me, and how she was always trying to help me with 'finding a middle ground.' When she said I didn't have to live up to Mom's expectations, it kind of messed with my head. Everything made sense before her, and after . . ."

Dad grunts like he gets it, still carefully keeping his eyes on his phone screen.

"I used our fight as an excuse. I tried to convince myself that it was good that things ended, but it doesn't feel like it. And then that umpire today still said I only made it as far as I did because Ivy was fixing the game."

"That's ridiculous." Dad's hand tightens on mine. "You know that, right?"

"Yeah, but it still hurt. That's why I started throwing all those fastballs to prove it."

"June," he huffs out, so quiet I almost don't hear him. "Why'd you guys even tell him if he's like that?"

"We didn't," I say, because why would we?

"Then how'd he know?"

"I . . ." I trail off, realizing I don't actually have an answer to that.

How *did* he know?

CHAPTER TWENTY-NINE

Ivy

JAVONTE FINALLY texts me around 1:00 a.m.

Just talked to her finally. She forgot her phone in the car. She's going to be okay. They're releasing her now. Needs surgery asap. Everything else TBD. She was pretty messed-up from pain meds. Just wanted to let you know. Sorry for not checking in earlier. I've been with the guys.

I stare down at the phone. I've been wearing holes in my bedroom carpet since I got home, pacing uncontrollably while waiting for word. I've texted her a hundred times, and him too. There was no chance I was going to sleep tonight.

I read his text a few more times, vacillating between being angry he ignored my texts, comforted that he waited until he actually had an update to write to me, and, selfishly, hurt that June must have her phone back if she called him, but she still hasn't called or texted me.

I know I'm not a priority, being the ex and all, but I just

thought . . . I don't know what I thought. I text back a quick **thanks** and fall onto my bed, pulling a pillow over my face to let out a quick groan of frustration.

I know we took a time-out for things to settle down. I know that we both agreed, but I thought maybe this would change something. Maybe we could have an injury time-out from our time-out. I want this "break" to be over almost as much as I want June to be healthy and happy. I want her back, and being scared only highlights how desperate I am for that.

My phone buzzes again, and I pick it up, expecting to see an alert from Javonte. Maybe a thumbs-up or a heart by my "thanks," like just the bare-minimum acknowledgment or something. I nearly drop my phone when I realize it's June.

Hey, I'm okay. Sorry to scare you. Saw you texted a ton.

I stare at the screen as those three little dots keep appearing and disappearing, hoping that what she says next is something like "we're being ridiculous" or "I miss you" or "I would also like to call an injury time-out from our stupid time-out," but instead she says something else entirely.

Did you tell Aiden about us?

I stare down at the words, eyebrows scrunched, half wondering if I'm already asleep and this is some kind of nightmare.

I can't figure out what that has to do with anything, and I can't help but feel a little annoyed if I'm being honest. Why does she want to talk about Aiden *now*, in the middle of the night, when she's just gotten out of the hospital? When she hasn't spoken to me in weeks. When I've been worried crying all night. Even though she doesn't know for sure that's what

I've been doing, I wasn't exactly being subtle with my dozens of panicked messages.

I debate responding at all. I could very easily put it off. Pretending I'm asleep would be a plausible thing, of course, given the time, but . . . she's on my phone. She's texting me, and even if it's not what I want to talk about, it's something. A little glimmer of a *maybe*. A tiny thread of hope that somehow, possibly, that fall formal can be back on.

No. Not really anyway. But yeah, he knows.

The three dots appear and disappear again, but then they disappear for good. I'm suddenly filled with concern that she's worried or upset. That she thinks he's going to tell, which is what I tried to prevent with this whole *taking a break* thing. I try to set her mind at ease.

It's fine, though. I took care of it.

Her response comes almost immediately.

Yeah, I think I'm figuring that out. Seriously, Ivy?

Wait, is she mad? I can't take it anymore. I pick up the phone and call her, holding my breath. Every ring feels like an accusation.

Her voice mail picks up, just the robot default one. It's not even her voice, which I really could have used after today. When it beeps, I unload.

"You were literally just texting me, but you won't pick up? The phone was in your hand, June. Maybe you fell asleep or ran to the bathroom or something, but I don't think so."

I take a deep breath, steeling myself to say the words I just can't keep to myself for another second.

"I can't do this break thing anymore, June. I need to talk to you. I'm gonna . . . fuck . . . I'm gonna come over tomorrow, okay? I get that you might not be up for company or just might not want my company, but I don't know what else to do. Don't open the door, or I guess tell your dad not to, if you really don't want to see me. I . . . I have to try, though.

"I was so scared when you went down today. Mia had to keep me from running onto the field, and I know that Javonte said you were okay, and so did you, but I can't just . . . I need to see you, okay? If you don't answer the door, then at least I'll know. I'll know it's not just a break; I'll know we're really done. I can't stay in this limbo anymore, and I can't . . . I need to see you, if you'll let me. Please."

I scrub my hands across my eyes as the little robot says, "Hang up or push 1 to send. Press 2 to rerecord." I'm about to hang up, but then think better of it. My grief is not her problem, and neither is my anxiety. I clear my throat and press 2, determined not to sound as desperate or tearful as I really am.

"Hey, June," I say, trying to sound nonchalant, even though I'm two seconds away from full-on losing it. "We need to talk, okay? Um . . . I'll swing by tomorrow around ten-ish? If that works? If you don't want me to come, just text me. It's . . . it is what it is. But if you don't text me, I'll be there. Okay, bye, I lo— Just, bye."

This time I hang up without even waiting for the robot to ask me if I'm sure. I've done the best I can, given her as much of an out as I can. There's nothing left to do but wait.

I BARELY SLEEP, and I'm relieved to see that June hasn't texted me not to come when I wake up. That feeling is quickly replaced by anxiety as I realize I still have two hours before I can see her, two hours in which she can change her mind.

But she doesn't, and soon I'm running downstairs to head over to her house. My mom stops me as I get to the door, because of course she does.

"Where do you think you're off to?" she asks, handing me a muffin. "We have a tour today, remember? We have to leave in twenty, so eat quick."

"I'm not going on a tour today, Mom." I look at her like she has two heads. What is she talking about?

"Yes, you are," she says, her tone not angry, but matter-of-fact, like I'm Sammy throwing a fit about day care and not an almost adult who should get a say in her own life.

"I'm not going on another tour, period. Please, I'm going to be late." I go to leave, but she blocks me.

"No," she says, crossing her arms. "I've been really lenient with you, Ivy, but you are under my roof, eating my food, wearing clothes that I bought you, and soon you'll be going to a college that I will be paying for! You don't get to tell me that you're done or that you're not going. You are still my kid, and I am still your mother, and I say *we leave in twenty*."

"Really? You're going to force me to go on a college visit. For what? You can't make me actually enroll anywhere, and even if

281

you could, you couldn't make me go to class! Mom, I love you, but this isn't how it's supposed to be, and I think you know that too."

"You're going to throw your life away," she says, her voice sounding almost plaintive. "You have your whole future ahead of you. Do you know how lucky you are? Nicky—"

"I'm not Nicky! Sammy is not Nicky! He died and nothing we do can bring him back. I could play the same sport, go to the same college he dreamed of, become an oncologist myself . . . I could live his whole future, and he'd still be gone, Mom."

"I know that. Do you think I don't?" she asks, her eyes filling with tears. "I could never forget that, even if I wanted to."

"I don't think you forgot, Mom. I think you miss him so much you can't stand it, and whether you realize it or not, I think you forcing this college stuff on me—his college stuff— makes you feel connected to him or like he's still here or like his dreams didn't die with him."

My mom gasps, actually gasps, like I just cut her or something, and maybe I did. Maybe I really did. But it needed to be said.

"Ivy," my dad says, stepping out of the living room with a napping Sammy in his arms. "You need to stop."

"Brian, don't," Mom says, so quiet I barely hear her as she steps forward to tuck some of my hair behind my ear. She rubs her thumb over the track of one of my escaped tears and offers me a watery smile.

"Mom, I'm sorry. I shouldn't have said that," I say, suddenly feeling like the worst person on earth. I hurt my mom. I know I did, even if it's true.

She takes a deep breath, studying my face. "You're right."

"I . . . What?"

She pulls me into a hug, and I crumple against her.

"Not about all of it," she says, her voice thick with emotion. "You still don't get to just tell me no, at least not without a discussion . . . but the rest? I probably needed to hear it."

I hug her back, scared to trust this is real, but hoping it is. "Does that mean you're going to get off my back about the college stuff?"

"No." She laughs, leaning back to wipe her eyes. "Education is important. You need a backup plan *just in case* you don't end up in the NFL." She holds her hands up in surrender. "I hope you do, and I'll support you trying, but in the meantime, that means good grades and SATs and all that. We can change the rest of the plan to look at community colleges or the local schools or any of the trade schools—but there has to be something. I want you to take your future seriously, but I recognize that it is *your* future, and I haven't been doing a good job of accepting that.

"Why don't we go sit down and talk a little bit more about what *you* want for yourself and go from there?" Mom asks, and it's reasonable, super reasonable. Pretty much the most ideal outcome I could even hope for. Except . . .

I wince. "Is there any way we could do that later? I'm supposed to be at June's right now, and I really, really want to talk to her."

"Oh, are you two back together?" Mom asks, and I raise my eyebrows. "What?"

"I didn't think you even noticed we broke up."

"I can always recognize a broken heart, Ivy. I was just giving you space to come to me and trying to keep you moving in the meantime. We still need to talk too, though," Mom says, but then Dad steps forward and wraps his free arm around her, kissing her on the temple. Sammy snuggles in a little tighter, and I can't help but smile.

"Let her go, Gigi," Dad says. "There'll be plenty of time to talk later."

Mom glances at him and then back at me. "Okay," she says, and I race to the door. "But Ivy?"

"Yeah?" I say, turning to look at her as I step onto the porch.

"I love you."

"I love you too, Mom," I say, pulling the door shut behind me and feeling lighter than I have in a long time.

UNFORTUNATELY, THAT LIGHTNESS is short-lived. All of my anxiety and doubt swirls back up the second I knock on June's door. I'm terrified that her dad is going to tell me to leave or that no one will even come to open it.

Both fears prove untrue when her father opens the door wide and welcomes me inside. "Ivy, it's good to see you again," he says, and he sounds genuine, which throws me a little. "Junie told me you were stopping by. She's in her room resting. I was just about to head up with this ice pack. Would you mind taking it for me?"

"Not at all," I say, squeezing it tight in my hands, grateful for the distraction as I climb the stairs to her room.

June looks like she's asleep when I get there. Her arm is in a sling, her eyes closed, her head resting on her pillows, which have her half propped up to sitting. I stand awkwardly in the doorway, not sure what to do. I could go or—

"Are you planning to stay in the doorway all day, or do you want to grab that chair by my desk and come sit?"

"Um, the second option, please." I give her the ice pack and then bring over the chair. It feels weirdly formal, sitting beside her, when I want to be crawling into bed around her.

She struggles to get her ice pack right, and I struggle not to do it for her since she hasn't asked me to and I don't know if I'm still allowed. She gets it situated soon enough, which puts us both out of our misery.

"You wanted to talk?" she asks.

"Are you in a lot of pain? Javonte said it was your rotator cuff."

"Right, he mentioned that he told you. Yeah, rotator cuff and biceps, and it's kind of all messed-up in there with old injuries and scar tissue and stuff, so it's not really positioned properly in the socket right now. It's not so bad, though. I'm on, like, really good meds until the surgery in a couple days." She gestures to the sling. "Apparently, like, my biceps can completely detach if I move it too much, so yeah, fun times."

"Sorry." I squeeze my eyes shut, trying not to cry at the thought of her being in pain, of her needing *surgery*.

"It's okay," she says, her good hand tapping my shoulder until I look at her.

I wipe my face. Why does this feel so hard, so heavy? "It's not really, but . . ." I sniffle, hanging my head, knowing that I'm going to cry for real if I keep talking.

"No, you're right. It's not." She sighs, resigned, as she reaches for my hand. "But it *will* be okay."

Neither of us says anything for a while. I watch the way she rubs small circles across my palm with her fingers, and then I slide my chair a little closer, right up against the bed.

"Ivy," she says, finally. "How did Aiden find out about us? You said you didn't tell him. I think I know, but . . ."

"I shouldn't have lied to you." I rub my forehead. "It was that day when you grabbed my hand. He confronted me after you left. He was going to go to Harry and—"

"And you gave him the tournament so he wouldn't. That's what happened, right?" she asks. I look away. "He made a comment yesterday, just to let me know he knew, I think. I didn't put it together until later."

"I wondered what he said. I saw that and I—"

"You were there yesterday?"

I bite my lip and then nod. I'm done keeping secrets. "I wasn't sure if Javonte would tell you. Yeah, I was there, June. There was no way I would miss it. I lost it when you went down. I was so scared, Mia practically had to hold me back from running on the field to you. I know we're on a break, or we're supposed to be, but . . ."

"But what, Ivy?" she asks, her hand stopping its movement

on mine. "Being on a break doesn't cancel out the lie you told me about Aiden finding out, you know. It's my life too, and you were my girlfriend. You didn't have to fall on your sword and then lie to me about it. It could have been something we figured out together."

"*Were?*"

"What?"

"You said *were*, as in 'you were my girlfriend,' past tense. Meaning, *no longer*. Is this break going to be permanent, June? Because you have to put me out of my misery, please, either way. Just fucking tell me."

June looks at me, and then looks away, her hand pulling back from mine as my heart plummets to the floor.

CHAPTER THIRTY

June

IVY TAKES a breath that's somehow both sharp and shaky, a gasp that's trying hard not to turn to tears. The sound sends my eyes snapping back to hers, almost as soon as they've left. She looks gutted in a way that I'm going to apologize for forever, because I realize too late that pulling back my hand, looking away right when she asked that question, implied an answer to her that I hadn't meant to give.

"Ivy," I say softly. She squeezes her eyes shut, her eyelashes going damp as she struggles to act stoic when she's so clearly falling apart. I reach out for her again, but she pushes the chair back out of my grasp, her eyes opening, frantic, like an animal caught in a trap.

"I . . . I have to go. I can't be here."

"Ivy," I say, more firmly. "Ivy, sit down."

She doesn't listen, and I can't even bolt after her, or I'll risk hurting myself more. She's almost to the door, and then she'll be down the stairs and gone all because of a misunderstanding.

"Ivy, please, don't go. Not when I can't chase after you. I'm stuck in this bed and . . . I don't want you to go, and I *don't* want us to be over. Sit down. Come back."

She hesitates right before she reaches the hall. "But you—"

"I'm right here," I say, holding out my good hand again. "I want you to be too."

She walks back until she reaches my hand, and when she does, I tug her even closer until she's sitting on my bed. She's so careful not to jostle me, and it makes me love her even more. Because yeah, *love*—that's what this is and has been for a while now, even if I tried to run from it.

"I thought, when you looked away . . ." she says quietly. "I thought you were done."

"I know, and that's not how I meant it *at all*, but everything is processing kind of slow right now." I nod toward the orange pill bottles lined up neatly on my nightstand. "I was just trying to think of the right words to tell you that I love you and I'm sorry. I didn't mean to make you think I wanted to be done."

"You're sorry?" she asks, scrunching up her eyebrows. "No, I'm the one who's sorry! I lied to you about Aiden, and then I got so resentful that you weren't reading my mind or even questioning why I wanted to give up the tournament when it was so important to me before. That wasn't fair of me."

"No," I say. "It wasn't. I had a right to know what was going on. It's really frustrating that you kept that from me, but you had a right to have a girlfriend who noticed that you were hurting too. It was weird that you suddenly wanted to drop out from something so big, but I focused on how much easier that made things instead. I'm not the only one who's dealing with a lot right now, and I've been a crappy girlfriend. I was so single-minded about baseball and my pain that I said hurtful things, and I lost sight of you and what you—"

"It's all right," she says, giving me a sad smile. "I get it."

"But you shouldn't have to," I say, shaking my head. "You should feel comfortable enough to tell me what's going on, and I should be there for you the way you always showed up for me. We might not have broken up if I had. And I might not be lying in this bed right now, about to have a frankly terrifying surgery, if I had really thought about what you were telling me about how I needed to find a balance. I didn't want to hear it. I didn't want to face that, and it was easy for me to make you the scapegoat and convince myself that you were in the way and that we should take a break, even though I didn't mean it. I know you're here because you still care about me, but you would be right to not give me another chance after that."

"There is no 'another chance,'" she says. "It never *really* ended for me, June. I know we said we were on a break, but I couldn't get you out of my head. I almost texted you every night. Javonte even caught me stalking your Insta when I was hiding at a party the other night. It was kind of mortifying, but . . . June, I don't want to get over you. I don't think I ever could."

And now it's my eyelashes that are going damp. Happy tears flood my eyes as I tug her down to kiss her. It's slow and gentle. She's being careful, careful, careful with my body, the way I wasn't with her heart, and it makes me feel sad that I ever took her for granted. She has a smile on her face as she leans back, and it feels impossibly good to know I'm the one who put it there.

"That probably explains the random heart on one of my really old Insta posts," I say as she wipes my tears with her free hand, never letting go of my good one, like I'm tethering her to this place, or like she's scared I'll disappear.

She looks baffled. "I didn't heart anything. I was really careful about that."

"Javonte," we say in unison, and I try to stifle my laugh because jostling my arm hurts too much.

"He took my phone for a second. I should have known." Ivy tries to turn her smile into a pout, but the corners stay up anyway. "He's a good best friend."

"He is. He's also clearly a devious matchmaker." I let out a sigh. I owe him an apology too. "I know Javonte's been as worried about me as you have. It's just hard because I know he's also counting on me to make him look good in front of coaches. Not just him but the whole team. He said they lost yesterday. I can't believe that I—"

x

291

"Who cares about the game?" Ivy groans, dropping her head back.

"A lot of people—recruiters, players, my team, my coach, I thought my dad, but no, definitely your boss, probably the colleges. Should I keep going?"

"No," she says, taking a deep breath like I'm testing her patience, which I probably am, I'm sure. "I take it back. I'm sure plenty of people care about that tournament, up to and including the popcorn vendors. But what I really mean is I wish you weren't worrying about that. You have to have surgery, June. Surgery! You're so hurt, and you're so amazing, and it kills me that you think all you are is a fucking pitcher."

"Shhh," I say, squeezing her hand. "I get it, and you're right. My dad and I had a great talk last night. Believe it or not, he blames himself. I think it's time we all stopped blaming ourselves and made some changes around here."

"What kind of changes?"

"I know my coach wants me to do an escalated rehab schedule so I'm ready by spring, but my dad and I turned it down. I'm going to do the surgery, and I'm going to do physical therapy for as long as it takes. I'm going to work on getting healthy and stronger; we're going to prioritize that for a minute. I'm going to try out that middle ground you told me about. It's really scary, and I don't know if I'm going to be able to keep it up, but I want to at least try. Plus, I'm pretty sure my dad will kill me if I don't."

"What does that mean, exactly?"

"It means it's time for me to figure out who I am aside from just my mother's legacy or the star varsity pitcher. Those things are awesome and I'm proud of them, but if I step back on the mound, *when* I step back on that mound, I want to be there just for me. Not because everyone's expecting it or forcing it or anything like that, and not because I want to open some more letters." I sniff. "My dad said he was really sorry about the letters, by the way. He didn't know how I felt about them. He said he always thought of them as wishes, like wishing on an eyelash or a shooting star. He never meant for them to feel like the expectations I saw them as. It's just . . . I think this change of pace is going to be good, even if it really scares me."

"Sometimes scary is good." She smiles.

I nod and tug her down until she's lying next to me in bed. I'm again awed by how gently she moves around me, like I'm made of already cracked crystal, and I suppose after the stunt I pulled yesterday, she might feel like I am.

"I'm sorry that I scared you," I say, "and that you had to see that yesterday."

"I'm sorry you had to feel it," she says. She's trying to hide her nerves, but I can see them. I can see everything now.

I tuck some hair behind her ear and meet her eyes. "What's wrong, Ivy?"

She shakes her head. "Nothing, it doesn't matter."

"We're not doing that anymore, remember? This is a fresh start for us, or at least we need it to be if we're really going to do this. I'm so, so happy that you're here, but you have to change too. Or I guess the way we work has to change. You can't keep things from me anymore, and you can't always be the one who's caring instead of being cared about. It can't be the one-way street it was before."

She nods hesitantly and then kisses my forehead. "I'm scared you're going to regret this after the pills wear off."

"Regret what? Stepping back from pitching a little or . . . us?"

Ivy shrugs one shoulder and takes a shaky breath. "All of the above?"

"Never." I smile, and I hope she can tell I mean it.

"You're really high right now," she says, "and you're in a lot of pain and probably didn't get much sleep last night, so . . ."

"Why are you in my bed if you don't believe me?" I ask, pinning her with my stare.

"Because I'm hopelessly in love with you, and I'm really, really crossing everything that you're in love with me too, even when the Percocet wears off."

I swallow hard, my eyes drifting shut longer and longer between blinks as the exhaustion and meds catch up with me again. "Shut up," I say, my voice barely above a whisper. "I've been in love with you since you gave me your Biofreeze that first day."

"Really?" she asks, in disbelief.

"You were so cute about it," I say. "I hated you, but I also thought you were pretty great. It was a very confusing time." I huff out a laugh. "So you don't have to worry about that. It might not predate the pain, but it definitely predates the Percocet and lack of sleep. I have a pile of letters in that desk drawer that can prove it if you don't believe me."

"You do?"

"Like mother, like daughter." I sigh, trying to stifle a yawn.

"Can I read them?" she asks, unsure.

I'm too tired to talk anymore, so I let my eyes shut all the way and I nod. "They're yours anyway," I say.

She shifts off the bed, and I want to ask her to stay, to read them later, but I'm too tired to form the words. She brushes some hair away from my forehead and kisses it gently, almost reverently. I feel warm, and loved, and content, and I chase that feeling all the way to sleep.

WHEN I WAKE up, it's dark out and she's gone, but my desk drawer is slightly ajar. It takes a minute of staring at it to remember that I told her she could take the letters, and I almost die of embarrassment. I grab my phone with my good hand and hit FaceTime immediately.

She answers on the first ring, her smiling face filling the screen. "You're awake," she says, like it's the best thing that's ever happened.

"Yeah, sorry for falling asleep on you."

"It was cute. You need your rest. I hope it's okay that I took off. Your dad came in and it got kinda weird. He said you're usually out for a while, which I took as a hint. I was going to call you a little while ago, but then I was worried you might still be out, and I didn't want—"

"I need a favor," I blurt out, cutting her off.

"Anything."

"Don't read those letters. Promise me. Seriously, it's so embarrassing I wrote all those."

"Too late." She grins. "And I'll try not to take it personally that you find being madly in love with me so embarrassing that you had to immediately try to stop me the second you returned to consciousness."

"It's not embarrassing that I'm in love with you. It's embarrassing that I wrote you a million love letters instead of just FaceTiming you and telling you that I missed you! Plus, they're, like, super sappy."

"First of all, there were only seven, not a million. And second of all, they were cute! I especially liked the stuff about how every day without me feels like loading the bases with walked hitters."

I groan so loud I'm worried my dad will come and check on me, and Ivy laughs.

"Hey," she says, "if it helps, I left you a long rambling voice mail after you got hurt."

"What? No, you didn't."

"Yes, I did, but I had the good sense to rerecord it instead of committing it to your inbox."

"Some girlfriend you are." I snort. When I look at the screen again, she's gone quiet, studying my face. "What?"

"Do you really mean it?" she asks.

"Mean what?"

"Girlfriend?"

"Yes, you goof. What else is it going to take to convince you that I'm not just hopped-up on pain meds, I really want to be with you?"

"Time, I think," she says earnestly, and then taps her chin. "And maybe some more love letters with terrible baseball metaphors."

"Time you can have, but my days of writing love letters are over." I laugh. "I love you, though, even if I don't put it in a letter."

"Say it again."

I smirk. "I love you."

"I love you too," she says, and it sounds like a promise, like a fresh start, like the best thing I've heard in a long time.

"Good, now that that's settled, wanna come over again and watch *Superstore*?"

"Now? It's almost ten o'clock at night."

"You got somewhere better to be, Ivy?"

"Impossible," she says, already grabbing her keys off her desk. "I'm on my way."

CHAPTER THIRTY-ONE

Ivy

A FEW weeks after her surgery, June asks me to take her back to the scene of the crime. I'm hesitant, not wanting to remember that day she fell and how useless and scared I felt to be on the bleachers, but I reluctantly agree. I know she'll go with or without me. She thinks it's "important to her healing," and maybe it is, even if my instincts are telling me to wrap her up in bubble wrap and shove her back into bed.

The doctors have cleared her—she's back in school and everything—so there's no sense in dragging it out any longer.

It's nearly 6:30 when I pick her up, dusk already threatening to take over the day, and I'm surprised to see her waiting on the porch with a giant duffel bag.

"Carry this for me?" she asks when I walk up to give her a kiss.

I toss it into my back seat and get into my car, lacing my

fingers through hers and using both our hands to shift into reverse.

The drive is over too soon, and I let out a nervous sigh as I park in front of the empty diamond. There are no games, and it's eerily still as I trail behind June, her heavy duffel bag slung over my shoulder. A part of me panics a little, like maybe she's filled it with balls and bats and is about to do something really, really stupid. She turns back to me and smiles in a way that tells me she knows what I'm thinking, and I bite my lip, hoping I'm wrong.

I set it on the bench in the dugout and watch her walk out to the mound, sensing she needs a second to herself. She toes the dirt and clay, doing the best approximation of her pitching stance that she can with her arm still in a navy blue medical sling. Then she turns around, staring out at the field. I watch her shoulders rise and fall as she takes long, deep breaths, and even though I want to run out there, want to hug her, want to be a part of whatever she's feeling, whatever she's going through right now . . . I wait.

Finally, she looks at me and smiles, her eyes a little more watery and red than they were before. "Will you bring that bag over here for me?"

My stomach twists with worry about what's inside of it, but I do as she asks, determined to see her through this the way she's seen me through countless talks and arguments with my parents—my mom is trying, but it's not an overnight change—and with Harry when we both came clean.

I didn't get in as much trouble as I thought I would—mainly

because I didn't work the showcase and could prove I swapped out any game I possibly could of hers—but Harry was definitely upset that I didn't come to him about everything from the start. In the end, he decided a stern lecture, along with a couple weeks off the field and on snack bar duty, plus sitting through some webinars he found about ethics and responsibility was a worthy enough punishment.

Aiden didn't make out quite as well. Harry was pretty furious about the whole blackmail angle. While Aiden still technically has a job, I don't think he's getting out of long days spent ironing jersey numbers on uniform orders anytime soon.

I know June was hoping Aiden would get fired, but honestly, her rubbing my back reassuringly when I texted him that he had nothing to hold over us anymore and then blocked his number was the next best thing. I'd like to think he's ashamed of what he did, but who really knows?

But none of that matters right now, as I set the bag down beside her, and she carefully drops to her knees and unzips it. She pulls out a giant blanket first and hands it to me.

"Spread this out?" she asks, and then starts lifting out various plastic containers and two giant Gatorade bottles.

"What's all this?"

"A picnic," she says, like it should be obvious.

"A picnic?"

"Yeah, you've surprised me with about a hundred stay-dates since I got hurt. It's my turn to spoil you," she says, referencing all the ways I tried to help her pass the time while she was stuck in bed recovering.

Besides our standard takeout-and-movie nights, I'd try to mix it up; like I'd throw in some red Solo cups full of parent-approved root beer and reenact the basketball team's house parties—which Javonte is now making himself a staple at, by the way. (We suspect it might have something to do with his now-obvious crush on Mia.) Or once I came over with a little construction paper fire that Sammy helped me with, and we microwaved s'mores. We even had our own little fall formal where I decorated her room with tiny disco balls and surprised her with a real corsage and a ridiculously cheesy playlist, since it was too soon after her surgery for her to be up and about much.

"If it's my turn to be spoiled, why did I have to carry the duffel bag?" I laugh as she goes about setting everything up.

"Oh, please." She grins. "Like you would ever let me carry it."

She's got me there.

I sit down beside the mound, staking out a corner of the blanket while she opens up containers full of fruit, candy, cheese, crackers—you name it and it's here. I'm tempted to help her; it's not easy doing all that when you're down an arm. But when I finally reach for one, she flashes me a look that tells me I'm risking ending up in a sling myself if I don't let her handle it.

When everything is set up, she passes me a plate and takes her place beside me. She leans in close and kisses my cheek just as the night sky forces on the field lights. It's kind of perfect.

"This is really great, June," I say, when she leans forward to grab a small piece of watermelon. She smiles and pops it into my mouth before taking one for herself.

"Yeah," she says, looking out at the field around us. "I know that day was hard for both of us. This is gonna sound so cheesy, but I wanted to make a new memory here, with you. A happy memory."

"It doesn't sound cheesy to me," I say softly, catching her lips when she turns to look at me. She tastes like watermelon. She tastes like June. And all the food is forgotten as I sigh against her skin, kissing my way to her favorite spot, right where her neck meets her jaw.

"You're trouble," she breathes.

"I've barely had you to myself between your dad taking time off and Javonte hovering like a nervous mother hen," I say as I place another kiss. "You can't blame a girl for taking advantage of finally having a moment alone."

"You're not playing fair," June says, running her fingers through my hair.

"No," I say, pressing my lips to her skin one last time before leaning back to look at her smiling, blushing, perfect face. "I'm playing for keeps."

EPILOGUE

June

"STRIKE THREE. You're out!" Her words echo down the field. She gives me a little wink, and I grin.

"Yes! You call that strike!" I shout, just to make her laugh. "That's some good officiating!"

A bunch of people turn to look at me, some agreeing with the call, some looking pissed off about it, but I don't care. My girlfriend is the best ump to ever ump. The official extraordinaire, and I am her number one fan.

Yeah, I know, it's weird to cheer for the ump, especially at a tournament this big—the last one of the spring season for my old team—but I am.

Yeah, *old* team. I said it.

While my arm is about as healed as it's going to get, it's not where it was or even close in terms of pitching abilities and fastball speeds. A lot of that is on me, for sure. An accelerated timeline, going back to my old practices and workouts immediately, visiting my multiple private coaches—all of that probably would have gotten me back there, or at least close enough to still have scouts banging down my door. We had more than enough get-well-soon cards from them after my surgery. I guess they liked what they saw last fall . . . aside from the whole existential crisis thing. The only problem was that I didn't want that anymore. I did my physical therapy, and yes, a lot of mental therapy as well, and I realized that I'm not just a life-support system for a pitching arm after all.

It was a big eye-opener. I'm not glad it happened, that would be going way too far, but I'm glad that it forced me to take some time off and evaluate things. I'm also glad that I used that time to figure out what I really want out of life. Plot twist: It isn't pushing myself to the brink—and then past it—to be a superstar.

I know that sounds obvious, but it wasn't for me. Not after an entire life of baseball being the main thing, the biggest thing that most people knew about me. It was my whole identity. And it's taken more than a couple calls with a sports psychologist to deal with the aftereffects of trying to craft a new self-identity after a dozen or so years of thinking I already knew who I was.

Dad and I have had a lot of talks these last few months too.

He offered to burn the letters or keep them locked up somewhere, but I couldn't do that to Mom. Instead, we made a big meal of all of Mom's favorite foods and then went through the box of letters together, so that there would be no more surprises. We set aside a couple that I might not ever open and a couple that I could already but am not ready to. He's going to keep them safe for me just in case, and it helps a lot knowing all the rest of her wishes for me in advance. *Wishes*, like Dad said, not expectations.

They live in the closet over Dad's flannels, because neither of us wants to look at them every day, but they're still there when I need them—when I need her. We even found one he was supposed to give me on my seventeenth birthday, but somehow missed. I guess it just slipped down beneath everything else. I thought I would be sad about that, but I felt relieved. It took some of the pressure off. We had already missed a letter and the world didn't end.

Baseball's not completely out of my system. It turns out that healthy balance Ivy suggested *is* a thing after all. I'm in a couple pickup leagues, and even a local rec team. It lets me keep my arm loose without fully unleashing the rocket. And if I do occasionally let it go, just for fun, that works too.

I've been offered a couple walk-on spots for next year at college, but right now I'm planning to just play for the school's club team and focus on my new thing: studying sports medicine, specifically focusing on pediatric athletes. I wouldn't be where I am today without all of the doctors and therapists I've worked with over these last few months. I want to be that person for other kids. It's a long road to get to where I'll actually start making an impact, but I'm determined.

Ivy, on the other hand, after several long talks with her mom, finally decided that she wants to go to school for business at the local college, with a minor in sports management—probably inspired by how much work she put into managing me at the start of our relationship. Ha!

Her real goal is still to keep working up the ranks as an official, and her parents are really making an effort to get on board with that. They might not fully get it, but they love Ivy enough to try. It's been really cool to see—they even brought Sammy to one of the games she was umping. I think he was a little confused that she wasn't the one *actually playing* the game, but it was still pretty awesome.

Plus, she's already making some pretty big waves on the officiating side. She's going to be the first woman ever reffing varsity football for her old high school in the fall. She's already umping high school baseball at the highest level, but I know football is where her heart is—her shrine to Sarah Thomas is a dead giveaway.

I watch the rest of the game, alternating between cheering on my old team and cheering for my favorite umpire, even when she calls them out, but my favorite part is when Ivy runs off the field, sweaty and dusty after calling a whole game, and I trot down the bleachers to meet her, dragging my own baseball bag behind me. We exchange a quick kiss, and I melt into her. She smells like sunshine and baseball and *Ivy*, and it's intoxicating.

"Okay, break it up," Javonte says a moment later. "We're already behind."

Because, yeah, he's my best friend, and he said if I was doing a pickup league, then so was he. Brothers in arms, always. A few other guys are joining up for the summer too, now that the regular season is almost over and the risk of injury is much lower.

"Five more minutes, Mom?" Ivy whines, and I smile against her skin. She sighs when I step back. "Fiiiine, I guess she's all yours."

"No, she's definitely all yours," he says, looking at the puppy dog eyes I'm currently making at the thought of leaving her.

She grabs my face and sneaks in one more quick kiss. "Go win, baby," she says. "I'm gonna hit the showers, and then I'll be back to watch you blow everyone out of the water."

Javonte warms me up while we wait for everyone else to get there, and before I know it, the game is on—sandlot baseball, just on nicer, better fields, with a bunch of players who actually have a shot at going pro.

Ivy comes back at the top of the third, right when Javonte and I are arguing over whether my last pitch was a strike or a ball.

"It was definitely a ball," Ivy calls out. "I was watching as I walked up."

"What's the point of dating an ump, if she won't even make calls for you in a pickup game?" I tease. Ivy throws her head back and laughs. And it's so nice that's something we can laugh about now. That our past didn't break us. That we made it out on the other side, in mostly one piece.

"Shut up. You love me," she says.

And I do.

I do.

ACKNOWLEDGMENTS

MY ETERNAL GRATITUDE to my agent extraordinaire, Sara Crowe, who is the best champion and business partner an author could ever wish for; and to my editor, Stephanie Pitts, who is always so excited and supportive when I say, "I've got this new idea about messy queer kids who fall in love . . ." And also to my friends and family, who know this job inevitably means I'll be locked up with my MacBook more often than not, and choose to love me anyway.

While they are always the first to know, they are far from the last! I am forever grateful to the entire team of people who help to make my daydreams a reality:

The fabulous Matt Phipps, who keeps us on track and somehow always makes sure I survive copyedits and pass pages. The entire Penguin team, including my publisher, Jen Klonsky, and my publicist, Lizzie Goodell (bonus thank-you to Lizzie for always finding me layovers long enough to not trigger my anxiety!!!), along with Felicity Vallence, James Akinaka, Shannon Spann, Alex Garber, and everyone at Penguin Teen! And of course, the Penguin Young Readers production editorial and managing editorial teams, including Cindy Howle, Misha Kydd, Bethany Bryan, Laurel Robinson, Natalie Vielkind, and Madison Penico.

Also, a massive, massive thanks to Jeff Östberg for creating another stunning cover illustration, and to Kelley Brady for pulling it together into such a gorgeous design.

And last but certainly not least, thank you to all the readers, bloggers, Instagrammers, BookTokkers, teachers, librarians, and booksellers—this community wouldn't be what it is without you. I'm more grateful than you could ever know.

© Amber Hooper

JENNIFER DUGAN is a writer, a geek, and a romantic who writes the kinds of stories she wishes she'd had growing up. She's the author of the graphic novel *Coven*, as well as the young adult novels *The Last Girls Standing, Melt With You, Some Girls Do, Verona Comics,* and *Hot Dog Girl,* which was called "a great, fizzy rom-com" by *Entertainment Weekly* and "one of the best reads of the year, hands down" by *Paste* magazine. She lives in upstate New York with her family, their dog, a strange kitten who enjoys wearing sweaters, and an evil cat who is no doubt planning to take over the world.

You can visit Jennifer at
JLDugan.com
or follow her on Twitter and Instagram
@JL_Dugan